IN THE NIGHT SEASON

a novel by
CHRISTIAAN BARNARD
with Siegfried Stander

PRENTICE-HALL, Inc.,
Englewood Cliffs, N.J.

IN THE NIGHT SEASON
Copyright © 1978 by Christiaan Barnard

Printed in the United States of America

The introductory section quotes are from Ecclesiastes 3:1-2.
Song lyrics reprinted by permission of Leonard Cohen,
© Leonard Cohen.

10 9 8 7 6 5 4 3 2 1

Library of Congress Catalog Card Number: 78-51825
ISBN 0-13-453654-1

O my God,
I cry in the daytime,
but thou hearest not;
and in the night season,
and am not silent.

—Psalms 22:2

To every thing
there is a season,
and a time
to every purpose
under the heaven.

A time to be born . . .

She lay on the couch, beneath a single glaring light. She held her body stiffly: shoulders back, arms down at her sides, in the touchingly vulnerable pose of a sacrificial victim. Her breathing was shallow. She was naked to the waist and with each shy breath her breasts swelled and lifted. Yet her lips were curved in a smile of distant amusement which belied the body's embarrassed posture.

They were shapely breasts, he noted. Full without being pendulous, high and well defined, with small nipples which diverged by only a fraction from complete symmetry. Her arms and shoulders and flat belly were still deeply tanned after a summer which was now moving to its close, but the demarcation between tanned skin and the paler areas normally covered by a swimming costume was less distinct than to be expected, giving an intriguing clue to her habits and thus to her outlook and nature: on occasion she sunbathed in the nude.

He had been leaning against the closed door and now he pushed himself into a standing position, flexing his shoulders and pushing both hands into the small of his back as if troubled by a vague ache. Nothing ailed his back, but this momentary hesitation and the grimace as he straightened up had become an odd reflex of moments of doubt, a social subterfuge by which he sought to distract other minds and gain time to think.

She looked up at him as he came toward her. Her smile became more frank, but she did not speak, as he briefly feared. He, too, said nothing. He began to rub his palms together to warm them. As he touched her she pulled her arms closer to her body in a small, involuntary gesture of withdrawal. Her eyes were alertly on him. He did not look at her face, but gently squeezed the right breast between finger and thumb. Finally he uttered a grunting sound of satisfaction.

He returned to the left breast, still conscious of her watchful eyes and of the slight frown which had now appeared between her eyebrows. Resolutely he ignored her unspoken question.

His testing fingers probed the soft tissue of the breast. There it was again. Small and comparatively smooth. He moved it around. There was no dimpling of the skin.

"Is something there?" she asked quietly.

He was still fingering the thing within her body. The consistency was firm, but he was no longer sure about the surface feel. Not as regular as he had believed at first. Was there infiltration?

"Hm?"

"A tumor?"

Whatever it was lay deep in the breast tissue, but superficial to the pectoral muscles. And yet it seemed to be mobile.

"Nothing much. There seems to be a small nodule."

Her right hand moved quickly to cover his, then to push it away, not discourteously but nevertheless with determination. She too began to squeeze with thumb and forefinger.

"Where?"

He guided her hand. "Here."

She found it. Her smile widened, but it became set, a mechanical showing of teeth. The brows had drawn together. Her eyelids had a bruised look and were half lowered, as always in moments of thought, giving her face an expression simultaneously indolent and cynical. With her long dark hair (he noticed a few strands of premature gray) brushed straight back off her forehead and those masked eyes and the fixed smile she had, briefly, the look of a lean wolf standing alone on windswept moorland.

"When did you last check your breasts for lumps?"

She reddened slightly.

"Not for . . . oh, not for quite a while. I can't positively remember, but it could be six months."

He shook his head and told her gently: "That wasn't very clever, was it? You, of all people, should know that."

She blushed more deeply. Her fingers were still working at the object below her left armpit.

"I know. But one gets careless. You have this foolishly optimistic idea that it can't happen to you."

He said quickly: "We don't know yet that anything has happened. You haven't felt this before?"

"Definitely not. Perhaps because it's a bit out of the way. Up in the axilla. And perhaps it hasn't been there long. Maybe it's just a gland that's come up."

He noticed the change in her face, the sudden charge of hope, and said carefully: "It's possible. Have you had any infection of your arm or your hand?"

She shook her head dubiously. "No. You don't think it could be ... "

Even she could not quite master the word, so he said it for her, with the same mixture of care and casualness: "Cancer?" He smiled. "As you've just said, one never thinks it can happen to you. But the moment anything does happen you automatically assume the worst. Don't worry. You're not the only one. I had the same experience when I was working down at the Cape."

"What happened?" Her interest was genuine, not that of social convention.

"Right out of the blue one day I discovered an enlarged lymph node here in the posterior triangle." He touched the back of his neck. "Of course I decided immediately it could only be a lymphoma or the start of a leukemia. Nothing less."

She smiled and he went on, dramatizing the telling a little for the sake of reassurance. "At the same time I was too scared to ask anyone to have a look at it in case it really was what I feared. I looked up all the causes of enlargement of the lymph nodes in the neck. By the time I was finished I could have been a world authority on the subject."

"You must have been very worried."

"I used to lie awake at night wondering what was going to happen to my poor wife and family. It was just after I'd started as surgical registrar and I was very broke. I'd lie thinking about who was going to pay for the funeral and then I'd palpate the gland and it would grow bigger by the minute. Anyway, finally I scraped up courage and showed it to the professor. He examined it and said: 'My boy, it's nothing. But I'll cut it out just to show you.' He was so reassuring about the whole thing that I felt quite foolish. The next day I was assisting him. I still remember, he was doing a resection of the stomach. When he finished he told me to get up on the table and he removed the gland under local. Then we went on with his slate as if nothing had happened. I'll tell you one thing I learned from him that day. Even if you're worried about a patient you should never show it."

She looked up sharply. "Are you worried about me?"

He smiled. "Of course not. I'll take this lump out too and I'll show you it's nothing more than a fibroadenoma or just fibroadenosis."

He could sense the ease which came to her. She asked: "And your lymph node? What was wrong with it?"

"You won't believe me. The pathology report said it was reaction to an insect bite. To this day I don't know how they made the diagnosis but they were right. I'd been stung by a bee about six weeks before but it had quite slipped my mind."

They both laughed.

He saw that his story had helped and asked cheerfully: "When can I book the theater to do this little job?"

"Are you going to do it under a local?"

"I think a general anesthetic would be better."

"You won't cut anything off while I'm asleep?" She was only half joking. Doubt had not been dispelled.

"Don't be silly. Shall we get it over with as soon as possible?"

"All right. Whenever you say."

He pulled up a chair. "Now sit up. Let's finish the examination."

She swung long brown legs over the edge of the couch.

"Left hand on the hips please." He located the lump again and moved it around with deft fingers as he went on speaking in conversational tones. "It's always an odd feeling to have the tables turned and be a patient for a change, isn't it? Makes you feel almost doubly helpless. You know what's going on, but there's absolutely nothing you can do about it." The lump was freely mobile in all directions. "Now press that hand into your side. Press hard. That's fine."

With a cheery evasiveness quite equal to his own she followed his lead. "Yes. And doctors make the worst patients, don't they?"

He laughed. "Geoff was in hospital last month with that

back of his and you should have seen him giving the nurses hell." As if he had been reminded by coincidence he asked: "How's *your* back, by the way?"

"Not much better," she began to say, but stopped short. She looked at him, her eyes opening wide. "Surely not." She searched his face with passionate attention. "You don't think there's a connection, do you?"

"No. No." He laughed again and held up a restraining hand. "There you go again. Now you've developed secondaries in the spine, all because of an innocent little lump. You mustn't let your imagination run away with you."

She smiled and he noticed that her alarm had passed. His assurances had apparently been convincing. Or perhaps it was simply that she had *wanted* to believe and thus *would* have believed, no matter how false the note he had struck.

He lifted her left arm, digging the fingers of his free hand securely into the armpit, then bringing her arm down to rest limply on his. She looked at him from nearby and he gave her a reassuring smile. He slid his fingers down the side of her breast. She turned her head. Her eyes fixed on something beyond his shoulder and her expression became impassive. His hand moved over the warm skin under her arm. He could smell her perfume, mingled with a faint smell of sweat.

He had gone back to his consulting room, leaving her in the examination room to dress and make the necessary adjustments to makeup and hair which were required to restore feminine composure.

He sat down at his desk, opened a file, and paged through the typed notes, the reports, the diagrams and graphs which constituted her medical record: all those bits of paper which told the story of a life, one-sidedly perhaps, over-emphasizing certain aspects, overconcerned with the physical, and yet a story which told a great deal to one who could read it. Not all the secrets were there, but the initiated could discover some of them and could make an educated guess about the existence of certain others.

Mens sana in corpore sano was what you prayed for. But inevitably that sound mind depended on the collateral of the sound body. If your body was sick the whole of you was sick and in time the body would betray the mind.

But not this body. The tale told here was one of vigorous health. A fractured tibia six years ago was the result of a skiing accident. A very correct Swiss doctor had treated her and had provided a set of X rays to bring home to her own physician, as if they were certificates awarded for achievement on the snow slopes. The jagged stylus pattern on a roll of graph paper was an electroencephalogram recording, also the aftermath of an accident, this time falling off a horse when it refused a jump. She had been concussed and had suffered from headaches, but the EEG had shown nothing abnormal and the symptoms had disappeared with time. Then there had been mild dysmenorrhea a few years ago. He had referred her to a gynecologist who had ascribed it to cervical erosion which he had cauterized. At the very back of the file was a copy of a medical report he had filled in for her when she had taken out an insurance policy. He picked it up with a half smile. The childhood diseases were all there: measles, chicken pox, mumps, whooping cough. Everything else was scratched out and under the heading "Remarks" was scrawled in his handwriting: "General health excellent."

He closed the file, pushed it aside, and leaned back in his chair.

The two rooms had formerly been one. They were divided by a wooden partition, skillfully constructed to match the original walls and antique moldings, with high bookcases on the consulting room side, glass-fronted shelves for laboratory equipment on the other. The rooms were light and airy and yet, with all that woodwork, from smooth-worn floor to beamed ceiling, there was an aura of solemnity too, as if nothing said or done here could be lightly disregarded. Even a mild caution to a patient to smoke less, or to avoid fatty foods, was hung around with a grave judicial resonance.

The interleading door opened quietly and he turned in the swivel chair, rising. One hand, casually resting upon his green-ruled writing pad, covered the notes he had taken. They smiled at one another, smiles of courtesy and friendship, and he gestured toward one of the pair of padded leather armchairs. He waited until she was seated.

"Now then," he said, still smiling, "I know you'll worry until it's been removed and proved benign, so we won't delay."

"Do you have to cut it out? Can't you do a needle biopsy?"

His smile stiffened slightly but he persevered with it. "I'm surprised at you," he said in mock reproof. "Don't you remember the golden rule? No woman shall harbor a lump in the breast."

"An undiagnosed lump," she corrected.

He decided to change the focus of the conversation a little. "You won't even see the scar in a few weeks' time. I promise you I'll do a neat job."

She was not to be diverted. "How long before we get the path report?"

"Well, as you know we don't have the facilities to do frozen sections. But in any event I'm sure it would be unnecessary in your case. It'll only be a matter of days before we know."

"It's not going to be any kind of fun, waiting."

"Of course it isn't. But, you know, once I've got it out and I can cut it in half I'll be able to give you a diagnosis as accurate as that of any microscope." He glanced at her. The tight look was still around her eyes, as if already a permanent feature of her expression. He had to try to placate her. "I think first we should do a mammography." He picked up his pen and held it poised over his appointment book. "Will this afternoon suit you?"

"I'll be free any time after three."

"Right." He began to write, then changed his mind and pressed a button on the intercom instead. After a moment his secretary's voice, made gravelly by some fault in the equipment, came from the speaker.

"Mrs. Haarhoff, will you get me Mr. Bicard at X ray, please."

"Mr. Bicard. Yes, Doctor."

While he spoke to the X-ray technician, making the appointment for the afternoon and explaining what procedure he required, she sat looking at the pictures on his walls, politely pretending not to overhear. But when he replaced the receiver she said: "Then that's arranged for three o'clock. And you'll let me know when you can do the op?"

"We'll do it as soon as we can. Tomorrow, if I can get a theater."

He saw her to the door and they parted with further smiles, only slightly strained. She stopped to speak to his secretary in her small office overlooking the waiting room. His secretary laughed with pleasure at something she said. He closed his door.

In a brown paper envelope in one desk drawer were X rays showing two different views of a spine. He took up the plate with the lateral aspect. There was a neon-lit viewing box on a stand in the corner but he ignored it and held the X ray up against the light from the window.

There. The third lumbar vertebra. Was there a spotty decalcification of the body? He could not be sure. He picked up the frontal X ray. Nothing showed. The body and pedical of lumbar three appeared normal. It was imagination. A lump in the breast, a backache. So you started looking for something which wasn't there.

Again he examined the lateral view. There was the bottom of the rib cage, there the spreading arch of the pelvis. Lumbar one . . . two . . . three. Was there a shadow where no shadow should have been?

He stood frowning, lips slightly parted, breathing through his mouth. He held the X ray up against the sunlight, which shone, gold and thick, through the tall windows.

PART ONE

And a time to die ...

1

The houses on this street were identical, small and square like drawings by a child with a passion for order, each with a door set in the center and equidistant windows on either side.

Toadstools, Charles de la Porte thought as he took the corner and the arc of the headlight swung from one drab building to another. There was the same air of squat impermanence, of things pushed up out of dark and moldering earth. He smiled faintly at the extravagance of the image, flicked a switch to change the headlights to full beam, and sat up erect behind the steering wheel. The house he sought was number 48. But, to compound the felony of dull duplication, the houses were poorly marked. There were few streetlights. He drove on slowly, peering from side to side.

Why was it that, in a land which was open and filled with space, people had developed this instinct to huddle, to breathe the same stale air as their fellows? The forefathers of the people who lived along this street had been pioneers to whom the sight of smoke from a neighbor's distant fire was a signal to trek onward, away from encroachment. But here they lived like chickens on a roost. Because of economic circumstances, clearly enough. But also because of fear of dark forces which now moved across the land, around the perimeter of their cluttered enclave?

A white square hung on a lopsided garden gate. He turned the car to bring the lights to bear. It was a sign of a kind but the paint had faded and he could not make it out at this distance. He fumbled in the glove box, found a flashlight, and, leaving the engine running, climbed out. His shoes grated over the gravel sidewalk. The sign was fastened with twisted wire, low down on the gate. Even with the aid of the flashlight he had to lean down close to decipher it.

"Beware the dog."

To lend depth and credence to the warning a dog began to bark at that moment; barking deeply and dangerously somewhere in the darkness. Startled, he leaped back. Something slid out of his breast pocket and fell with a tinkle of breaking glass. There was a pungent smell of Formalin.

He swore under his breath and hastily shifted the beam of light to where a wet stain and bits of broken glass marked where the test tube had fallen. He kneeled and began feverishly to scratch around in the gravel. After a moment, holding the flashlight close to the ground, he found the object he was hunting. He examined it briefly.

The dog was still barking and there was an ominous switchblade sound of a chain sliding along a length of wire. As he retreated other dogs from neighboring houses took up the challenge in a shrill and mounting chorus. There were always too many dogs in these townships of the poor, black as well as white. Was that also a symptom of their fears?

He switched on the dome light and opened the black bag which lay on the back seat. He found a half-empty plastic container, shook the remainder of its contents of tablets out into an envelope, and then dropped the object he had retrieved, a brownish-white bit of tissue, into the container. He wiped his hands. The skin of his fingers felt thick.

He had traveled halfway further down the street before something sparkled redly in the headlights. Numbers against a fence on the right, a "2" and a "5" formed with reflector buttons like those on the rear mudguards of bicycles. Not in the most elegant taste, perhaps, but helpful enough. He started to count the houses.

Number 48 Seringa Street was in darkness, except for a glimmer of light which showed behind drawn curtains at the side of the house. He grimaced in annoyance. Typically inconsiderate, he thought. People call you out at all hours but they can't even be bothered to switch on a light for you. He pulled the car

15

up across the curb, reached for his bag, and climbed out without switching off the lights. Carrying the bag, he crossed an overgrown patch of grass, keeping to the floodlit tunnel provided by the lights behind his back. As he stepped onto a minute cement-tiled porch and rang the bell he could hear a distant mutter of voices. After a time a light went on overhead and the front door opened. The sound of voices continued more loudly.

A man stood in the doorway, frowning suspiciously. He was in his shirt sleeves. His face was flushed, as if from exertion. As he took a step forward, squeezing up his eyes and peering at the intruder, he breathed out the smell of liquor.

Charles de la Porte suppressed feelings of distaste and asked, as courteously as he was able: "Mr. Erasmus?"

The other stared up at him. He swayed slightly and reached a steadying hand towards the wall. Then he nodded. "*Ja.*"

"I am Dr. de la Porte."

"Delport?"

The mistaken but not uncommon contraction of his surname brought to Charles de la Porte's mind a fleeting memory of his father and of the pained expression with which similar solecisms were always received. Correction made with dignity, he would afterwards confide: "They do not know any better, my dear Charles. And yet the fact remains that it is a corruption of the old name, forgivable perhaps when you consider the circumstances of a hard frontier life and the absence of civilization and its graces. All they had was the Bible, for God's sake. But a corruption it remains and it is one's duty to put them right." Poor Father.

"Yes," Charles de la Porte said disloyally. He said: "The doctor. Your wife called me."

"Doctor? Oh. I thought ... The other doctor ... "

"Dr. Hutton? He is away. He's my partner, so I am taking his calls tonight."

"He's away." Slowly, as if thought was a dim-eyed fish swimming in murky waters. "But he's the Railway doctor." Suspicion sharpened the dulled senses. "We don't want a private doctor."

"You don't have to pay private fees," Charles de la Porte said patiently. "Dr. Hutton and I work together. Now will you please let me see the child? Your wife left a message that her baby was sick."

The first sign of animation. "Yes, she's sick. I told her to call the doctor. What do I pay money to the sick fund for, hey?"

Charles de la Porte followed the man inside without comment. He had little to do with the Railways side of the practice these days, for the appointment had been taken over by his younger partner. He had surrendered it gladly, mainly because of the attitude personified by this belligerent and half-inebriated man: that a doctor was at the beck and call of all gangers or flag-waving shunters merely because they had a small medical aid contribution deducted from their wages each week. He made a mental note to discuss the problem with Geoff Hutton.

The railwayman Erasmus led him into a cramped, darkened sitting room where gray images on a television screen explained the source of the voices. Erasmus reached out for a switch at the door. A woman looked up, blinking, from her seat on a couch drawn up in front of the set.

"Wife," Erasmus said. "The doctor has come."

She was young, not far past twenty, and attractive in a pale, wilting way. She continued to blink drowsily at the stranger. She had been drinking too. There were two glasses and the remains of a bottle of cane spirits on a side table.

Anger stirred. "You called me to attend to your child," Charles de la Porte said brusquely.

She rose slowly from the couch and showed vague awareness of his anger. She seemed alarmed by the realization that this very big dark man was cross with her. She looked nervously at her husband.

"The child," Erasmus said with an appearance of briskness. "Show the doctor." He passed her and turned down the volume of the television but did not switch off the set. On the screen were two men who alternately mouthed soundless sentences at one another. They were obviously in a historical play, for both wore period dress. The woman's eyes turned mechanically back toward the screen.

17

"Where is the child?" Charles de la Porte asked her.

The baby was a little girl of ten or eleven months. She lay asleep in a metal frame cot in a room off the passage. Another child, a boy of about two, was sleeping on a mattress on the floor. He whimpered when the lights went on and put an arm over his face.

How much was the installment they had to pay each month for the new toy of TV, Charles de la Porte wondered. More important than a bed for their child. He leaned over to examine the baby, thrusting the irrelevant from his mind. She was slightly flushed and felt hot. Her pulse was fast and her nose blocked. Probably nothing more serious than a cold.

"What symptoms did she have?" he asked the mother.

She stared at him.

"What's wrong with the child? Why did you call me?"

The woman looked at the baby as if perplexed. "She's sick," she said after a moment. Her voice was surprisingly deep.

"I know that. But what made you think she was sick?"

The husband had stopped in the door and was leaning against the frame.

"The child wouldn't go to sleep," he volunteered. "She's been crying all the time. Crying and, you know, moving around. Like she was sick."

"She's asleep now."

"Yes." Defensively: "But she only fell asleep a little while ago. Just before you came."

"My secretary received your call only after six. If the child has been ill all afternoon why didn't you bring her to the surgery?"

Erasmus looked accusingly at his pale wife. "I told you," he said. "I told you to take the child to the doctor's office."

Charles de la Porte shrugged and turned back to the baby. Obviously there was nothing to make a fuss about. But he might as well finish the examination. He took a thermometer from his bag, shook it down with a flick of the wrist, and placed the bulb in the axilla. As he lowered the child's arm he noticed a raised patch of red on the thin upper arm.

"Did something bite her?"

He watched the woman's face prepare to show the predictable pattern of bewilderment and then incredulity and finally rejection of responsibility. She peered closer to follow his pointing finger. But, surprisingly, her expression changed.

"That's the injection," she said.

"Injection?"

"I took her to the clinic yesterday for her injection."

"What injection?"

"You know. The one the sister said she must have."

"Do you mean the inoculation for diphtheria, whooping cough, and tetanus? She should have had that at the age of six months."

She nodded and became voluble. The clinic sister had been cross with her about the child and its injection. She had even been sent a letter about not taking the child to the clinic. But these nurses didn't seem to realize people had other things to do. The sister had come to the house yesterday morning and threatened her with the law so she had taken the child to have the injection in the afternoon.

He listened to the familiar lame story in expressionless silence. It was a symptom, he thought, of a disease which had deep and profound origins. But it was incurable; an ill within society itself for which no medication would serve.

There were people who should not be allowed to have children.

But at once conscience cringed away from the barren intolerance which lay behind the thought. Was there, in its essential prudery, not an echo of the jackboot? And yet. Faced with evidence of Mrs. Erasmus's lazy-minded fertility, of Mrs. Erasmus's neglect, of Mrs. Erasmus's lack of concern, would not even liberal thought throw up its hands in horror and join the disapproving chorus of sour old virgins in exclaiming: "It shouldn't be allowed."

The inescapable fact remained. Some people were inadequate and Mrs. Erasmus was among them.

He could guess at the rest of the story. The child, showing a slight reaction to the DWT inoculation, aggravated by her cold, would have been fretful all day. The mother had done

19

nothing about it. It would have been too much trouble, just as taking the infant to the clinic had been too much trouble and in the same way all the other responsibilities of parenthood were too irksome.

She had not thought to do anything about the child until the husband had come home from work. A little drunk already, probably. The Railway Institute lay between this township and the yards where, presumably, he worked. Beer was a couple of cents cheaper at the institute than at any other pub in town. He would have been under the influence and the child's crying would have annoyed him. He would have shouted at the woman to take the child to a doctor or, if it was too late, to call the damn doctor. That would have been when he started on the bottle of cane spirits. Clearly she was afraid of him; she had gone to a neighbor or to a telephone booth down the road to make the call. By the time she returned and with two or three more drinks inside him he had probably mellowed; had perhaps even forgotten about the child altogether. Again, she had chosen the line of least resistance. She had sat down with him in front of the television and they had set out to get drunk together.

Charles de la Porte pulled the crumpled cover sheet around the child's shoulders and turned to face the parents.

"There is nothing wrong with this child," he said sternly.

The woman gave him a terrified smile and nodded her head repeatedly.

"She has a bit of a cold, for which I'll give her medicine, and she is a little unhappy because of the injection. But that's all. Now let me tell you that I think it is disgraceful that two adult people should behave like this. You have been totally irresponsible. Apart from wasting my time, calling me when it was clearly unnecessary, it's quite obvious that both these children are being gravely neglected."

The man took on a drunkenly stubborn look and Charles de la Porte knew that he was about to say something aggressive. He stared the man down coldly, tightening his jaw. Erasmus swallowed and looked down at his feet. He might have liked to assert himself, to maintain that he was as good as any man and no one had the right to tell him how to behave. But the stranger in his house, with a big man's air of utter assurance and his massive head and cold eyes and graying hair, had the advantage of age and authority and class superiority. There was no contest. The doctor was master of the situation; was right and righteous and therefore unassailable.

Charles de la Porte maintained his disdainful look for a moment. But then it wavered, as doubt returned.

Who are you to judge? he asked himself. How can you claim to know so certainly what this man thought and did? How can you decide for yourself that his concern was not genuine?

My child is sick, he had said. Call the doctor.

It was true that he had shown poor judgment and little sense of responsibility. His truculent bearing made it clear that he regarded the services of that doctor as a right to be demanded whenever it suited him. He showed no gratitude; no awareness even that gratitude was owed. It was this attitude which antagonized many doctors. But one should be fair and recognize the converse: that many doctors regarded indigent patients of all races, for whose medical needs the state provided, as no more than cyphers on the official forms they filled in to claim their monthly allowances.

Erasmus, the railwayman, could not call the doctor of his choice. Was it any wonder that he was churlishly suspicious about the attention he received? Did he believe it to be indifferent, careless, and inferior? And did his manner indicate a shapeless rage within him, an inarticulate resentment of the fate which made him as he was?

Who are *you*, to judge?

2

Charles de la Porte pulled his car up under the great oaks which stood sentinel around the paved square. Streetlights shone on the paleness of new leaves. He thought briefly of the miracle of rebirth which, in due season, restored to these gnarled trees, planted at the command of a Dutch colonial governor two and a half centuries ago, the face of youth. He was reminded, too, how the Town Council, planning a new ring main for its sewage system and persuaded by an economy-minded engineer that a direct course over the square would be least likely to result in a rates increase, had voted for the removal of two of the seventeen oaks. He had been a member of the deputation of protest.

Now, walking past the reprieved trees toward the long-fronted white building which covered one end of the square and was, in its utter simplicity, a logical extension of the square itself, a charmingly balanced composition of which the oaks formed the frame, he thought with fond appreciation of Frank Edelstein, who had led the deputation and had played the only speaking role. Frank, as befitted an attorney, was both eloquent and persuasive. Too eloquent, in fact, for the taste of some of the more dour members of the deputation, who could not be expected to understand that Frank's mincing manner was a calculated mockery of itself. Charles de la Porte had persuaded them to accept Frank as spokesman, for he knew that, behind the affectation, there was a steely intelligence and an ironic wit.

Frank had spoken of history and the nation's legacy and the town's not-inconsiderable contribution to that legacy, while the mayor had sat toying awkwardly with his gavel, occasionally looking under his brows at two of his fellow councilors sitting attentively on either side. The gavel, as a small plaque on its carved wooden stand proclaimed, was a gift from the distilling company which was the town's largest, indeed dominating, industry.

Gradually, Frank had worn down resistance. All three councilors had seemed gratified by the reminder that Frank knew the difficulties and frustrations of municipal service, for, as they would recall, he had himself been on the council for several terms and had retired only for reasons of health. (A myocardial infarct several years previously; Charles de la Porte had been called at four o'clock in the morning by the distraught Coloured man who was Frank's man-servant and majordomo and jealous guardian; he had found his friend gray-faced in his bed, but alive to the grim humor of it, looking at death with a side-of-the-mouth smile.) The whole of the speech had been delivered with grace and a grave sincerity which filled out the emptiness of the formal words and gestures, which gave form to the ritual and made it more than its reality.

A rerouting of the pipeline was recommended and accepted without comment at the next council meeting.

Charles de la Porte climbed the flowing flight of steps which led to the broad veranda, feeling in a pocket for his key to the massive wooden door. Standing before it, holding the key, his approving eye wandered over the door's elaborate design of antlered deer and other animals of the European forest which had, with singular inappropriateness, been carved into its African yellowwood. Frank again, for it was he who had spotted the warped old door lying discarded in a loft on a wine farm in the district, who had been amused by the contradiction, who had bought it and paid for its restoration.

The carved door turned silently on huge brass hinges. He went inside, reaching for a switch. Light sparkled from a chandelier which had been his own contribution to the reinstatement of former glory. Frank once more. Councilor Edelstein at the time and deputy mayor, he had headed the subcommittee which had blocked the sale of the old Drostdy, long derelict and an eyesore and a disgrace in the opinion of many townspeople, to the distilling company, which wanted the ground for a multi-story office block. But Frank had spoken tirelessly at meetings and at the club bar (he had been elected a temporary member for the duration of his term of office, in the face of opposition: "What's the place coming to? Now they allow a Yid to join. And as if that isn't bad enough he's a bloody queer too!"). Finally he had found the support to form a syndicate of professional men which had bought the ramshackle place from an indifferent state department and had it restored. The Drostdy, seat of district government two hundred years before, now belonged to the town, but the partners were entitled to lease the office suites established in some of its magnificent rooms.

Charles de la Porte went through the hall with its gleaming floor of broad planks and the grandfather clock built by a Dutch master craftsman. He turned down a long passage, leaving the public rooms behind. He passed the signboard which announced the offices of Edelstein, Lewis, and Meyerowitz, attorneys, notaries, and conveyancers; then the single door which led to the rooms of Eric Shaw, architect; an imposing suite which housed Drs. Botha and Cronje, dentists; two rooms for Mr. Leicester Edwards-White, surgeon; finally his own rooms, Drs. de la Porte and Hutton, general practitioners.

He used another key and went swiftly through the waiting room and the reception office beyond it, with covered typewriters and empty desks, chairs squared off, cabinets locked and anonymous. Although Mrs. Haarhoff, the chief receptionist and his own secretary of long standing, had resigned and left he was pleased to see that her near-military discipline appeared to have rubbed off on the other girls.

His own consulting room now, with the familiarity and warmth of books which rose from floor to ceiling on both sides of the ancient fireplace. He sat down on the padded swivel chair behind the leather-topped desk, switched on the desk light, let his eyes go lingeringly around the room. Here, surrounded by known and certain things, by the homely trappings of his work and daily life, surely he must regain confidence? Here, surely, there could be no doubts?

On the wall facing him were the framed certificates which, conventionally posted there, proclaimed his status and degrees. He supposed it was somehow reassuring to patients to see them hanging and to learn that this man, this doctor whom they had come to consult about the slower or faster but certainly inevitable processes of decay which assailed their flesh, was legally licensed to advise or dictate or scold or sympathize or even to force them to face the ultimate brutal truth of death.

Despite this visible evidence of his competence, doubt at times assailed him. What real qualification did he possess to calm the fears of a woman who suspected her husband of infidelity, or to advise the young man who came to him with a stammered story of real or imagined sexual inadequacy? Where did they teach a doctor how to give advice to a prominent merchant facing bankruptcy or to a middle-aged teacher facing charges under the Immorality Act?

He pushed back his chair and crossed the room to where the certificates hung. Leaning close to the glass which fronted the frames, he examined the documents with solemn interest, as if they were puzzling evidence which contradicted a theory he had long held. One announced that Charles Michel de la Porte, having satisfied the examiners, was awarded the degrees of bachelor of medicine and of surgery by the University of Stellenbosch. It was dated twenty-six years before. The other conferred on the same Charles Michel de la Porte the additional distinction of fellowship of a College of Surgeons, with all the obligations and privileges which this entailed.

He thought wonderingly about those two distant figures, those two Charles Michel de la Portes of twenty-four and thirty-five years of age. Impossible to believe and yet reason proclaimed it so: he had been that young and all-knowing new doctor and also that wry, world-wise surgeon of early middle age. And now? At fifty?

The obligations and privileges of this new qualification had never been set forth. He began to phrase a certificate in his mind. "Know all men by these presents that we do hereby admit Charles Michel de la Porte to the fellowship of fallibility, thereby entitling him to anguish and doubt. . . ."

Slowly he removed from the wall the earlier document, the one which conferred the degrees of M.B., Ch.B, so revealing the front of a small built-in safe which it had effectively concealed. He put down the frame and its certificate, mentally re-

25

cited a sequence of numbers, spun a dial through its set pattern, and opened the safe door.

He used the wall safe principally for personal documents, a copy of his will, bank statements, private correspondence, and the occasional more than ordinarily confidential patient record. Now he searched among these and took out a bulging folder on the red cover of which was noted, in his own sprawling hand, the name Janice Case. Carrying it carefully, half opened, gently juggling the letters and copies of letters which it contained and which were threatening to slide out of sequence, he returned to his desk.

He put down the file, but did not sit down at once. He felt absently in his jacket pocket, took out a packet of cigarettes, lit one and drew at it without really thinking. He had stopped smoking several years ago, more as an example to his patients than out of conviction. For a little while he had missed the habitual gestures, like that of automatically reaching for a cigarette whenever he needed to sit back to consider a problem, or the ritual of a cigarette with the evening drink. After that he had found it tolerably easy to do without tobacco. However, he had started smoking again a month ago.

He began to page perfunctorily through the voluminous correspondence in the Janice Case file. He had no real need to do so, for it was all inside his head, as fresh as the day it had started. For that matter there had been no need to return to his rooms. He had completed his hospital round before dark and the Railways family in Seringa Street had been the last of his evening calls. He could have gone directly home from there.

Memory was jolted and he reached for a scratch pad, selected a pen from among the half dozen in an antique copper bowl his wife had unearthed at an auction sale, and made a brief note: "Railways. See G."

Geoff Hutton would be back in the morning from his hasty one-day visit to Cape Town on the urgent family business about which he had been, perhaps deliberately, perhaps merely not wishing to bore others with his problems, more than usually uncommunicative. They would meet tomorrow and he would mention the question of the Railway practice and whether it was really worth their time. But there would be no hasty decision. They would look at figures on time spent and comparative income and then decide, after next week perhaps.

He winced. Next week. There was always the possibility that next week would alter the whole situation beyond recognition; that the Railways post would then be a lifeline he dared not let go. And yet he must not even consider the possibility. He must hold steadfastly to the vision, to the unalterable fact that he was right and that this must never be in doubt.

Then why had he come here, to paw once more through the all-too-familiar sequence of papers which told the story of his present predicament? To refresh his mind, as he had pretended to himself? To search again, among the long-winded but inexorably advancing course of the correspondence for that one word, that sudden insight, which would make all else clear, which would sustain his defense, strengthen his cause beyond danger, and confound his enemies? Or merely because he was in search of comfort and, like any other wounded animal, was driven by instinct to crawl to the familiar den where no one could reach him?

Impatiently he shrugged away the renewed onset of doubt and, as was his habit during emotional stress, tried to calm his mind by retracing his thoughts to that kernel moment, the start of the series of impulses which had brought him here. He recognized after a moment's reflection that a small event, the accident with the test tube on the sidewalk in Seringa Street, had been the trigger.

Equilibrium was restored and at the same time memory received another signal. He took the plastic container out of his pocket and went over to a store cupboard in a corner. He found a rack of test tubes similar to the one which had broken and a brown glass-stoppered bottle beside it. He filled a tube from the bottle. Again there was the smell of Formalin. He transferred the gray bit of flesh to the tube and set it in the rack.

It was a lump he had excised from a woman's breast during an operation late in the afternoon. He had himself brought away the specimen so that it could go to the pathologist for analysis first thing in the morning and not be subject to the

27

inevitable delays of hospital routine. But analysis was hardly necessary. He had known at once, immediately he had the cyst free and had handled it, that the news he would bring the unconscious woman under his hands would be good. The soapy feel, like cutting into an unripe pear, which was characteristic of cancerous tumors, had been absent.

The news was good.

It had not been good on another occasion.

He returned to his desk and the file which lay on it.

He opened the folder at the beginning, at the first wad of stapled papers. The top sheet bore the letterhead of a firm of attorneys in Cape Town and was dated six weeks ago.

"We address you on behalf of our client, Mrs. Janice McOwen, also known as Dr. Janice Case. Our client instructs us that on February 16 this year she consulted you in regard to a growth in her left breast. Our instructions are that on February 17 you performed an operation on our client for the removal of the said growth on the understanding that you would have the said growth examined by a suitably qualified person to determine whether it showed signs of malignancy."

There was a noise at the outer door, a combination of scratching and thumping which ceased expectantly at that moment. He put the letter aside, frowning and aware that the weird sound had been in progress for some time without really registering. It was not loud, but persistent: the efforts of some creature to gain attention and entry.

A dog whined behind the closed door.

He sighed in exasperation. Of course. Major! Obviously he had neglected to close the street door properly and the damned dog had found its way in with its usual dumb determination. He went through into the outer offices. The thumping of a heavy tail on the floor rose to a tattoo of delight and the dog gave a single deep bark.

He opened the door, planning to scold and if necessary to beat and send the unwanted visitor on his cringing way. The big tawny bull mastiff grinned up at him, lolling its head in its usual toy-dog attitude of amiability. He sighed again and held the door open. Major padded in past him with an air of calm triumph.

The dog belonged to a young couple who lived in the street behind the Drostdy. It was the second mastiff they had owned; its predecessor had been named Captain and its owner liked to joke that he was planning to continue the military promotions until the last dog achieved the name of the then Minister of Defense. The dog was a roamer by nature, however, and since puppyhood had preferred the Drostdy to its own home. Jacob, the old Coloured man who by day grumpily guarded the front door and the public rooms, hated the dog and chased it on sight. But it had learned to wait for the moments he was called away from his cubicle or when he dozed in the afternoon sun and would then sneak past with an outrageous air of furtiveness, like a blond shadow, then progress with waggling bottom down the corridor, calling on each office in turn. It was a public nuisance, but tolerated by most of the tenants, petted by most of their female employees. He went back to his room and the dog followed him, its toenails making quick click-sounds over the bare floor. It made a circuit of the room before selecting the most impossible place to settle itself: a narrow corner between wall and bookcase. Squirming and wriggling, it wedged itself here and then lay flat on its belly, golden eyes staring placidly at Charles de la Porte.

He sat down again; took up the letter.

"We are instructed that you duly caused this examination to be performed and that the pathological finding, conveyed to you on or about February 21, was to the effect that the said growth was an invasive duct (scirrhous) carcinoma.

"It is our client's contention that a legal obligation resided with you to inform our client or her husband or some person interested in her welfare about her condition, alternatively that a legal obligation resided with you to ensure or advise that she should immediately receive the appropriate treatment.

"This, we are instructed, you failed to do."

The dog had casually fallen asleep and was apparently dreaming for it now gave forth a number of strangled, high-pitched barking sounds and its hind legs jerked spasmodically.

Charles de la Porte said sternly: "Major!"

The dog opened its eyes and beat its tail a few times on the floor, with difficulty because of the cramped space. Otherwise it did not move.

What phantoms had been on its mind? A dream of pursuit; of being pursued? A vision of sexual gratification? A fight? Did it dream of food, of endless rows of Coloured caretakers armed with broom handles and stones, of countless successes in evading its master's attempts to keep it cooped up at home?

A high-revving car went raucously across the square and the dog turned its head sideways while its face took on a comical imitation of human perplexity. He laughed aloud and the dog thumped its tail again.

The noisy car went away and the square, which carried little nighttime traffic, fell silent once more. And in that instant Charles de la Porte, the faint remains of a smile still lingering around his mouth, knew himself to be totally alone.

Silence was a wasteland, an infinity of emptiness which surrounded all creatures. He was set apart from this dog by silence, equally as from Frank Edelstein, from Jacob, from Geoff Hutton, from his wife, even from Jay Case. Communication was the frantic gesticulation of deaf-mutes; not even the thinnest whisper of sound reached across the universe.

He realized that he was sweating, although the early summer's evening was no more than mild, and ran a hand distractedly through his hair. His thoughts ran on death. Not impersonal, abstract death, which he knew well enough, but horrifyingly, his own. How could he not think about it? How could any thinking being contemplate anything except its own certain and impending end?

With a determined effort he went back to the letter. The Cape Town attorneys claimed, on behalf of Janice Case, that she had suffered reduced expectancy of life, shock, pain and suffering, disfigurement, future disability, and loss of amenities. It was her intention, the letter concluded, shortly to institute legal action for damages.

He read the next letter, too, from Frank Edelstein, formally acknowledging the instruction to act on his behalf, then a photostat of Frank's reply to the Cape Town attorneys, other copies of correspondence between Frank and Patrick Bachelli, the young barrister who had accepted the brief, and of papers which had been served on either party. The cumbersome clutter which recorded the prescribed moves of the game made it all seem almost innocent at times; merely a symbolic ritual in which solemn men of learning took part, but which had no power to harm either life or livelihood.

He had himself spoken bitterly about this, sitting with Frank in Pat Bachelli's chambers a week ago. He and Frank had traveled to the Cape together, driven efficiently by Amos, Frank's servant, for a final conference before the impending court hearing. Frank and the barrister had been discussing legal strategy, Frank with cool assessment, Bachelli apparently laconic. Charles de la Porte could not bring himself to like the young man, who had a supercilious manner and a sarcastic tongue.

Interrupting them, he had said: "To listen to you one might almost believe I had no choice. And that interpretation of my motives and my way of thinking is utterly incorrect. What I represent is a concept which is often forgotten, that of the doctor as friend. His concern is to prevent suffering more than to conquer death. And what I insist on is that the doctor must have a free hand to make his choice."

The others were both silent. They were sitting in sumptuously padded armchairs in Bachelli's very modern, very slick-magazine rooms. The barrister crossed his legs at the ankles and leaned back in his chair, contriving to look both bored and faintly amused.

Frank lifted a dark eyebrow slightly and looked out through the window. It was a beautiful, still Cape Town morning. From here one could see the harbor and the blue sweep of Table Bay beyond. A tug moved busily on some unknown errand, trailing a line of black smoke.

Finally Frank said: "You see, what they're claiming is that your acts constituted abuse of that freedom. No one is denying a doctor's right to make a choice."

"But the whole point is that the motive for my choice was to avoid suffering for my patient. It seems perfectly simple to

31

me. Why tie it up in legal mumbo jumbo?"

"Motives play a lesser role in the operation of the law than outsiders are perhaps aware," Frank said. "The law's principal function is the orderly assembly and organization of a series of facts. It is on facts that the judge will judge."

It was as close to a rebuke as he had come.

"If this was a case of 'Did you pick up that gun and pull the trigger and kill that man?' or of 'Did you forge that check and steal that hundred rand?' I would agree with you," Charles de la Porte told him obstinately. "But the central aspect of this case is a question of interpretation, of how one's judgment should be used. And if my motives are not taken into account it all becomes meaningless."

Bachelli uncrossed his legs, but maintained his expression of quiet scorn. "Most people who come into contact with the law reach that conclusion sooner or later, Doctor. That it consists of rigmarole, most of it meaningless."

"It seems like that to me. Everything is so"—he searched for the word— "studied. All these conventions one has to go through merely serve to confuse the issue. It's as if you're trying to force this case to alter shape, to conform to the pattern of all other cases, so that you can solve it by the same means. Well, it bloody well isn't like other cases. The law has arbitrarily decided that it has a right to give judgment on a question of medical ethics and as a result doctors from now on will have to bear this thought constantly in mind: Apart from what is right for the patient, what is right in the eyes of the law? I think that is an intolerable burden to place on them."

Frank rubbed his eyes tiredly. For some reason the gesture irritated Charles de la Porte. He thought briefly of their different lives: Frank's cosseted bachelor existence in the glass-walled penthouse of the apartment block which he owned, with Amos to cater for his every wish and the wealth and time to enjoy the leisurely processes of the law which he practiced; his own—hurried, congenitally sleepless, always only minutes ahead of the next urgent call, the next emergency, the next hurried decision. He forced the envious thought away and listened to what Frank was saying.

"To my mind one of the advantages of the law is that it removes such difficult matters from their setting, from the emotional frame into one of pure reason."

Bachelli had not been listening. He broke in, sounding very confident. "That's precisely what I maintain, Doctor. A court of law is not the proper forum for this. It's an improper action, improperly brought. That's one of the weapons up our sleeve. Medical ethics should be the sole concern of the Medical Council. I'll force the judge to recognize that."

"Medical matters seem to have become the concern of a lot of bright young lawyers these days," Charles de la Porte said.

Bachelli looked uncertain. He pulled at his drooping moustache, which was gingery in spite of his presumably Latin ancestry. "How do you mean?"

"There's money to be made from lawsuits against doctors, isn't there? A doctor is easy meat. He's often overworked. At times he has to treat patients under conditions far from ideal. Often he has to make instant decisions. But one mistake, the least little slip"—he mimed a downward swoop with one hand—"and down come the vultures."

Bachelli looked ruffled but did not say anything. Frank was silently contemplating the view.

Charles de la Porte addressed his friend directly. "It's an unpleasant thought, Frank, but one can't escape it. Look, I'm not saying everyone in medicine is perfect. But most of us are reasonably decent people, trying to serve our patients, trying to give them a little comfort, a longer life expectancy, a modicum of dignity when they die. And in contrast it seems to me there are a hell of a lot of lawyers out for all they can grab. They've even infected the patients. Trust is gone. There was a time when a doctor was your last ally. Now he seems to be the first source for easy money. Do you realize there's a full-scale crisis in medicine in the United States because of the threat of malpractice suits? Some doctors simply refuse to tackle any risky procedure whatsoever. And who suffers? The patients."

"I don't think you can fairly say that applies here in South Africa," Frank said with a touch of disapproval.

"I concede that. But it doesn't basically alter the fact that the law is being used to paralyze medicine. Let's take the example of a doctor driving past an accident scene. Out of a sense of humanity he stops. The victim has had a leg half torn off and the doctor has a battle to stop the bleeding. At that moment the bleeding is the gravest threat to the patient's life. But when they get him to the hospital and there's a chance to take X rays they find he also has a fractured skull. And it's not uncommon for doctors to be sued for missing that fracture." He shook his head. "To my mind medicine represents the valuable things in society, stable values, regard for others, that kind of thing. And what really sets my nerves on edge is that its destruction is being accomplished by this very civilized"—he put bite into his voice as he pronounced the word, then repeated it— "civilized process of civil actions. The law takes its course while the jungle waits."

"Have you considered that there are medical malpractice suits because there is medical malpractice?" Bachelli asked coldly.

"I'm not trying to seek protection for the fool or the incompetent who maybe reads an X ray back to front and removes a healthy kidney or who misses a subdural hematoma because he didn't bother to take an adequate history. But what about the man who missed that fractured skull because he was saving a patient from bleeding to death? Does he deserve to be thrown to the wolves?"

There was a brief, palpably hostile silence. Bachelli seemed about to say something hurtful, but Frank Edelstein held up a hand.

"You've obviously given this a lot of thought, Charles, and I understand why. The law is no more perfect than medicine, when it comes to that. If society is sick then the law will reflect that sickness."

"I understand that," Charles de la Porte said. "I suppose we're all victims of our times, aren't we? Doctor and patient alike."

Frank Edelstein looked at him with warmth and sympathy. The brittle feeling of discord was no longer in the room. Bachelli, as if anxious to make clear his own appreciation of a doctor's dilemma, leaned forward and gave a quick smile and said: "I'm still rather vague about Dr. Case's reasons for starting the action. All we really have to go on is her affidavit and that, as you've pointed out, follows the usual legal formula. Could you tell me a little more about her, Doctor?"

Charles de la Porte looked uncertainly at Frank.

"Has Mr. Edelstein not ... ?"

"Mr. Edelstein has given me information about her marriage and the amount of good work she does in your town and so forth. And of course it's a terrible tragedy and a great loss to the community. But you were her family doctor. You must know more about her than most people."

"Jay Case is a marvelous woman," Frank Edelstein said flatly.

Bachelli nodded, looking disconcerted at receiving an opinion from an unasked source, and said: "Quite so. I understand that. Nevertheless I would like Dr. de la Porte ..."

"And we'll get nowhere by attacking her character or integrity," Frank said in the same toneless voice. "It would only hurt the side which started it."

"Nevertheless," Bachelli said, obviously nettled and determined to reassert his position. "This has nothing to do with my conduct of the brief. I am simply interested in hearing Dr. de la Porte's assessment."

Frank was silent and after a hesitant pause Charles de la Porte said: "Oh, but I agree with Mr. Edelstein. Dr. Case is a marvelous person."

"In what sense?"

"How do you mean?"

"You say she's marvelous," Bachelli said with an irritating air of great patience. "But in what way? Her personality? The work she does?"

"Certainly. In both those ways."

"She's attractive, is she?"

"Attractive?"

"Yes. She is ... how old is she? Thirty-six, not so? Of course I have only seen a photograph, but ... ah ... I would say she is a long way from being repulsive. Would you agree?"

Charles de la Porte hesitated again, aware of the young

man's insistent stare. Then he said acidly: "Janice Case is a dying woman."

Bachelli started to make a gesture of waving aside the irrelevant but Charles de la Porte went on. "She is riddled with cancer. Her body is wasted beyond recognition. But for drugs being constantly administered she would be in great pain. She has suffered and is still suffering. But yes, I would say"—he imitated the barrister's faintly sneering tone— "she has always been a long way from being repulsive."

Bachelli, caught unprepared, had blushed deeply. He bit his lip and looked away. "Yes, quite. I beg your pardon. I . . . "

"And for your information I have always found her personally attractive, too."

Utterly routed, Bachelli made a gesture of shuffling together invisible papers and changed hurriedly to a safer line of questioning.

"The other side have made a big play of her good works. What exactly does she do?"

"Well, as you probably know Dr. Case's husband is a wealthy man. Mr. McOwen owns a large printing works as well as a chain of country newspapers. He is himself owner-editor of our little weekly paper."

"So I have been informed."

"Both of them are very charity-minded people. Dr. Case has done a great deal for child welfare and feeding schemes in the town, but her particular interest is geriatrics. Some years ago her husband helped finance the founding of a hospital-home for the aged which is one of the best in the country. She has been medical superintendent there since its foundation."

"Surely geriatrics is a strange choice for a comparatively young woman?"

Charles de la Porte exchanged glances with Frank. Then he shrugged. "That's hard to say. But I would think she was drawn to geriatrics precisely because it's a rather neglected field. Old people tend to get shoved aside. And Dr. Case has always been on the side of the underdog."

"You know her well?"

Charles de la Porte shrugged again. "I was the McOwens' family doctor. And I also acted as honorary surgeon to her hospital."

"Quite. That of course was why she came to see you."

"Yes."

"It still seems strange that she should have instigated this action. It seems out of character. Judging by the way you've described her, I mean. Everyone describes her as good and loving and so forth. And yet, facing death, she becomes vindictive. It's strange."

"Who's to say?"

"Could it possibly be the husband's influence?"

"I honestly don't know."

"Yes. And if you do know you're not telling." Bachelli smiled, and for the first time it was a smile of genuine amusement. It illuminated his blunt, rather fleshy features and made him almost handsome. The illusion, Charles de la Porte thought, was due to the gloss of youth, but that made it no less vivid. "Forgive me, Doctor," the young man was saying, "you must take me for an awful prying young prick." He paused, and it was hard to tell whether he was waiting for reaction to the deliberate crudity of his admission or for recognition that he had already turned the scale and changed his earlier defeat into victory. "Well, I won't get on my high horse and tell you to stuff your case if you won't take me into your confidence. Everyone is entitled to the privacy of his own thoughts."

Charles de la Porte stirred uncomfortably. "I've told you all I know."

"I'm sure you have," Bachelli said easily. "Then that disposes of that. Now I would like to deal with the circumstances around your decision not to tell Dr. Case that she had cancer. Your reasons, and so forth."

"Look, we've been through all this. My affidavit covers it very fully."

"The affidavit has been admirably well drawn up, certainly." Bachelli made a complimentary bob in the direction of Frank Edelstein, who did not respond. "But there's an element of . . . well, let's say I want to fill in the personal element. You will probably have to face cross-examination. I want to try to find the traps the other side might set for you."

Charles de la Porte made a grimace of reluctant acceptance. "Very well."

"Let's start with the report from your local pathologist. How did you react to it?"

"You've seen it, haven't you?"

"It's part of the court record."

"Well, it was brief and very specific. The diagnosis was invasive duct carcinoma."

"I have of course read quite extensively about this and other forms of cancer in the last couple of weeks. But I'd like you to tell me what you know about the disease."

Charles de la Porte decided it would be pointless to test the young man's claim to expert knowledge. He said: "It's an extensive subject. Would you like to know about the pathology or the clinical presentation?"

"Just some general features."

"Perhaps your reading will have informed you that it is the most common cancer in women. So if a woman presents with secondaries in the bone the first place one looks for the primary is the breast."

"That was why you were suspicious of those spine X rays?"

"Yes. Another feature is that it is usually the patient herself who discovers the lump. Frequently this happens while she is bathing."

"So it was unusual that you should first have detected it?"

"Very unusual. Especially as Janice Case is a doctor."

"Even a woman with no medical training could have done so?"

"Oh, yes. There are cancer detection clinics nowadays, you know. Women are taught how to check their breasts for abnormalities in the appearance of the nipple or the contour of the breasts. And for the presence of lumps, naturally."

"Would you tell me how this is done?"

"It's quite simple. They are taught to divide the breast into four quadrants and then to examine each quarter, first between the fingers and then with the flat of the hand. This is done both lying down and then sitting. It's best done while having a bath. A lump is identified more easily when the skin is wet."

"Dr. Case did not take these precautions?"

"No."

"So in the final analysis she could herself be blamed for her present condition. There was a degree of negligence on her part."

"Negligence? Well, I don't know. As she said to me herself one always feels it will never happen to you. For example, I see you're a heavy smoker. When last did you have your chest X-rayed?" He smiled to take the sting out of the comment.

Bachelli looked guilty and quickly stubbed out a newly lit cigarette. Then he smiled also, and relaxed. "Well, perhaps it's not very important, Doctor. Let's get back to the point. I take it the pathologist's findings confirmed your earlier suspicions."

"My fears, yes. Because of what I had seen on the X rays."

"Those X rays. I can see they're going to be an important factor in the case, so let's deal with them now. What were the circumstances?"

"What happened was that Dr. Case had mentioned to me in passing that she was troubled with backache. What a layman would term lumbago."

Bachelli asked quickly: "But she did not actually consult you about this condition?"

Charles de la Porte hesitated. "Not in a formal sense, no. She just happened to mention that her back was hurting."

"This was purely as part of a conversation? She did not come to your rooms complaining of backache?"

"No. In fact it happened while we were doing a ward round at her hospital."

Bachelli nodded, looking content. "Very well. And your suggestion on this occasion was that she should have an X ray done. But you had no means of knowing whether or not she followed your suggestion?"

"I had no idea. And she didn't mention it to me again. As a matter of fact I forgot about it, too, until, early in February, I happened to be in the X-ray department at our hospital, talking to the chief radiographer about something. I think Dr. Case's name was mentioned, and then he asked me whether she was my patient. I told him she was and he went to his files and hunted out those plates. What apparently happened was that she had examined them herself and passed them as NAD."

"What does that mean?"

"Nothing abnormal detected."

"I see. That was a slip on her part, obviously. You will have noticed that the other side say nothing about this in their replying affidavit. And of course it's doubtful whether we will have the chance to question her about it."

There was a degree of callousness, of calculating the chances, about the comment which, for a moment, both startled and silenced Charles de la Porte.

"Please continue, Doctor," Bachelli said. "The radiographer showed you these plates."

"Yes. I had a quick glance at them and superficially there seemed to be nothing wrong. Then he asked whether I wanted them for my records. He didn't have space for them and the alternative would have been to destroy them. So I took them."

"And then, when you looked at them again . . . "

"I looked at them again in my consulting rooms."

"And you spotted what everyone else had missed." The barrister's voice had risen, as if with deep satisfaction that a worthy climax had been reached and virtue had triumphed.

"It wasn't quite that, really," Charles de la Porte protested. "Besides myself only Dr. Case and the technician had seen the plates. There was the merest trace of something amiss. I might easily have overlooked it as well."

"The fact is that you did not, however. What you had detected was evidence of the spread of cancer, the metastases. Is that the correct word?"

"Yes. But naturally I could not be sure at that stage that it was a secondary, or even that I was dealing with a carcinoma at all. All I had was a faintly suspicious shadow on the X ray and a history of backache. It could have been any of a number of things."

"But you pinned it on carcinoma."

"Eventually. The correct thing to do under these circumstances, that is if you find a suspicious lesion in a bone, is to look for the primary source. The most common cancers which do spread to the bone are those of the breast, lung, and kidney and in the male the prostate and in women the uterus and cervix. So I persuaded Dr. Case to let me examine her."

"How did you manage that without explanations?"

"As I've told you I acted as surgical consultant to her hospital. During that week she happened to bring one of her patients to see me, an old gentleman with prostate trouble, and after I had examined him I suggested that she might as well have a checkup, too."

"And you found this lump?"

"Yes."

"You then decided to perform this operation, this"— Bachelli glanced at his notes— "excision biopsy."

"Correct. I did it the following afternoon."

"The operation went normally?"

"The operation procedure was perfectly normal, yes. But of course the result was not so good. As soon as I had cut the tumor out and was able to examine it I was sure it was cancer. A scirrhous carcinoma cuts with a characteristic gritty feel and the cut surface has a very characteristic appearance. It looks rather like cartilage, with white strands running through it."

"Nevertheless, you sent it to the pathologist."

"I took it to our local firm of pathologists myself the next morning."

"And the report came back and it said that Dr. Case's condition was malignant. Now, what is the usual procedure in confirmed cases of carcinoma of the breast?"

"Radical mastectomy, usually. Complete removal of the breast and nipple, as well as the two pectoral muscles and the lymph nodes which drain the breast. However, I must point out that there is a difference of opinion about this. Some authorities prefer to do a simple mastectomy, which of course is still a

41

mutilating operation, and then follow this up with irradiation therapy."

"Radium, is it?"

"No, no. Not radium. X-ray therapy. Or a cobalt bomb is used. But it's called irradiation as a general term."

"However, you did not follow the usual line of treatment?"

"No."

"Why not?"

An uncanny feeling of already being in the witness box, already facing the barrage of hostile and guileful questions, mastered Charles de la Porte. So intense was the fantasy that he could almost smell that depressing odor which clung to old courtrooms, as if long contact with life's petty defeats produced secret and noxious gases found nowhere else. He put his hands on the padded leather of the armchair rests to reassure himself that he was not sitting on a hard wooden bench.

"Because bone metastases were already present," he said.

"In other words, the cancer had already spread to the spine, so surgery was out of the question?"

"That about sums it up. If I had discovered it earlier I would have removed the breast. Then there would have been hope. Even at that stage, when I did the operation, there had been no clinical evidence of lymphatic spread. But obviously the cancer had already spread through the bloodstream to the bones and, God only knew, perhaps to other parts of the body. No, it was too late to do anything about it. Too late to ... " He forgot what he had intended saying and instead said again: "Too late."

"Now tell me, Dr. de la Porte, what were your first reactions on reading the report?"

"It only told me what I already knew. But I had been hoping against hope that I was wrong. It seemed a very cruel thing to have happened to someone so young and full of life."

"Quite. But what did you do?"

"I looked through all the latest literature on carcinoma of the breast. All the articles in the medical journals I could lay my hands on, hoping I could ... I don't really know what I was hoping for."

"You make a practice of keeping up to date with medical literature?" Bachelli's tone was approving and Charles de la Porte wondered if the young man knew how patronizing he sounded.

"Yes," he said shortly.

"Then, I remember from your affidavit you asked for a second opinion. Why?"

"I suppose I was reluctant to accept the finality of the findings. At my request our pathologist sent the slides to the professor of pathology at the medical school."

Bachelli put his fingers together in a judicial pose. He said: "It seems to me that Dr. Case has little to complain about. You obviously had her welfare very much at heart. I don't believe the most demanding patient could have expected more than you did."

Charles de la Porte looked away.

Obviously slightly disappointed that his performance had received no better response, Bachelli went on. "The second report was negative, too?"

"Positive. Positive for carcinoma."

Again Bachelli looked flustered. "Yes. Quite. I meant negative in the sense that ... Anyway, the news was bad?"

"It was a confirmation of the first report."

"And your next step?"

"I consulted various colleagues. A surgeon in Cape Town who actually specializes in breast cancer and also members of the breast clinic at the university hospital. I wanted to know what they would have done, placed in my situation."

"What was their advice?"

"Oh, they were definitely opposed to surgery. No mistake about that. But on further treatment opinions differed. Some favored irradiation. But most of them, especially those from the breast clinic, preferred hormonal treatment."

"And that was what you finally decided on?"

43

"It was the form of treatment which could best be disguised. I did not want Dr. Case to discover what was wrong with her. And of course, being a doctor herself, if I had ordered her on X-ray therapy she would have known at once what was going on."

"Ah. Now we come to the point at issue. You did not want her to know she had cancer. Why not?"

"I thought about it very long and hard and came to the decision that it would be more merciful to say nothing."

"Not to tell her?"

"No."

"Nor her husband?"

"Cliff McOwen is a peculiar man. He would not have been able to keep it from her."

Bachelli looked at him with an air of sharp triumph. "Peculiar? Why do you say that?"

Charles de la Porte considered his reply. "Perhaps 'peculiar' is putting it too strongly. But he has very strong feelings about certain things. Secrecy is one of them. He is apt to go up in flames at any suggestion that something is being kept from him. Perhaps it's part of his journalistic background. I don't know. I've heard him expound on this very subject, that of whether or not to tell a man he is dying. It was at a hospital party a couple of years ago and naturally there were a number of doctors present. Cliff didn't mince words. He called us the new priesthood. A cabal who resented truth and relished being able to deal in life and death. That kind of thing. He'd had a few drinks and he was very eloquent."

"So it was because of his views you didn't tell him?"

"Yes. If he had followed his declared philosophy he would immediately have told her. And I wanted her not to know."

Bachelli looked faintly incredulous. "But surely? If the welfare of his wife was concerned?"

Charles de la Porte gave a dry cough. "You would need to know him to understand. He is a very . . . emotional man."

"Sounds unbalanced to me."

Charles de la Porte shrugged.

"We'll leave it at that," Bachelli said. "Now, you've said you believed it more merciful not to tell her. Could you elaborate on your reasons, please?"

"I don't believe anyone should be told he or she has cancer. People who can take that news with equanimity are very rare indeed."

"Don't you think a patient has a right to know?"

"I prefer to consider the *need* to know. You might find someone with complicated arrangements to make and in such a case I would make an exception. But even then I'd be hesitant, especially if I had little or nothing to offer. And as far as Dr. Case was concerned there was no doubt in my mind. She had no need to know."

"Can one treat someone with this condition without telling him?"

"Naturally it depends on the intelligence of the patient. And on the form of treatment. If you subject them to a course of irradiation there's no way to hide it. They get very sick, you know. And it would be quite impossible to keep the truth from a doctor."

"Your idea was to keep her under observation without her realizing it?"

"Yes. I put her on androgens. That is, treatment with a male hormone."

"Is this a recognized form of treatment?"

"Yes, certainly. Especially when there are bone secondaries. Quite often one is able to arrest the spread of metastases and with luck you even get regression of the growth. But of course it's not a cure. And in her case I fear it had no effect."

"I assume Dr. Case asked you about the pathological finding?"

"She telephoned me two days after the operation and asked about it. I had then not yet made up my mind what to do and I put her off by saying I had not received the path report."

Bachelli stroked the side of his nose contemplatively. "I see. And after you received the report?"

"I went to see her. I lied to her. I told her it was negative."

"You believe your decision was the right one?"

"Implicitly. You see, Jay Case continued to live without dread for a while at least. It's sad that it could only be for six months. It might easily have been a year or two or even longer. But at least she's had those six months."

"While you carried the burden of secrecy."

"Better me than her."

"You think it's part of a doctor's duty to carry that burden?"

The barrister's dramatic tone irritated Charles de la Porte. He said, deliberately emotionless: "Look, it's quite simple. It's all very well talking about the patient's right to know. Perhaps it is true that knowledge is better than doubt. But it's my experience that the only things we really want to be told are the things we'd like to be told. Tell us the news, by all means, provided the news is good."

Bachelli was undeterred. "Fine, Doctor. I know I can make the judge see it that way. It's the doctor who must decide. If he's willing to shoulder the burden he must be left free to make the choice." He turned to Frank Edelstein and shook his head. "They don't stand a chance. And they know it. The proof is in the way they've brought the action. Obviously they saw they had no hope to prove negligence. Nor could they claim *injuria* on the grounds of lack of informed consent. So the best they could do was this nebulous claim. There's no basis for it in law." His manner had become brisk, as if victory was already in sight. "Now, Doctor, please let's go into the circumstances of Dr. Case's discovery of the truth and subsequent events."

Charles de la Porte said: "How she discovered the truth. Yes."

3

The deviation was marked with red triangles and a row of oil drums on which red lights winked warningly. Charles de la Porte slowed his car to a crawl as he left the tar and jolted through the first of the series of potholes. The headlights moved searchingly across the clutter of big machines pulled up alongside the road. Bulldozers, graders, ditchdiggers, and other yellow-painted hulks of indeterminate purpose stood there in random confusion, as if abandoned at the onset of sudden catastrophe. Immobile in the dark, lit in passing by the car's lights, they seemed to him doubly sinister. Irritation at the state of the road was reinforced until it became genuine hatred.

Ridiculous, of course, to make machines a personification of human folly and to vent your anger against a bulldozer. But there it was.

The great hills above the town were particularly lovely. Vineyards covered the lower slopes and beyond them were granite cliffs where cedars grew. The road machinery had come to change all this. A freeway had been designed to pass through the hills and to cut across the valley where the town lay. The road would carry six lanes of traffic between the coast and the North. In spite of an intensive protest campaign and a press hue and cry the roads authorities were unmoved. The road would be built exactly as and where the engineers had decreed.

He gained the tar at the far end of the deviation and drove faster.

The road department's intransigence was typical of the situation in the country, he thought. Bureaucrats made the decisions and were astounded when the people disagreed. But the hell with the people. The planners always knew best.

47

Uneasy doubt wormed into his mind. Was that not your attitude toward Jay? Did you not also claim to know best?

Surely it was not comparable? He had been moved by regard for another's feelings, by grief and compassion, not by stubborn desire to exert power.

He buried the thought hurriedly and concentrated on the road ahead. Its winding way followed the irregular boundaries of the farms on either side and it was narrow, for the old wine farmers who had driven their wagons along it had been reluctant to waste precious acreage on a profitless road. Now it was in poor repair, for, lulled by the prospect of the freeway, the local board had cut the funds for upkeep. And yet the twisty little country road had charm which its ruler-straight successor would never have.

But, Charles de la Porte thought, I suppose that once the thing is there, I, like all the others who are so vociferously shocked by its coming, will drive on it, too. We'll be seduced by its smoothness, its engineered curves, by speed and comfort, by the luxury of being only five minutes from town, less than two hours from the Cape. That's why the bureaucrats always win in the end: what they offer us seems so reasonable, so sweet with promise, that we lose the capacity to judge.

He had been a founder member of a group with the belligerent acronym SOC, standing, somewhat ambivalently, for Save Our Cedars. Composed mainly of landowners who saw the projected road as a threat to peace and serenity, the organization had led the protest. Meetings had been organized at which scientists and conservationists had preached to the converted; the press campaign had been launched; a fund-raising drive had proved almost embarrassingly successful.

At times he had felt awkward, even ashamed, about the untiring effort and devotion to a cause which really aimed no higher than the rescue of a couple of square miles of natural hillside. One could not help but note that the old road up the valley passed the monotonous rows of boxlike houses, painted in rainbow hues in a futile attempt to make them appear individual, where the town's Coloured people lived their separate lives. Were a handful of cedars or an unspoiled stream, some bird and animal life, a couple of waterfalls, and trout in a still pool more important than the thousands of mortals who rode a daily bus along the narrow road? Should SOC find a nobler cause and change itself to Save Our Coloureds?

He imagined, with a certain grim pleasure, the discomfited and even genuinely indignant response such a suggestion would evoke from the worthy workers for cedar trees. Indignant, perhaps, with good reason. It was a fact that most of those who best served the committee were correspondingly earnest in their attitude toward people of a different color. John Cilliers, for example. It was no secret that he was a supporter of the Nationalist Government. But he was also a leader in the campaign among agricultural associations to improve housing for black farm workers. Then there was Clark Denisson, ex-British Army, ex-Kenya Highlands, with a manner to match. And yet it was he who had donated most of the money for the public hall in the Coloured township where cinema shows were held every weekend with the use of a projector given by Bob French, a third member of the committee. All these were good men with good intentions, who did practical things to improve relations between the races. Then why did one always come away with that feeling of unease, with the taint of distant guilt which no nobility of purpose ever quite eradicated?

He tried consciously to state his own feelings, but his thoughts became a contradictory jumble in which for some reason there loomed large the image of a Coloured woman whose name he could not immediately recall, a methylated spirits addict who had been his patient and who had died six months ago of cirrhosis of the liver.

And finally he thought about Janice Case, who was dying.

But she had seemed very much alive to him on that day. She had been wearing a short-sleeved linen dress with a pattern of crimson blossoms and there was an air of youth and vitality about her. She had walked beside him along a graveled path lined with real blossoms and her impatient, long-limbed stride had kept her constantly half a pace ahead.

They came to a fork in the path and she gestured to the right, toward a many-windowed building set back a little from the line of other similar buildings.

"This way. We've had to move her to the Annex."

Charles de la Porte glanced up quickly and caught the faint grimace.

"Oh? Is it that bad?"

"It's not so good. I inserted an indwelling catheter to try to do something about her incontinence. But it seems as if she regards it as a sexual insult. She's taken to smearing feces all over her face. We had to put her where the nurses can keep an eye on her."

He made a sound of distress. "Poor old girl."

"Yes. And what makes it especially sad is that one remembers what she was like when she came here. Do you remember, Charles?"

"I do. I saw her then for a fractured femur, didn't I?"

"That was why she was admitted. But even so she was an absolute fashion plate, even at the age of nearly ninety. Had her hair done once a week. Nothing delighted her more than a new dress."

"I remember when I came to see her she was having her nails manicured by one of the nurse's aides."

"The stroke changed all that. She's as helpless as a newborn infant. Worse than that, for at least a baby has life ahead of it. Mrs. Barrett has nothing. Not even the memory of the life she's had. She would be better dead." She shivered slightly and smiled at him as he stopped to allow her to precede him up the shallow steps which led to an enclosed sun terrace. "Am I being morbid on a beautiful day? Cliff would say that. He believes that contemplation of death is morbid at any time."

"You can't really escape it here, can you?"

"No."

A handful of old people sat in a sun-filled corner of the porch and she moved toward them. Two were in wheelchairs; the rest sat in a row on a padded bench. She talked to them

50

animatedly, rounding her words to make them distinct.

"Good morning, Mrs. Brink. How do you feel this morning? Good morning, Mr. Webster." She bent to retrieve a blanket which was slipping from arthritis-twisted hands. "Morning, Mrs. Potgieter."

Charles de la Porte watched as the faces of the old people were turned toward her. They showed, beneath the surface similarity which age created, a variety of expressions: welcome, curiosity, a childish pleasure, petulance, the blankness of incomprehension. But there was a further common factor which lay deeper even than the wrinkles and minor disfigurements and loss of hair pigment which they shared. It was a stillness which was more than placidness. It was the attitude, he recognized with a small shock, of people who were waiting.

Janice Case came back to him.

He said to her in a low voice: "Are they always like that? Do they always sit so still?"

She turned to look wonderingly at the small group and then at him. "Why, no. They move around. Those who are able." Then she appeared to grasp the meaning of what he had asked. "They are quiet, aren't they? But you must remember that ours is a small world, Charles. The world has shrunk around us."

They moved out of the sun's heat into the cool foyer.

"Are they afraid of death?" he was forced to ask.

She gave him her ambiguous, hooded look.

"Who isn't? I don't think they are any more afraid than any of us."

"Still. I wouldn't like to end up like that, with nothing left to me except to wait. Doesn't it depress you, always being with them?"

"I get depressed at times. But you know it isn't the thought of death itself. The awful part is the process of dying. When it comes to me I hope it comes quickly."

He shied away from the subject. "Is the Lions Club still running a film show for the old folks?"

"Yes. They look forward to it all week. Mind you, attendance has dropped since TV started. I'll have to persuade them

51

to bring *Gone With the Wind* around again."

They laughed, but he returned to his sudden obsession as if it were a fresh scab at which his fingers could not keep from picking.

"Anything to keep their minds occupied, I suppose. After all, what are their needs, apart from bed and food? Isn't it ironic how one goes back full circle, back to the only things that mattered when you were a child?"

"There are a few who are reduced to that kind of existence. But the number isn't really all that high. You'd be surprised how much fun a lot of them get out of life."

"Do you ever have cases of old people committing suicide?"

"You know, it's a funny thing. That's very rare. When I was working at the geriatric hospital in Durban we had one case, one old lady who talked about throwing herself out of the window. But she never actually tried it."

"It's the young who kill themselves."

"Perhaps they think they have a prescriptive right to despair. Whereas old people can come to terms with it because they must."

"True."

"We did have one old lady here a couple of years ago who decided that the time had come for her to die. And what she did was to starve herself to death."

"Good grief. You didn't tell me about that."

"I was upset about it. But later I came to see things more clearly and I could see that she was right."

"What was wrong with her?"

"Arteriosclerosis. Well, that was the diagnosis we wrote down, but she was simply very old. Nevertheless she knew what was going on around her. You could get through to her. But then she developed a wound on her arm which became infected in spite of everything we did and eventually she developed cellulitis and when that happened she decided it was time to go. The sisters wanted her to eat and drink but she refused. Finally we decided: No, we wouldn't force her. She hung on for a day and a half, almost two days, and in that time she had no more than a cup of milk. And finally she died."

"That was what she wanted."

"Yes. She knew what she wanted."

They turned a corner and came to a room where a woman in a starched uniform sat writing behind a desk. She smiled a welcome.

"Good morning, Doctor. Good morning, Dr. de la Porte."

"Morning, matron," Janice Case said. "Dr. de la Porte has come to see Mrs. Barrett. Have you got the admissions list for me?" She turned slightly, holding the form so that he could read it over her shoulder. His eyes skimmed past names, which were merely labels, and hunted for the facts of disease, which were important.

Age ninety-one. Right hemiplegia and fractured right humerus.

Age seventy-seven. Congestive cardiac failure.

Age eighty-nine. Ischemic heart disease, colostomy, and CA rectum.

Janice Case and her staff would never cure these. They were all dying, with the only distinction that some were dying faster than others.

They turned to go and he said to her, casually, almost as if it was an afterthought: "Oh, by the way, that path report came in this morning."

She stopped. She did not look at him.

"And?"

"It was as I told you. You've got nothing to worry about."

Her expression did not change but, briefly, her lips parted as if she had snatched at a breath. She turned toward him at last.

"Thank you," she said. "Thank you, Charles."

"Nothing to worry about," Charles de la Porte said again, with a careful smile.

Until a moment before he had not known whether or what to tell her.

4

The living-room curtains were drawn and his wife was sitting, very erect and poised, in a straight chair opposite the empty fireplace. She had the slim, controlled body of a natural athlete and the ability to look relaxed even in attitudes of physical discomfort. She looked up as he came in and put down the book she was reading.

"Hello, darling. I didn't hear the car."

He kissed her on the forehead.

"I had to come around the back. There was a wheelbarrow in the middle of the drive."

She uttered an exclamation of annoyance and got to her feet.

"That damn Jan. I've told him a million times to put the tools away before he knocks off work."

"Leave it. I'll put the thing away before I go to bed."

Always acutely sensitive to mood, she read his voice accurately. "Difficult day?" she asked with sympathy. She crossed the room toward a built-in cupboard with high, arched doors. "I'll get you a drink. Scotch?"

"Please. Soda, if we have any."

She brought his drink and her own glass of sherry to where he was leaning against the mantelpiece. She rested a hand briefly on his as she gave him the glass. "We'll eat fairly soon, shall we?" She glanced at the clock over the mantelpiece. "At half past. I'll warn Dora."

"Whenever you like. I'm not particularly hungry."

"It's very light. I managed to get a couple of fresh soles in town today."

"Sounds tempting."

"Oh, and your new Paul Scott novel has come. I left it in your study with the rest of the mail."

"Good. I'll have a look after dinner. Was there anything else in the mail?"

"Nothing much. Advertisements and junk."

The calm domesticity of their conversation soothed him, as she had known it would. She talked on, of the state of the rose garden and the pool with cascade she had designed and planned to build with the help of one of the two Coloured men who cultivated their small remaining vineyard. Charles de la Porte sipped his drink slowly and listened to her clear, beautiful actress's voice and felt weariness drain away like muddied water in a pond into which a fresh stream had begun to flow. He started to make observations and suggestions of his own.

"What was the wheelbarrow doing in the drive?" he asked.

"I had Jan put a couple of loads of gravel on it. It was in a bit of a mess near the gate."

"The road up from town is in a state, too. Especially where the freeway people have their deviation."

She looked momentarily startled and bit her lower lip. "Gosh. Just as well you mentioned the road. I saw John Cilliers in town this morning. He wanted me to remind you there's a SOC meeting on Wednesday evening."

"Wednesday? Of next week?"

"Yes."

He looked doubtful.

"I don't know. I may still ... I may be in Cape Town."

"I told him you might be away."

"Anyway, it's probably best if I stay away. Cliff will probably be there."

There was a strained silence between them, an unease at being obliged to face an awkward and unwanted topic, but one which refused to go away altogether.

She asked: "Is it likely?"

"Knowing him, he's not going to be daunted into staying away."

"I suppose not."

Again that silence. Gillian de la Porte broke it eventually. "I met other people in town, too."

Alerted by something odd in her voice, he looked up. She had a stubborn, almost defiant look.

"Hm?"

"I said I met other people. And everyone is on your side, Charles. You're not to think differently. They all think the McOwens have done a mean thing."

"You're neglecting the human tendency to enjoy a scandal."

"Now you're crawling in behind that sardonic, surprised-by-nothing shell of yours. Do you think people don't realize you do it simply to avoid being hurt?" She half-laughed and made a gesture of despairing acceptance. "Oh, Charles! After ten years. Do you think I don't know you by now?"

Taken aback, not so much by the insight as by its essential misdirection, he said: "I suspect public opinion will eventually depend largely on the outcome of the action." He shrugged. "People prefer others to make their moral decisions for them."

She was watching him with the cat's-eye scrutiny which he knew by experience to be the prelude to her most devastating salvoes.

Then she asked: "Are you worried, Charles?"

He feigned nonchalance. "Not particularly. I believe I did the right thing."

She shook her head. "Nevertheless, I can see you are. Well, you musn't be. You'll see."

"Everything will come right on the night, eh?" He laughed. "You theater people are always either down in the depths or wildly optimistic." He knew that it irritated her to be teased about her stage career and he added quickly: "I'm not really worried. Frank and young Bachelli believe we have a sound case. But I suppose I can't help thinking that the outcome might depend on whether or not the judge likes my face."

"What will happen if you lose?"

He had ceased to wonder at her ability to change direction in midstride or to make hard, even callous calculations.

"It won't be pleasant."

"Don't try to put me off. What exactly would the implications be?"

"Well, for one thing I couldn't continue to practice here. Geoff and I would have to dissolve the partnership and I'd have to go somewhere else. But I don't know whether I would care to go on with the practice of medicine at all, anywhere."

"Don't be absurd, darling."

"Do you think that's absurd? Do you think I could live with a kind of medicine which is a negation of everything I've always believed in?"

"One only lives with oneself."

Was there a subtle shadow to her voice, a veiled reproof which, persisted with, forced into frank recognition, would lead to a scene he did not wish for? He was disinclined to find out, so he said: "And of course the financial aspect is not inconsiderable. Let's assume the court awards them half their claim. Legal minds seem to dwell on large sums these days. Let's say they get fifty thousand. And there would be costs for both sides. I don't really know, but let's put it at another ten. That's sixty thousand."

"Doesn't your insurance cover this kind of thing?"

"I've never carried malpractice insurance. I've never believed in it. My feeling is that a doctor can't be guilty of malpractice if he has treated a patient to the best of his ability." He gave a short, humorless laugh. "Now it seems everyone is at pains to prove me wrong." He regretted the note of self-pity at once. "Frankly, the notion that I might have to face this kind of court action in this country never even occurred to me."

"How much money do we have?" she asked calmly.

He laughed, not without effort.

"We're not fabulously wealthy, Jilly my love. And there are drains, of course. This place, for instance, has never shown a profit. And then there's Paul to think about. Let's put it this way: I'm not in a position where sixty thousand, either way, won't make a difference."

"You could always borrow it from Frank. He wouldn't miss it."

He pretended to give the thought serious consideration. "It's a lot of money, even to Frank. And one has to consider whether he would want to lend it to me. Not to mention whether I would want to borrow it from him."

"If you can't carry on practicing here I suppose we would have to sell this place."

She seemed unalarmed by the possibility and again he realized that he would never fully understand the processes by which she reasoned. Women's nerves run deeper, he thought. And their minds prepare them for the suffering their natures anticipate.

"I would fight damn hard to avoid having to sell Hoog-in-het-Dal," he said evenly, as if he had long ago dismissed the possibility. "For one thing, it would be a terrible blow to my mother."

"Yes. Of course."

Mercifully, mention of his mother put her thoughts on another tack.

"You haven't told me when you're planning to go down to the Cape."

"Sunday evening, I think."

"Wouldn't you rather leave early on Monday morning."

"I dare say I could. The court only sits at about ten. But I thought it would save you a rush on Monday."

She waved away the idea of a rush on Monday being inconvenient.

"Are you staying at the hotel or with Mother?"

"At the Mount Nelson. It's just a walk from the Supreme Court. And I wouldn't like to bother my mother at a time like this."

"Your mother thrives on being bothered."

He smiled at the thought of his mother's encumbrances: the secretaryship of the ailing Poetry Society, the Mountain Lovers Club (irreverent fancies of orgies on the slopes of Table Mountain always intruded into his mind when she spoke about the latter), and all the other obscure organizations which had replaced the great causes of her youth. Small, spare, and immensely energetic, at seventy-nine she still drove herself in her own car to one meeting after another; still stood on street corners rattling coins in a tin at reluctant passersby; still led startled guests on foot tours of the beloved city where she had been born and, on her husband's death and her son's remarriage ten years ago, had happily returned as if the intervening decades in a country town had been no more than an interlude.

"I know. Nevertheless, I think it would be best at the hotel."

"All right. I'll do your packing on Sunday morning in any event."

"There's no need. I'll do it myself before I leave."

Gillian nodded and rose, putting down her glass. "Get yourself another drink while I'm in the kitchen. I won't be long."

He poured a small tot of whisky, filling his glass to the top with soda water. He balanced the glass on a chair rest while he reached for the cigarette packet. He hesitated, then put the cigarettes away unopened.

Glass in hand he walked through to his study, a long narrow room opening off the hallway, with books on both longer walls, windows, now shuttered, on both the others. He knew in his mind's eye what he would see in daylight, with the shutters open: at the front, the long descending slope of the valley with the white buildings of the town at its foot; at the back, the upper vineyard of Hoog-in-het-Dal and then other vineyards, rising in layer after layer until the final sharp demarcation where green ended and the blue hills began. Two views familiar to the point of being commonplace since his earliest remembering, they had never paled for him. Of all the rooms in the old house this was his favorite. His grandfather had left the original beams when he rebuilt the house and in the study, a kitchen long ago, they were smoke-blackened and ran transversely, giving an illusion of even greater depth. His father had used this room, too, and he left it unchanged when his own turn had come. There were no pictures or any other decoration: only the two walls of books and the windows facing on two magnificent views.

On his desk was the novel Gillian had spoken about,

holding down a pile of mail. He picked up the book, looked at the glossy dust cover, read the publisher's blurb, hefted its promising bulk with the pleasure of anticipation.

The telephone rang.

He was long inured to its shrill summons, but was nevertheless startled and slopped his drink. He put down the glass, mopped hastily at the puddle with a handkerchief, and reached for the receiver.

"Hello. De la Porte."

There was the sound of distant connections, then a high-pitched humming.

"Hello," he said again.

"Hi," his son's voice said immediately.

"Oh, hello, Paul."

"Hi, Dad."

They went through the conventions of "How are you?" and "Fine, how are you?" then Paul asked: "Did you get my letter?"

"Unless you're speaking about the one you wrote at the start of the winter term, no, I haven't."

Paul laughed, but there was an edge of tension. "I guess you wouldn't have got it yet. I posted it yesterday."

"Perhaps that's asking a bit much of our superefficient postal service." The jocular tone was a strain and he abandoned it. "How are your studies?"

Paul laughed again, with the same awkwardness. "That's what the letter was about. Sort of."

"Was the subject of the Navy mentioned by any chance?"

"Well, yeah. Actually that was what I wrote about."

"And I assume you said you would prefer to give up medicine and go back to the Navy?"

"Yeah, that was it, more or less."

"Look, son, we've been through this before. All I'm asking is that you should give university a fair trial. You've got a good brain and I think it would be wasted in the Navy." He heard his son, at the far end of the line, make sounds of incipient interruption and probable disagreement and he hardened his

60

voice. "Getting you into medical school wasn't easy and, frankly, you'd be a damn fool to quit now."

"I've heard all the arguments, Dad, but damn it, I'm over twenty-one. I have a right to live my own life."

"No one has suggested that you have not," Charles de la Porte said stiffly. "All I ask is that you don't quit before you've even written your first-year exams."

"I'm going to fail. I know it."

Charles de la Porte picked up the trace of panic in his son's voice, remote and machine-borne as it was. Immediately he was reminded of Paul as a small boy, trying to appear impassive in moments of trepidation, when only a squeak in his voice would betray his real feelings.

"I'm sure you won't fail," he said more gently. "Your test results have been very good. Everyone gets into a flap before the exams."

"I bet you never did."

If there was an acid note about the comment, Charles de la Porte pretended not to notice.

"Look," he said, "I'll be down in Cape Town next week."

Paul's voice changed again, to alertness and concern. "Oh. For the court case?"

"Yes."

"They haven't withdrawn?"

"No. It's going ahead."

"And I think *I've* got problems!" Paul said wryly. "Anyway, good luck with it."

"Thank you. As I was saying, I shall be in the Cape from Monday onward. We can have dinner one evening and talk about this again."

"Okay, Dad."

"I'll ring you, shall I? After classes on Monday."

"That'll be okay."

"Good. Good-bye, Paul."

"Bye."

Charles de la Porte stood holding the receiver for a moment after the connection was broken. He heard his wife's voice calling. He replaced the receiver.

"Aren't you too tired, darling?" she asked.

"No," he said.

There was a teasing, below-the-surface chuckle in her voice. "I'm sure you're much too tired."

The night was warm and they had thrown off the blankets. They lay covered only by a sheet. Her hands moved under the sheet. Suddenly she laughed outright.

"Gosh! You're not tired at all!"

He laughed, too. Her occasional private shamelessness was part of their life together, evidence of their self-sufficiency and indifference to outside opinion. Tonight he perhaps needed it more than usual and she had sensed this and knew how to fill the need.

She came to him with warmth and loving kindness which soon became transformed into passion. They made love and afterward talked gently in the dark.

He woke, and he had been dreaming about his first wife, Antoinette, and he had been making love, too, but without joy. Their bodies were contorted in some freakish position, but he could see her closed eyes which at that moment had opened and looked darkly into his. Time and again, frustratingly, they had reached the point of orgasm, only to have it flow away like a tide ebbing over ribbed sand. They had beat their bodies together in sadness and remorse and then her face had changed into that of another woman with short-cropped blond hair and unknown to him. As he woke he knew that the dream had started far beyond the lovemaking episode, that there had been a labyrinth of doors opening on other doors, and that there were profound reasons for his being there. But the memory slipped beyond reach and all that was left to him was making love with Antoinette and her despair.

The wind had started to blow; he could hear the sad sea sound of it in the trees. Gillian had rolled away from him, far over to her side of the bed. He pushed himself up onto an elbow and looked at the luminous hands of the clock. Just after two. When he woke like this it was often around four. He thought of a phrase he had once read or heard: In the dark hour of the human soul it is always half past four in the morning. He could not be sure of the origin or the accuracy of the quotation, but certainly the thought was close to the mark. Many nurses, and doctors, too, for that matter, believed that this hour of the night was the low ebb of human life, that it was in the dark hours before dawn that most patients gave up and died. Was there any truth in the legend? Could there be a physiological or a psychological explanation?

He hoped he would not lie awake now, plagued by night phantoms. The trick was not to think. Not to think. Especially not about Antoinette. Or about Janice Case.

He felt himself slide toward oblivion and, perversely, his mind brought itself back from the edge, into full consciousness.

He remembered a day he had spent on the beach with Antoinette and her daughter. It was before they were married and the child had been small then, three or four. They had been very happy, sitting on the beach while the child, totally engrossed, played with a handful of shells. He had taken them for lunch at the ramshackle little beachfront hotel and Antoinette had wanted to sit outside, on the terrace overlooking the sea. There had been a low hedge of some brambly plant along the edge of the terrace and as they walked to their table they alarmed a bird which had been inside the hedge. He was uncertain what species it was but it was very small, obviously a fledgling of some kind of land bird, a robin perhaps, or a wagtail. The startled bird flew out of the hedge and flapped away over the rocks. There was an offshore wind. They saw the bird turn and try to fly toward the beach. But the wind was too strong for its unskilled wings. Already it had been blown out over the sea. Antoinette made a small sound of pain. They stood watching the bird struggle vainly against the southwesterly wind. Soon it was out of sight. They did not see it go down into the ocean.

Antoinette had put the incident into a poem two or three years later but had never showed it to him and he had only read it in her second collection, the one published shortly before she died. "Bird Falling" was the title piece of the volume and the instant he saw the name on the unpretentious dust cover he was jolted back to the hotel terrace in the moment before the bird had flown. He could feel the sun on his neck and the trickle of sweat down under his shirt and hear the slow hiss of surf on the rocks beneath the terrace. He remembered that he had been pleasantly hungry. The child was holding his hand. They had rinsed the sand off her hands in a rock pool and he could even remember the cool stickiness of the small hand in his. Then the bird had flown out of the hedge.

He and Antoinette had been living in Cape Town when her book appeared. He was doing his fellowship then and was in his final year as surgical registrar. A month later she had been killed, traveling with Marianne in a car through the mountain passes south of the Karroo. The car had left the road on a hairpin bend and had fallen almost vertically two hundred feet down a cliff face. She and the child must both have died instantly.

He had gone to the place himself. He had stood beside the road, looking at the fresh scars over the gravel verge and the gap in the low parapet. Then he had looked down the long drop at the distant, crumpled wreckage. Antoinette's brick-red Volkswagen was smashed beyond repair, and retrieving it from the awkward position where it had come to rest would have been difficult and pointless. He looked down into the valley where his wife and his stepdaughter had died. It was a place of stone and silence.

That night in a hotel in the village at the foot of the pass he had read "Bird Falling" again. It was hard to avoid allegorical interpretations, for they persisted. But in truth the poem contained nothing of this; no premonition, no chill insight. It was a very simple poem about simple joy darkened by a small tragedy.

5

He had been dreaming again, this time of being a passenger on a ship which had been overcome by a vaguely comprehended disaster. He kept asking questions, but in the general pandemonium no one stopped to give answers. Alarm bells were shrilling and people ran from him.

The clamorous bells dissolved into the insistent ringing of the telephone at his bedside. He groped for it, fumbled with the receiver, registered sleepily what the clock told him: a quarter to five. There was gray light behind the bedroom curtains.

"Hello," he said. "De la Porte."

A woman's voice, strident and peremptory.

"Dr. de la Porte, this is Mrs. Anderson."

A mental picture of a big and blustering woman. Mrs. Anderson lived in an old house at the edge of town with her middle-aged spinster daughter. The daughter played the organ at services in the Dutch Reformed Church.

"What's the problem, Mrs. Anderson?"

"It's about Marietjie."

"What's wrong with her?"

"She's run away."

"Oh, God! What happened?"

"She wouldn't take her pills last night, but I thought it would be all right so I let her go to bed without them. But I suppose something must have warned me because when I went to look in her bedroom she was gone. She's nowhere in the house or the garden. You must come out and help me find her."

"But, my dear woman, why don't you phone the police?"

"Because you're her doctor."

"That may be so, Mrs. Anderson. But you must agree that the police are the best people to organize a search party."

65

"No. Think of the scandal."

He said firmly: "Mrs. Anderson, you must telephone the police. Your daughter is in a serious condition and she must be found as soon as possible."

"Oh, please, Doctor, won't you come out? You're the only one who knows what is best for her." Imperiousness had changed to pleading and the woman sounded near hysteria. He could not refuse.

He sighed. "Very well. I'll be there as soon as I can."

But he did not get out of bed immediately. He lay back and stretched his legs, savoring the comforting feel of the sheets for a few more precious moments.

I should have gone in for some other line of occupation, he thought with half-humorous resignation. Do plumbers or carpenters get called out in the early hours of the morning at the summons of people like Mrs. Anderson? Where could her crazy daughter have gone?

The Andersons were new patients. Until recently they had been attended by a partner in the opposition firm of general practitioners. Charles de la Porte had not questioned the reason for the shift, although he could guess it.

He tried to recall Marietjie's age from his examination notes. Was she forty-four? He remembered her vaguely, from his own youth, as a child not yet at school, with dark ringlets around a pale, plump face. Her father had been the Dutch Reformed Church dominee, descendant of one of the generation of Scottish ministers who had been brought to South Africa to preach to the old Boers. Over the years the families of the shepherds had been assimilated by their flocks. Dominee Anderson had hardly been able to speak English. He had been a small, ineffectual man with thinning red hair who doted on his daughter and was dominated by his wife. There had been gossip about his death, but the stories were long forgotten.

Marietjie, dutiful daughter, had stayed at home to care for her widowed mother. A good child, people said. She never looked at men. Had men ever looked at her? Probably not. She had grown into a stout woman with a muddy complexion and a sweet tooth. Her mother spoiled her with cakes and pies and pastries. And her hair was still shaped in the hanging locks of her childhood.

She was intensely religious. Her passion was the church organ, which she played with fair skill and many tremolo effects. Who could tell what other passions raged within that dumpy body with its incongruous little-girl hairstyle?

Marietjie's crisis had come unexpectedly, only a fortnight ago. A much-publicized revivalist preacher had brought his mission to the town and, to the chagrin of Marietjie's own minister, had been responsible for a spate of evangelist fervor. The DRC dominee had preached against it and Mrs. Anderson had disapproved but Marietjie, in a rare show of independence, had attended several of the services. She had quite enjoyed them. The ardent voice of the preacher and the hypnotic cries and clapping of his followers had stirred something in her. She had listened to his hellfire warnings, snug in the knowledge that she was immune, that she was already saved and safe. Until the night he had quoted thunderously from St. Mark: "But he that shall blaspheme against the Holy Ghost hath never forgiveness, but is in danger of eternal damnation."

Mrs. Anderson had called Charles de la Porte the following morning. She had met him at the front door, her face a mask of tragedy, as if there had been a death in the house. An organ was playing somewhere, muted at times, then swelling into tumultuous chords which drowned her voice as she told the story. She was both horrified and obscurely excited by its drama. Marietjie had been playing the organ most of the night. She was demented. She raved about her sin against the Holy Ghost. She had cut off her hair. There was nothing to be done with her.

He had reluctantly followed the old woman down a passage toward the source of the music. There was a musty smell and framed Bible texts on the walls. He felt embarrassed and out of place.

The organ notes ceased abruptly. The woman who had been seated at the old-fashioned instrument whirled around at their entrance. In that wild creature with its raggedly shorn hair he hardly recognized fat and placid Marietjie. She backed away from them, against the wall. She made her fingers into claws.

67

"Jesus sal my red—Jesus will save me," she snarled at them. "Even if you kill me I shall still believe," she snarled at them.

He knew when he was out of his depth. He had prescribed a sedative. Obviously, he said, psychiatric help was required. Mrs. Anderson objected because of the shame of it, but he overrode her resistance.

He had himself made the appointment for Marietjie to see someone at the mental health clinic, but now, finally forcing himself out of bed, he wondered: Did the damn old woman keep the appointment?

He began to dress in the half dark, sliding on the trousers which, as always, hung neatly draped in readiness over the dressing stand beside the bed.

Gillian's even breathing changed. She stirred; turned over. She woke.

"What is it? A call?" Her voice was soft with sleep.

"Yes."

"What time is it?"

"Not five yet."

"Put on the light if you like."

He sat on the bed to tie his shoelaces. "It's all right. I've finished dressing."

"Shall I get you some coffee?"

"Don't bother. I'll get something in town later."

"Poor darling."

The sympathy in her voice was genuine, but there was also more than a trace of relief at the knowledge that she did not have to get up and could snuggle deeper into the blankets. He smiled to himself as he knotted his tie.

"It's Saturday. With luck I'll be home by lunchtime. Have we anything on tonight?"

"Yes, darling, don't you remember? The Shaws are having a party."

"Oh, hell. Do we have to go?"

With faint reproof: "I'm afraid so, love. It's Derek's birthday. And I promised Hope I'd help her with the food."

"All right, Jilly. I'm on my way."

68

"Bye, darling. Don't be late."

Outside, a sickle moon showed briefly, then was obscured by fast-moving, tumbling gray clouds. A few stars still shone in the patches of pale sky. The row of blue-gum trees which shielded the house from the west wind rustled, bowing their tops.

He drove fast, handling the car with unthinking, near-automatic skill. Mrs. Anderson was waiting at her garden gate. She had been hidden behind a gatepost (in case of being seen by curious neighbors, he guessed) but she stepped into the open as the car stopped. She was a bulky, shapeless figure in a man's brown overcoat. Without getting out he leaned across to open the door for her. She scrambled in and banged the door. He winced.

He waited for her to speak but she was panting, trying to catch her breath.

"Have you called the police?" he asked finally.

She protested at once. "Please, Doctor. I couldn't. I'm sure you'll find her. But if we had to go to the police . . . The disgrace . . . *You* know."

Suspicion was confirmed. Mrs. Anderson's simple reasoning had persuaded her that he, himself a victim of gossip, was better to be trusted with a shameful secret than her own doctor.

"Where do you suggest we start looking?" he asked coldly.

"I think she would have gone toward the mountain. She seems to want to get away from people."

"How will we ever find her there? You must call the police. This is quite futile."

"We will find her. God will help us."

The search, predictably, was fruitless. He drove several miles out of town along the mountain road. But the woods were dense here, and the dark cedars kept their secrets. When they turned back there was already a flush of dawn light above the hills.

"What pills have you been giving her?" he asked. "Did the psychiatrist prescribe them?"

"No, Doctor. It's the same pills you gave her."

"Did you take her to the psychiatrist?" he asked sharply.

The old woman drew her coat around her as if suddenly conscious of the morning chill. "No, Doctor. I . . . I couldn't. If people heard about it . . . they would think Marietjie was mad."

Words of accusation and reprimand formed on his lips but he did not utter them. What was the use? They drove the rest of the way in silence.

He stopped in front of the Andersons' house and walked around the car to help the old woman. He saw, as he held the door open for her, that she was quietly weeping, and felt a spasm of pity. The situation was beyond her. He would have to take control, telephone the police, make arrangements for a committal order.

She leaned her sad, sacklike weight against him as he steered her up the brick-edged path and slowly, one foot at a time, up the steps onto the front porch.

And there, hunched in a chair in a corner, was Marietjie.

His first reaction was flooding relief. He would not have to become involved, after all. But then he noted the unnatural stillness of the woman's posture. She sat with her white nightgown pulled up to her hips. She did not look up at them. She was muttering to herself, the same phrase over and over.

"Al maak julle my dood sal ek nog glo."

Her mother, at his side, gasped and took a pace forward. Marietjie looked up then, beyond them at first and finally, focusing as if with difficulty, at the old woman.

He anticipated the attack and was already bracing himself for it, but could do nothing to prevent it. Marietjie had flung herself at the mother, clawing and screaming, before he could move to intervene. Mrs. Anderson was knocked over, falling heavily on the paved floor, and instantly Marietjie had her by the throat.

"Maak my dood maar ek sal nog glo," she shrieked.

He tried to circle behind the threshing bodies and succeeded only after Mrs. Anderson had become ominously still. Marietjie had both hands fiercely around her mother's throat. He grabbed her from behind, pinning her arms to her body, and

70

managed to break her grip. But although he held her immo-
bilized she fought him with a terrible, mindless fury. She
twisted in his arms and lunged backward with her head, snap-
ping at his face like a dog. And through it all she made an
unearthly sound, midway between scream and howl.

Mrs. Anderson groaned and rolled over. The whites of
her eyes were showing.

He shouted at her: "Help me!"

She sat up and said angrily: "Don't you dare hurt her."

He was beyond tolerance for the single-mindedness of
mother love and shouted angrily: "Go and open the car door, you
silly old bag. I'm taking her to hospital."

His anger penetrated and she obeyed hastily. He lifted
Marietjie bodily and, staggering under her frenzied weight, carried her down the path. He saw that there were lighted windows
in a house across the street and movement behind the windows.
By now the screaming must have roused the whole neigh-
borhood.

"Help!" he shouted again. "Someone come and help
me."

The lights went out.

"Bastards!" he swore at the unknown, uncaring spectators, and stumbled into the street with his burden.

Suddenly Marietjie stopped fighting. Wearily grateful he
carried her the last few paces to the open car door. She opened
her legs and set them astride, one foot on either side of the door.
He struggled, trying to force her inside. Her body jackknifed,
then straightened out violently.

Caught off balance, he staggered backward. A foot
hooked on something and he fell, with the woman on top of him.
Winded, and struggling to control her flailing arms and legs, he
heard Mrs. Anderson's plaintive bleating as if from an enormous
distance. Furious, frustrated, and with the sting of sweat in his
eyes, he managed at last to pin Marietjie down on the ground.
The practical solution was to stun her with a fist blow, but even
now he could not bring himself to hit her.

Then, with utter relief, he heard the high whine of a
vehicle approaching at speed. Brakes screeched and then, around

71

him, was the normality of uniforms and gruff male voices. Someone with sense had called the police.

A young man said: "Hey! What do you think you're doing?" and at once, more respectfully: "Oh. It's the doctor."

"Help me," Charles de la Porte panted. "I must get her to hospital."

The young constable retreated a pace. "Is she mad?"

"Not mad," Mrs. Anderson objected shrilly. "She's only upset."

"Hold her," Charles de la Porte said. "I'll give her something to calm her down."

Hesitantly the policeman, aided by a colleague who had appeared at his elbow, took hold of Marietjie. She tried to fight them off and they handled her more firmly, pinioning her arms.

"Jesus!" the young constable said admiringly. "She's strong."

"Hold her," Charles de la Porte said. He rummaged in his bag. Good thing he always carried paraldehyde. Eight cc would do it. By the time he was ready with the syringe the policemen had forced the still struggling woman back to the ground, face down. Mrs. Anderson protested volubly but they ignored her. He knelt and jabbed the needle into an ample, squirming buttock.

"Hold her. I want to give her something else, too."

Fifty milligrams of largactyl, also given intramuscularly.

"Don't let her go. It'll take a few minutes to take effect."

The jerking body started to relax.

"All right. Help me."

With the aid of the policemen he stretched the drugged and now docile woman out on the back seat. Mrs. Anderson got in beside her daughter. She was weeping again and she covered her face with her hands.

Several people had come into the street to watch. Seeing them, Charles de la Porte was filled with rage.

"You can go back to your beds," he shouted. "The circus is over."

They stared at him blankly, unable to understand the reason for his anger.

72

Halfway to the hospital he overtook one of the elderly municipal buses, on its way from the township. The Coloured driver was ramming his frame-rattling vehicle along at reckless speed, occupying more than a generous part of the road. Charles de la Porte passed him with a blare of the horn. Faces behind the bus windows turned to look incuriously down at the car as it sped past.

The hospital, towering, modern, anonymous, could as well have housed the offices of an insurance company or a mining house. A square of light showed here and there against its gray bulk. Other unlit windows caught and reflected the soft rose of the day now gathering in the east.

He drew up at the admissions entrance and a nurse and a porter at once appeared with a stretcher. Marietjie was wheeled inside and he followed with Mrs. Anderson. The familiar procession evoked no more than casual glances.

"I'll help the porter put her to bed, Sister," he told the nurse. "I need some intravenous Valium. She's recovering from the drugs I gave her."

She nodded and was gone.

Only when, with the porter's assistance, he lifted Marietjie onto the bed, did he notice that she was covered with sand and dirt and was bleeding from a number of abrasions.

"Put screens around the bed, please," he said. "Then tell Sister Groenewald we'll have to wash her and dress these wounds."

The man stared at him owlishly. "Yes, Doctor."

"And I want some antitetanus serum as well."

"Yes, Doctor."

Marietjie stirred.

"Ask her to hurry with the Valium. I'll stay here and watch the patient."

He went to the window, behind the head of the bed, and leaned his elbows on the high sill, looking out. The window opened on an inner courtyard, treelined and divided into rectangles of paving and grass. As he watched, two nurses, capes around their shoulders, made their way across the courtyard, walking swiftly. It was too early for a change in duty shifts; perhaps they had been for a cup of coffee. He must ask Sister if she could get him some. He watched the nurses idly, thinking about the woman on the bed behind him.

What happened within the human brain for it so suddenly to lose contact with reality? Macroscopically, histologically, and even biochemically there was no distinguishable difference between his brain and hers. And yet she had cracked.

A man in the white coat of a technician (Charles de la Porte recognized him as one of the staff of the maintenance department) came out through a side door, passing the nurses. An eddy of wind swirled round the courtyard at that moment and both the girls clutched at the hems of their short skirts. The man said something to them, grinning. One turned her back on him haughtily but the other nurse made an unheard retort which caused both to burst into laughter. The man shrugged and went by.

A phrase from a popular song he had heard somewhere recently (on the car radio earlier? No; he had not switched on the radio. The song must have made its insiduous entry into his mind on another occasion) jangled within his head.

'*Life goes on.*'
Something, something
'*Life goes on.*'

He turned away from the window. Life, indeed, went on.

It was at times difficult for hospital patients to accept the varied and cheerful way in which life continued all around them. To them their diseases were all-important and it was incomprehensible and even irreverent that life's normal parade of flirtation between the sexes, of preoccupation with money, with holidays and time off duty, of food and drink and hopes and dreams, should be conducted within the hospital as if sickness was no more eventful than health.

Some patients became peevish, so that a couple of nurses laughing in youthful exuberance were seen to be mocking the dying, or a doctor was lacking in compassion if he did not have the time to listen to every petty complaint.

Totally wrong and self-centered, of course.

And yet, was it?

Did those patients (people, he reminded himself, people) who sullenly resented hospital routine which was not centered solely around them possibly express, inarticulately and for the wrong reasons, the misgivings he himself felt at times?

He remembered something the professor of medicine at university had said long ago, when he was still a student. He had said: "I have often suspected that real sympathy and understanding would have been worth more than any pill I have ever prescribed."

Very noble-sounding, but impractical when you thought about it.

Marietjie whimpered and he turned to look at her.

Compassion toward her was marvelous and praiseworthy. But her mind could not recognize it; could not even recognize love. And neither emotion would go very far in curing her mania. What was called for instead was electroconvulsive therapy. A charge of one hundred volts would be flashed through her brain for one tenth of a second and would set off an epileptic fit. Immediately after the electrical stimulation there would be a tonic seizure phase of between five and fifteen seconds. All the muscles of her body would go into tonic contraction. Her limbs would go rigid and her back would arch. This would be followed by clonic movements lasting between ten and sixty seconds, during which her whole body would convulse.

Compassion? Yes, in a way. For she could only benefit from an impersonal, scientific approach, from thinking which was not swayed by emotion. He could not allow himself to be influenced by the thought that here was a poor middle-aged woman who had been given little by life, except her mother's overpowering influence. She had never experienced the love of a man or the excitement of a sexual encounter. She had been taught to suppress her instincts and to subjugate herself to her mother and her religion. But he did not dare think: poor Marietjie. Instead he had to remember that this was a mentally disturbed patient who had to be kept sedated until her straitjacket and padded cell had been prepared for her.

He had long ago worked out his own ethic toward suffering. At first he had adopted the usual cynicism of medical students. But in his fifth year he had spent several months in a ward for terminal cancer patients and the students' gallows humor had proved a callow sham. Nevertheless you had to find a screen. His had been that of being friendly and gentle and very slightly aloof. It had served him well, so, without conscious choice, he had maintained it.

Perhaps, he now admitted to himself, he had allowed the screen to grow thicker and taller over the years. It was inevitable when those whom you treated and advised and tried to heal began to number in the thousands; when all the names and personalities ran together and a multitude of patients became one Patient, suffering from diseases of every conceivable organ, from seborrheic dermatitis of the scalp to rheumatoid arthritis in the toes. He remembered what Frank Edelstein had said: "Medicine has become indifferent to the people it treats."

Was there a warning concealed in the generalization? If so, was it warranted? Had the hedge grown too high; was he in fact isolated from those he sought to heal?

But if you allowed yourself the weakness of anguish and sorrow the river ran deeper, until eventually you were forced to start questioning God and His purpose. What questions had he, Charles de la Porte, been asking? And, receiving no answers, what answers had he made up for himself?

Unfair of Frank to charge him with indifference when it was precisely the opposite, an excess of compassion, which had landed him in a malpractice suit and in the hands of the attorneys. The thought was flippant enough to provide a refuge from further thought and he dwelt on it for a moment longer with ironic pleasure.

Sister Groenewald pushed a stretcher in through a gap in the bedside screen, lifting the curtains carefully to avoid them touching the sterilized dressing tray. She drew them again as if making a ritual gesture. They were isolated within their cloth-walled tabernacle, an age-old trinity: doctor, nurse, and patient.

76

"Ready, Doctor," she said. Then, nudging his attention a little: "I've brought a basin of hot water if you'd like to scrub here."

They worked together with speed and efficiency. He administered ten milligrams of Valium intravenously and Marietjie slept again. Then they washed her and carefully cleaned each wound with hibitane solution in water. Fortunately none of the injuries required stitching.

"Where's the ATS?" he asked.

"I didn't know you wanted any, Doctor."

"I told the porter."

"Oh. He did tell me you wanted something, but he didn't know what."

"Why didn't he tell me?"

"Probably scared of you."

"Well, you'd better get some for me. With all this muck in the wounds she's a candidate for lockjaw."

"I'll get it when we've finished here, Doctor."

When, finally, Charles de la Porte looked at his watch, he puckered his lips in an incredulous whistle. Time had gone by unnoticed. The bustle of washing patients and serving breakfasts and changing from night to day staff was already in process. Behind the cloistering curtains he and Sister Groenewald had remained aloof from the increasing bustle and noise outside: the deliberately cheerful voices of the nurses, the banging of stretchers and trays. Once a young nurse had pushed in through the curtains, to vanish very much more quickly at a glare from the sister.

It was too late now to return home to clean up, only to have to dash back to his rooms in time for the first patients of the morning. He kept a change of linen at the Drostdy. He decided he would shave and shower there. But first a cup of coffee at the snack restaurant opposite Drostdy Square. He seldom had more than this for breakfast on a working day, one of the means of keeping his weight under control. His large six-foot-plus frame had a tendency to fill out easily.

Sister Groenewald came with him to the door.

"What shall I tell Mrs. Anderson? She's still waiting."

"Hm? Oh . . . tell her I'll give her a lift home. I'll talk to her on the way."

She turned toward the waiting room, but stopped and glanced at him sideways.

"Doctor . . . I . . . "

Her agitation was so transparent that he almost smiled.

"Was there something else, Sister?"

"Yes, Doctor. You're going to think I . . . it's none of my business really, but I wanted you to know."

He remained patient. "Know about what?"

She made a flustered gesture. "I think you have a right to know. You know what this town is like. A small town. You know how stories get around."

He continued to regard her, his face impassive.

"Stories," he said at last, scornfully.

She misunderstood the distaste he was trying to convey.

"They're about you and I know they're not true. That Mrs. Haarhoff has been spreading them."

This time he was genuinely taken aback, "Mrs. Haarhoff? The sister who used to be my secretary?"

"She calls herself that, but she's not entitled to. She never did her training. She was just a nurse's aide here. Crause was her name then."

What obscure beginnings of envy or resentment or just or unjust indignation had this had? He listened, wondering, as the woman poured out her sour tale.

"But she calls herself sister and some of the other sisters are foolish enough to believe her stories. They're all very pally because they belong to the tennis club and all that. She's poison, Doctor. Pure poison."

Was there a shade of gloating about this? Was there a degree of calculation? Was his response under observation, so that she could find out for herself the truth of the rumors she was so indignantly repudiating? His view of Sister Groenewald shifted a little; became firmer in some ways, more ambiguous in others. Another lesson in the folly of adopting first impressions simply because they were the easiest.

" . . . and I said to them: I know nothing about that

business, but if you want my candid opinion it's nothing but a pack of lies," she was saying.

He interrupted her firmly. "Thank you, Sister. It's kind of you to defend me. But, really, there's no need. And it's best to avoid passing on these unpleasant and probably actionable stories, even with good intent." He paused long enough to allow the message to sink in, then smiled disarmingly. "Thank you for your warning. Now please fetch Mrs. Anderson. And don't forget to give the ATS."

The sun was hidden by a bank of dark clouds over the eastern hills. The wind was blowing harder now, bringing occasional squalls of rain slashing across the water-shiny tarmac of the car park.

Charles de la Porte made a dash for his car through one of these showers. It was going to be an unpleasant day, he thought as he climbed in behind the steering wheel. More muddy-looking clouds were rising in the west. An indoors day. He would spend the afternoon watching sports on television, snug in the knowledge that there was no need to be out in the rain trying to sail a boat or play golf or cricket.

He pulled up at a side door where Sister Groenewald, with a display of tact, had taken Mrs. Anderson rather than expose the now trembly, crushed-looking old woman in her absurd clothes to the ridiculing glances of people at the main entrance. The nurse was shielding Mrs. Anderson's head with an open umbrella. He opened the passenger-side door. She was helped in, wheezing and wet and miserable, bringing with her a smell of defeat.

He drove off slowly, waiting for the wipers to clean the windshield. Gently, he told her what he had arranged. Marietjie would be admitted to a psychiatric hospital in Cape Town. She needed specialized treatment.

Mrs. Anderson nodded her head but said nothing. They did not speak again all the way to her empty house.

He drove away and the wheels made a thin, hissing sound over the wet road.

What would Mrs. Anderson do now? The cozy nest she had built had been ripped apart. Would she try to patch it, like a mindless mother hen frantically adding bits of straw to the ruins? Or would she accept that the chicken would never again return to the nest?

The sense of desolation which lingered in his mind was not due only to the old woman and her fate.

Mrs. Haarhoff, he thought. The paragon. The flawless secretary. The tactful receptionist. The disciplinarian with the outlook of a drill sergeant. Never complaining, always cheerful, always able to produce a file or an X ray or a record instantly.

What had she said to him when, tearfully, she had handed him her letter of resignation? (Typically, it had been beautifully typed, even-spaced and without erasures.) "Doctor, I can't stay. I feel like a traitor. I couldn't bear to stay."

He had tried to reason with her and, failing, had called in Geoff Hutton. But nothing could change her mind. In a frenzy of unnecessary guilt she had insisted on leaving, and so she had left.

Could you believe such a woman capable of slanderous gossip?

Sadly, half a century's experience of life, and half of that again spent in the practice of medicine, had taught him that there was nothing humans, by their nature, that very human nature, were not capable of doing. So it was possible that Mrs. Haarhoff, seeking to erase guilt for treachery no worse than that of momentary indiscretion, had now turned traitor indeed, and was enthralling audiences of her newfound peers with tales about the funny goings-on in the secret inner chamber of her ex-employer.

Did it matter?

Again. Human nature being what it was, the sting of being held in public disrepute (and blamelessly at that, his mind reassured itself after a rapid scramble through incidents and situations now almost forgotten) was sharp, even if his judges were only a bunch of gossipy middle-aged women. Ridiculous, but undeniable. Pride had taken its due fall.

A traffic policeman on early duty at the entrance to the square recognized him and beckoned him through with a gesture which was half wave, half salute. The token of respect was childishly gratifying at the moment and he smiled a greeting as he drove past.

He turned the car in at the rear of the Drostdy, where a gray-haired African in a makeshift khaki uniform hurried from a tin shanty to shift the chain which guarded his unofficial, private enterprise parking lot from invaders. Charles de la Porte tipped him generously, knowing that failure to do so sometimes had awkward repercussions such as slashed tires or broken windshield wipers, calamities blamed on roaming bands of "bad men." The old pirate had no rights over the vacant lot, but for peace of mind it was safer to pay him.

He crossed the square swiftly, stopping to buy a newspaper from an urchin at the street corner. The owner of the cafeteria, a morose Italian, greeted him with a nod. A disinterested, yawning waitress took his order. He opened the newspaper on the table while he waited and glanced with distaste at the headlines.

There had been renewed outbreaks of violence in Soweto and the East Rand. Buses had been stoned and, nearer home in Cape Town, children had attempted to burn down a school. A Cabinet Minister had defended police action against rioters.

The bad news depressed him further. Why? Why? Why?

Why did the background to his own agony have to be the sounds of riots in which children were made the victims of two sets of intransigence? Extremists on both sides were using the children, of that he had no doubt. For radical African nationalists they were expendable skirmishers in a war which had as its goal the complete destruction of the white barricades of apartheid. But the state and its police saw them as young black thugs who had to be taught a lesson with batons and, if necessary, bullets. He had the somber feeling that the world was invading his cloister. It was no longer good enough to proclaim: "I do good by practicing good medicine, therefore I am blameless."

He sat thinking bleak thoughts about the future. But in due course personal considerations outweighed the problems of the troubled world outside. With clammy repugnance he remembered the conversation that day in the doctors' changing room.

From the start he had been suspicious about the invitation. Mr. Leicester Edwards-White requested Dr. de la Porte's assistance at an operation, that morning, on a patient of Dr. de la Porte's. It was conveyed with typical flamboyance, written out in the surgeon's slanting handwriting on his headed notepaper.

Charles de la Porte, about to start his morning round and in the process of putting on a white overcoat when a porter brought him the note, had studied it for a moment, frowning. He was certain that none of his patients had been referred to Edwards-White, and fairly confident that none had deserted his practice for the surgeon's. An emergency perhaps? But even then it seemed unlikely that Edwards-White would seek his help.

Dr. de la Porte was regarded as a rival, and therefore an enemy, by Mr. Edwards-White. (He insisted on this style of address, surgery's mark of status, the mock-humble reversal to a layman's title, dating back to the days of the barber surgeons and their poles striped with blood and pus.) He had his own supporters and sycophants among the town's medical fraternity, that supposedly tight-knit brotherhood in which, in fact, brother's hand was often raised against brother. A young man of mercurial temperament and insatiable ambition, he had clearly felt himself thwarted and frustrated ever since coming, a not very long qualified surgeon, to the town eighteen months before. He was skilled if somewhat impulsive in the operating room and had obviously expected to take the town by storm. The only conceivable opposition could come from a source he immediately disregarded: Dr. de la Porte, a surgeon who valued his own skill so lightly that he had chosen instead to work as a general practitioner.

Edwards-White had misjudged both his place and his man. Most of the town's GPs were essentially conservative. They held the old-fashioned point of view that a patient was best treated by someone who knew him well. They believed in seeing a patient all the way through an illness. They did not like to refer bits and pieces of him to remote and impersonal experts. They themselves carried the considerable volume of routine surgery and when something more complex was involved there was Charles de la Porte, a little rusty perhaps and not so slick, but steady as a rock. He would advise and where necessary operate himself, with the GP as first assistant. He made a point of never making the assistant feel like a bumbling idiot, which was appreciated. And his patients, quite a few of them, lived. Which was the important thing, wasn't it?

White, who despised old-fashioned thinking and methods, had been outspoken in criticism. His only reward was a further drawing-in of heads under obstinate shells. He was disliked and written off as bumptious. Vindictive tongues whispered that even the hyphenated surname was a pretense, that it dated back no further than one generation. His exhortations met the averted eye of embarrassment. His attempts at innovation ended in confusion because of lack of support. Even his praiseworthy and eventually successful campaign for the establishment of an intensive-care unit at the hospital had resulted in the enmity of the medical committee. White, in typical jump-in-with-your-boots-on impetuosity, had taken his appeal directly to the director of Hospital Services. It had needed Charles de la Porte's intervention to smooth ruffled dignity, and this perhaps, as much as anything else, had rankled.

It had only been a question of time before they crossed swords.

The patient had been a man of fifty-five, a tourist passing through town. He and his wife had stopped for breakfast (fried eggs and sausages; he ate fried eggs only on vacation, he confessed with a smile) and afterward he had developed indigestion. He had gone to a drugstore and the pharmacist, thinking that his customer looked rather gray, had suggested he consult a doctor. The man had come to Edwards-White's rooms.

83

After an examination the surgeon had diagnosed acute inflammation of the gallbladder, which was in imminent danger of rupturing. The impression was left that the man had been very fortunate indeed that chance had brought him to the only qualified surgeon for miles around. Edwards-White would admit him to hospital, whip out the gallbladder, and within a week he would be fit enough to resume his vacation.

The patient did not have the same enthusiasm for surgery. Somewhat plaintively he pointed out that he had experienced previous attacks of indigestion. This, said Edwards-White implacably, definitely confirmed the diagnosis. The symptoms were conclusive.

The stranger was still reluctant. He would prefer a second opinion. Was there another surgeon available? Edwards-White had hardly troubled to hide his anger. Yes, he said coldly, there was a doctor next door who had some surgical experience. If the patient insisted . . .

The patient insisted.

Charles de la Porte was called. Questioning produced the information that the patient had been suffering from indigestion off and on for the past six months. The attacks often came on after heavy meals, but had occurred in the early morning and once during a game of golf. No, he never vomited, but on occasion he felt nauseous. Did the pain radiate to his back and the left shoulder? He had not really noticed, but it could be so. Examination showed no abnormalities of the chest. There was no jaundice present. His temperature was a fraction above normal and his pulse rate ninety-five. There was rigidity of the abdominal muscles but no definite area of tenderness.

Edwards-White stood at the window, radiating disapproval. When the examination was done he left the patient without a word and led the way back to his consulting room, his back stiff and indignant. The door was hardly closed before he demanded: "Do you confirm my diagnosis of acute cholecystitis?"

"I would like to see some other tests done."

Edwards-White's raised eyebrows made his thoughts

clear: Typical physician's approach to an emergency: carry on with tests until the patient dies.

"Murphy's test is positive. That's all I need to recognize cholecystitis."

"I'd like to examine the urine, do a white cell count and an electrocardiogram."

"An ECG? There's nothing wrong with the man's heart."

"Look," Charles de la Porte said patiently, "if the condition is as you suspect there still would be no harm in putting the patient on drip and suction and watching what develops."

Edwards-White was furious. "Watch how he perforates, you mean. All right, then. Do as you wish. I wash my hands of this case."

But Charles de la Porte had suspected a degree of bluffing behind the apparent anger. Edwards-White had already started to think, and to doubt.

The ECG tracing had shown a telltale Q-wave and S-T changes over the chest lead. Acute antrolateral myocardial infarction.

Thereafter they had treated one another with icy politeness.

So what the devil did the man want now? What patient could he possibly be operating on? He was angered by the impudence and tempted to ignore the summons. And yet, if a patient of his was really involved . . . He thrust Edwards-White's note into a pocket and went back into the foyer, to where a handful of people stood waiting at the double bank of elevator doors.

The operating block was on the top floor and, as usual before the start of the morning's surgery, there was a sense of contained excitement. Masked nurses in green coveralls moved behind the glass swing doors which barred the outside, unsterile world. A porter wheeled a loaded stretcher past with a muttered apology.

There was no sign of Edwards-White.

Still angry, he went into the dressing room. From the showers came the sound of running water. A baritone voice was humming. The tune changed to slightly breathless whistling as the unseen musician rinsed himself under the cold tap.

Charles de la Porte picked a pair of linen trousers and a singlet out of the heaps which were sorted, not always accurately, according to size and carried them to his locker. A rash of inexplicable thefts had forced the hospital board to provide private lockers for each of the town's doctors. Even old Dr. Collins had one. His practice, it was true, consisted largely of malingering distillery workers who came to him on Monday mornings for the precious medical certificates which would prove to the foreman that what ailed them was not alcohol but something exotic and alarming. Acute fibrositis was the customary verdict. Or when the doctor was feeling fancy he might enliven the day with a diagnosis of anorexia nervosa or cephalalgia. There was even the story, probably apocryphal, that he had once booked off a forklift operator he had found to be suffering from hyperemesis gravidarum. It was perhaps as well that no one had ever told the burly, stubble-bearded workman that the bouts of vomiting he experienced were due not to the cheap brandy he drank to excess but, miraculously, to morning sickness. Dr. Collins had never, and if the medical committee had anything to do with it, would never, use the operating theater. But he had insisted on his rights and there, in a corner, was a locker with his name on its door on machine-embossed plastic tape.

Charles de la Porte took off his jacket and undid his tie.

The water sound and the whistling came to a simultaneous end. Leicester Edwards-White, towel in hand, walked out of the showers.

The room was long and narrow and, briefly, the two men faced one another at close quarters. White was startled. The color in his face, product of exertion and steamy hot water, faded a little. He looked suddenly very young and even guilty. But at once he regained composure, lifted an ironical eyebrow, and went past to his own locker.

"Morning," he said. "I assume you got my message."

Charles de la Porte returned the greeting curtly. "Perhaps you'll explain what it's all about. Who is the patient?"

White pulled on a pair of very brief underpants with a

design of green fleurs-de-lis on them. He was tall, almost as tall as Charles de la Porte himself, and broadly made and, as befitted a man only barely past thirty, his belly was flat and rigid with muscle. He did not answer the questions directly.

"I particularly wanted you to assist with this operation."

Charles de la Porte had half-unbuttoned his shirt, but now he stopped. "Look, Mr. Edwards-White, you should know that I never assist with an operation. Who is the patient?"

A slow, scornful survey. But in the depths behind the eyes there dwelt, also, a wicked triumph, a joyous gloating.

"The patient is Janice Case, Doctor."

A start of surprise, despite himself.

"Dr. Case?"

"Yes."

"What are you operating for?"

"Do you need to ask? I'm doing a mastectomy and an oophorectomy. The operation which should have been performed six months ago."

Charles de la Porte drew a long breath and then released it wearily.

"Are you seriously asking me to assist you?"

"I've invited you, haven't I?"

"You must realize that I cannot."

"May I ask why not?"

"Firstly because I don't believe in what you're planning to do. There is no local recurrence as far as I am aware. So there is no need to remove the breast. I assume you know I have had her on testosterone?"

"I am aware of that."

"Well the spine secondaries did not respond to that so it's highly unlikely that removing the ovaries will be of any benefit. All you will achieve is to increase the poor woman's suffering."

"I must be the judge of that."

To save self-respect he had to leave. He turned to do so. But again he stopped. Again he turned to the other man. He asked: "I saw her last week, a couple of days ago. Then she was all right. When did she find out?"

White acted the part of the pitiless avenger nevertheless

moved by pity; touched by his awareness of common humanity and the obligations of decency to spare a kind word for the groveling wretch who had been discovered in his crime.

"Two days ago," he said. Then, spoiling the performance by overacting, he added vehemently: "You knew it was carcinoma. Why the hell didn't you tell someone?"

Charles de la Porte ignored the unanswerable (how answered except by complexities which were not for this place and this moment) question and asked instead: "How did she find out?"

The waitress put down his coffee cup with a careless clatter. He pushed aside the newspaper at which he had been staring unseeingly and she put a plate with a single bread roll before him. There was no butter and she looked surly when he pointed out the omission. She went back to the kitchen with bad grace. He added one carefully rounded teaspoon of sugar to the coffee. Why did he keep coming to this place? It was not very clean, the owner was unfriendly, and the service was sloppy. The food was mediocre. Then why did he keep coming? Habit.

Habit was disaster. Habit robbed life of adventure, of a sense of the unexpected. Habit was for the dull-witted, who found security in sameness.

Or was habit, the customed order of life's daily events, the only way to achieve sanity in a bewilderingly senseless world? The question presented itself, as to any other concerned mind: Was everything going to blazes in a barrel? The newspaper he had been reading contained its usual quota of aimless horrors which he could only regard with utter incomprehension.

But reason and his own sense of history reassured him that chaos had always been a condition of life, that throughout the centuries men and women had slaughtered and been slaughtered in vain. The stability and calm routine which he remembered to have ruled his childhood world had been illusion, too.

What then did that child, grown adult, do to compensate for a lost world which (he now discovered) had never been? What else but to adopt a pattern of stable behavior and calm routine; to impose order on life's disorder? In that constant war between the visionary and the practical he said not "If I compel men to live by my ideals life will become ideal," but rather: "This is the way men are and this is how I am and only a fool would be persuaded to try to change either."

He thought, savoring the irony, how strange it was that all lives, even those of nations and large bodies of men, should always contain that gap between promise and performance, between young ideals and aged second thought. And, best irony of all, that he too should have fallen victim to this cliché.

Victim? No. Arbiter of his own fate. For the civilized adult, choosing not to impose his tastes on others, demanded also that the tastes of others should not be imposed on him. He ordered his own life, formed his own habits. And if this life in consequence became settled and predictable, what of it?

He felt a surge of anger at the unfairness, the essential haphazardness, of the whole sorry affair. Why had *he* been chosen. Why should this have come to disrupt *his* established attitudes.

But, protest to the contrary, was there a touch of spice about it? Was there excitement at the thought of again facing the unknown; of not knowing for certain what the day might bring?

Into his mind's eye came an image of a big bare room on a hill which faced a quiet sea. The room was furnished only with a table of rough board and a bed and a chair. Along one wall was a bookcase fashioned from planks and piled bricks. A girl sat at the table, writing, and on her left was the small pile of foolscap paper which represented the morning's work. It was late in the morning (it was always late in the morning in that dream) and down in the white village beside the sea the air was like the inside

89

of an oven. But it was cool up on the hill. The young woman was slim, with long dark hair. Her eyes became faintly hooded when she smiled, as she was smiling now, and her brows drew quizzically together. She had a generous mouth over slightly uneven teeth. He thought her very beautiful and loved her. Yes, he was in that picture, too, but without the gray in his hair and without the breathlessness which, now, would probably be the consequence of the climb up the hill from that village by a far-away sea.

He smiled, a little sadly, at the naïveté of the vision and sipped at his coffee. Living dangerously might be as exhilarating a prospect at the age of fifty as it had been (say) at midthirty. But some of the essential dexterity of both mind and body was lost in the intervening years. One's sense of "the hell with it" grew corpulent as the waistline thickened. Could he really demand that Gillian give up her small comforts and small luxuries and go with him into an uncertain future? Then he remembered her matter-of-fact attitude last night, her easy acceptance that Hoog-in-het-Dal might have to be sold. Was the apparent lack of dismay an attempt to reassure him? Or was that what she secretly believed: that the old homestead was merely another house, to be given up without too many pangs when necessary? She was younger than he by almost twenty years; did age make the difference? Was he, creature of habit, unable to contemplate not only the consequences of change but the simple thought of change itself, in fact the weaker vessel? Had habit unmanned him?

And that was the ultimate irony.

"How did she find out?" he had asked numbly during that dressing-room confrontation almost three months ago, and: "How she discovered the truth," he could remember saying in answer to a question from the barrister Bachelli.

Edwards-White had told him.

Three nights before, Janice McOwen had woken from deep sleep with her neck aching from being held too long in one position. She had reached up to massage the cramped muscles. At the base of the neck, just above the left clavicle, her fingers discovered a swelling. In a moment of cold horror which had driven away all vestige of sleep she had felt for it again. Unmistakably: an enlarged supraclavicular gland. Lying there in the dark she had linked together a chain from what had seemed until now merely a random clutter of incidents. There had been the backache. Then the lump in the breast which Charles de la Porte had removed. And the tablets, unmarked and anonymous, which he had insisted on giving her as part of a "trial" among patients with undiagnosed pains of the back. Then the pain had spread to her neck. And now the gland.

Quietly so as not to disturb her husband, sleeping in his own bed, she had got up and gone to the adjoining bathroom. She had closed the door and switched on the light and pulled off her nightgown. Then, naked in front of the big mirror over the washbasin, she had examined herself. First the smooth, pale skin of her left shoulder (it was July, midwinter; the golden brown of summertime had long faded), then her left breast and the neat pinkish scar down the side of it where Charles de la Porte had excised a supposedly benign lump (then it *had* been summer; she remembered his joking guarantee of a bikini—there would be no need for the neck-high 1900-style bathing costume of her pretended fears), and finally her armpit, catching her lower lip between her teeth as she felt the string of swollen lymph glands running up to the apex of the axilla.

She had gone out onto the terrace. Cliff McOwen, too, had built his house high up in the valley, but along the slopes opposite from Hoog-in-het-Dal. There had been vineyards here as well but it was all suburb now, covered with the large new houses of the wealthy. She had smoked a cigarette and looked down on the lights of the town. Finally she had gone back to bed, but not to sleep.

The following morning she had telephoned Charles de la Porte's rooms. For some reason she had not called during his normal surgery hours. Perhaps the explanation was that in the end, toward dawn, she had fallen into thought-obliterating sleep and that McOwen, considerate in his turn, had not disturbed her before going to the office. Left to sleep on that gray, wintry morning, she might well not have woken before half past ten.

Whatever the case, Mrs. Haarhoff had answered the telephone and had reported with regret that Dr. de la Porte was out doing his calls. Could she help in any way?

Perhaps one could understand the temptation. Perhaps there had been no calculation beforehand. Perhaps the need to know was so consuming that she was unable at that moment to resist the small deceit. This was Dr. Case, she had said. She had run out of the tablets Dr. de la Porte had been giving her, but he had never written a prescription and now how on earth was she to check it?

Mrs. Haarhoff had been all kindness. Dr. Case's voice had already been recognized. It would be a pleasure to help. Perhaps there was something in the records.

But, puzzlingly to Mrs. Haarhoff, the file was not where it should have been. She had perhaps clicked her tongue in annoyance (after all the trouble you went to, teaching these girls proper filing methods!) and checked back to BU, BO, forward to CE, CI, then double-checking all the MC and MACs. Without success. But then she had an inspiration. Dr. de la Porte, she knew, kept his own card index system on patients of special interest. He was planning a series of articles for the *Journal* and was meticulous about keeping his private records up to date. As it happened she knew where he kept the key.

And so the scrupulous locking away of Janice Case's file in the wall safe had proved of no avail. For Charles de la Porte had indeed filled in information on the card, as was his habit. Not only the prescription for testosterone which Dr. Case was seeking but something else which Mrs. Haarhoff read over the telephone in a confiding yet puzzled voice.

A date and then the notation: CA+ T:3 N:0 M:1.

Final irony. If "Sister" had been a nurse, would she have recognized the meaning of that not-over-cryptic shorthand and the significance of the hormonal treatment? And if so, would she have had the presence of mind to keep silent?

To her the scribbled note had meant nothing in particular. But to the woman on the other end of the line it signified, with the irrevocable certainty of an ax stroke, that there had been a finding of positive carcinoma and that, classified by the TNM method, the tumor was of Class 1; it had not at the time of diagnosis invaded the lymph glands; but, most terrifying of all, there were distant metastases. She had known, then, her own doom.

He had finished shaving and was adjusting the shower taps, testing the temperature with the flat of his hand, when he heard the telephone ringing in his consulting room.

He said: "Oh, hell!" and stood irresolute. The telephone continued to ring. With a sigh he turned off the shower. He looked at the wristwatch he had balanced on the glass shelf below the mirror. Twenty past seven. At least there would be no one around to observe him in a state of undress. He tucked a towel around his waist and padded through on bare feet to where the telephone was still shrilling.

A woman spoke.

"Dr. de la Porte, this is Sister Fry from Casualty. I tried to get you at home but they said you were here at the hospital and then I spoke to Sister Groenewald and she said you'd already left so I thought I'd try—"

He interrupted impatiently. "All right, Sister. What's the problem?"

"I have a patient of yours here, Doctor. At least, I think she's your patient. It's a little baby girl. The father says a Dr. Delport saw the child yesterday, but I don't know any Dr. Delport. It's a Railway case and seeing Dr. Hutton is away I thought—"

Again he was forced to cut her short. "Is the name Erasmus?"

"Yes, Doctor."

"She is my patient. What's wrong?"

"The parents brought the baby in because she was having fits. She had a convulsion while they were waiting and the Casualty officer doesn't come on duty till eight so I thought you might want to see her first and perhaps admit her. . . . "

Sister Fry was a compulsive talker, but at least there was nothing wrong with her common sense.

"Did you notice anything else?"

"Her temperature is very high. It's one oh four."

He said thoughtfully, more to himself then to her: "Could be just the high temp causing the convulsions. It can happen. Have you tried to bring down the temperature?"

"I gave her a disprin suppository and a tepid sponge-down."

"Right, Sister. I'll be there as soon as I can."

While he hurriedly finished his shower and dressed he thought with disquiet about the Erasmus baby. He had diagnosed a cold. Had he completely missed some symptom? And, worst of all, had he done so because of prejudice? He had been angry with the parents because of their neglect. Had he been negligent in his turn?

Sister Fry appeared at his side the moment he went in through the Casualty Department door, as if she had been waiting in ambush. But now she did not waste time on words.

"Morning, Doctor. This way."

The Erasmus baby was in a cot with the sides down. She was unconscious and her jaws were held apart by a wooden block. Her breathing was irregular.

With the nurse at his side he began his examination, following the routine which had become so much a part of his life, drilled into him by a hundred, a thousand, a hundred thousand repetitions, that he could probably go through the motions in his sleep: first inspect, then palpate, then auscultate.

Mucous membranes were pink. No jaundice. The pupils reacted to light. The pulse was racing but full. The skin was dry and hot. There was a rash on the upper part of the body. He leaned over to examine the irregular pink blotches more closely, then put a hand behind the baby's head and flexed the neck suddenly.

There was resistance, a stiffness. The child pulled up her legs. Then she screamed.

He released his hold and the scream changed to a sad wailing.

"We're going to need a lumbar puncture tray," he told the nurse without looking up. His hands were still going swiftly through the rest of their appointed tasks. "But a sedative first. I'll give her Valium intravenously. Right?"

"Right, Doctor," she said crisply. She hurried away.

He straightened up and pulled down his stethoscope. Who could you blame? Only yourself.

Nonsense, he told himself angrily. You cannot load yourself with responsibility for everything under the sun.

And yet.

Sister Fry was back with a stretcher and with a junior nurse in tow. He scrubbed in a hand basin for the second time that morning and gave the Valium injection.

While he waited for it to take effect he asked Sister Fry: "Where are the parents?"

"I told them to wait outside." She tightened her lips. "The father isn't very sober."

"Hm." He hoped he could avoid a scene. "Are there beds free in the Children's Ward? I'll want to admit her."

"I checked, Doctor. There are beds."

"Good." He looked at the sleeping child. "Turn her over, please. On her side. That's right. Arch her back and hold her like that."

He cleaned the skin over the lumbar spine with iodine in spirits and isolated it with sterile towels. He took up the long lumbar puncture needle and felt for the space between the third and fourth lumbar vertebrae. A quick jab through the skin and then, holding the needle at a slight angle, he slid it between the vertebrae and through the dura into the spinal canal.

The child squirmed and he flashed a worried glance at Sister Fry. Her lips were tight and she breathed slowly and determinedly.

He withdrew the stylet. At once there were drops of spinal fluid. It was not clear like water, as it should have been, but turbid with inflammatory cells.

No doubt now about the diagnosis: purulent meningitis.

No time for delay either. Already the diagnosis was nearly twelve hours late.

"I'll put up a drip and start her on intravenous penicillin. We'll give her a million units every six hours. And, Sister, will

95

you please get a good nurse to special her. I don't want to lose her."

Without meaning to he had glanced at the outer door, where Mr. and Mrs. Erasmus would be waiting for him. And the thought came to him that death, too, was waiting behind that door. Why? Because he had been concerned about the child, or about Mr. and Mrs. Erasmus? No. Because he had been concerned with himself.

"Did you manage to get through your business in town?" Charles de la Porte asked with polite interest. "I told you there was no need to hurry back."

"No, no," Geoffrey Hutton assured him with equal politeness. "I had plenty of time. Anyway I didn't feel like being stuck in the Cape for the weekend."

"Good," Charles de la Porte said warmly, for no particular reason.

He and his partner had met in the passage outside the children's isolation ward, to where the Erasmus baby had been transferred. Now they were sitting at one of the Formica-topped tables in the doctors' common room, each with a cup of coffee in front of him.

Hutton played abstractedly with his teaspoon, looking down at the floor. He was a lean man with very light, thin hair and the skin showed through under the hair. He now treated his companion to an extended view of that pale scalp, as if reluctant to meet his eye. Charles de la Porte wondered briefly. Geoff had an agreeably gentle manner, but he was seldom shy.

They broke the overlong silence simultaneously.

"I wanted to speak to you about . . . " Charles de la Porte said.

"I hope you had no . . . " Hutton said.

They laughed and Charles de la Porte made a yielding gesture. "You have the floor."

"No. No. I . . . "

"I insist."

"Nothing much," Hutton said in embarrassment. "I was only going to ask if you had any problems while I was away?"

"Nothing really. Only this meningitis case. And that touches on what I was going to discuss with you. I've been wondering whether . . . "

He was interrupted by voices and the sound of laughter at the door. Both he and Hutton looked up inquiringly, but with faint, expectant smiles on their lips. Two other men came in, still laughing, but checking their laughter when they saw they were not alone. One of them, a short broad man with vigorously curling black hair, whose name was Charles te Water, stopped in the doorway, but the other advanced into the room, grinning.

"Hello, Charles. Hello, Geoff."

"Morning, Sol," Charles de la Porte said, and Hutton said: "Hello, Sol."

Sol Levy took off his white coat. Under it he wore a perfectly tailored and expensive-looking dark suit. He was a gynecologist and by a long way the town's most fashionable and busiest doctor. His happy-go-lucky manner and the contrasting great gentleness of his long freckled hands were reputed to be the secret of his ability to charm women patients.

"What's so funny, Sol?" Hutton asked.

Dr. Levy shook his head disbelievingly and chuckled. "Something that happened in the men's medical ward last night. Sister was telling me. You know these new power beds?"

"The press-button things?"

"That's right. They lift and lower and tilt and do just about everything except take out the patient's tonsils. Well, Sister had a death yesterday afternoon, an elderly guy who had given the nurses nothing but trouble. She moved the body to a private ward to lay him out before the family came to pay their last respects. And in the ward was one of these power beds."

He paused and like an orchestra responding to the conductor's baton they all grinned simultaneously. Even the black-haired man, listening to the story for the second time, lost his expression of disapproval.

"They all came trooping in," Sol Levy said. "Ma and the children and all the aunties and uncles, all looking appropriately disconsolate, although I don't believe any of them had much time for the old guy. He was a real reprobate, one of our bottle-a-day men. You know. Anyway, they stand around mournfully for a bit and then Ma leans over to give the old chap a farewell kiss. And by accident she presses down on the control panel. And at once the top of the bed starts to lift and the old man begins to sit up, with his mouth coming open as if he's about to start cursing them. So Ma flops down in a dead faint with the body on top of her and the rest of the tribe make for the door, yelling blue murder."

The picture evoked, ghoulish and tragic and comic all at the same time, was irresistible. They began to laugh.

"But Sister says that what she suspects *really* frightened the hell out of them," Sol Levy said, "was the prospect of having the old devil alive again."

They laughed again, more moderately this time. It really was no subject for laughter. But what else could one do, faced with the essential absurdity of the dictum "The only certainty in life is death"? How else could one respond to the cosmic jest but with a wry smile and a nod of acknowledgment: Yes, that's a good one.

Sol Levy hung up his coat and left with an affable greeting. Charles te Water made a stiff motion of the head toward Charles de la Porte.

There was another strained silence when they had gone. To break it, Hutton asked: "Another cup of coffee?"

"Lord, no!" Charles de la Porte said. Sensing that he had expressed the refusal too forcibly, for reasons which had nothing to do with the invitation, he added quickly: "I'm awash with the stuff. I must have had five cups already this morning."

They laughed together with an appearance of ease. But the constraint caused by Dr. te Water's barely concealed hostility was still there. A hollow feeling of distress and incompleteness mastered Charles de la Porte. To him one of the many tragic consequences of the Janice Case issue was the knowledge that it had caused a split among the town's doctors. When the rumor that she had started legal proceedings against a colleague was first confirmed there had been little sympathy for her. She had been persuaded by outsiders to breach the closed society of medicine. Wherever doctors met the case was debated, with as much concern as if a priestess had been caught betraying the secrets of the temple. Naturally he had never been involved in these debates, but he knew, he knew. He had noticed the sudden silences or the clumsy changes of direction when he chanced on conversations. He knew also who sympathized with him and who hoped he would be brought down. Ranged against him in the beginning had been only Edwards-White and a few of his close followers. He did not for one moment believe that the disapproval of the majority of her colleagues would sway Janice Case. Nevertheless, there was a scrap of comfort in the thought that, at least, most people understood.

But attitudes had changed.

It was difficult to tell why. Impossible perhaps, for there were probably as many reasons, and more, as there were people involved. Charles te Water was one of those who had switched sides.

They had bought the boat three years ago. It was Te Water who had discovered her, lying half derelict above a slipway at Cape Town docks, and who had proposed that they form a syndicate between the town's two firms of general practitioners, he and his two partners on the one hand and Charles de la Porte and Geoff Hutton on the other. His enthusiasm overrode all reservations. It was a once-in-a-lifetime bargain, he assured them: only six thousand for a thirty-eight-footer with twin diesels, enclosed wheelhouse, state-room, and two cabins with sleeping accommodation. The picture he painted was of a vessel which would not have shamed minor royalty or the less flamboyant kind of multimillionaire. All this for only twelve hundred each. Not forgetting the tax angle. If they used her for charter work they would be able to write off a generous portion of the expenses.

Charles de la Porte, peering in under the barnacle-crusted hull, stumbling after Te Water over rusty lengths of steel cable and unidentified bits of metal, had wryly diagnosed an acute case of myopia brought about by an attack of deep-sea fishing fever. But he, too, succumbed after they had climbed a ladder up the boat's side and stood on the deck, looking up at the flying bridge. Then, in imagination, he saw her riding long blue swells and felt the strain of the line at the end of which a great marlin was leaping.

Against his better judgment he had found himself fifth owner of a seagoing fishing vessel which swallowed money as if there was a hole down in her bilges. Both engines proved in need of expensive overhauls. Dry rot was discovered in the deck planking and this had to be replaced. The steering gear was faulty and the generator packed up on her first sea trial, while she was being brought around Cape Point to Simonstown. Painting her cost a fortune. Te Water's faith in being able to find charter work proved misplaced. The Malay skipper had to be paid a salary for sitting at home all week.

But despite the expense and mishaps they had a great deal of pleasure from the *Boa Esperança* that first summer. They had made up a fishing party of some of the partners practically every weekend. At times the competitive spirit was fierce, as if the rivalry between their two firms had been transported from land out to sea. The traditional chaffing of the man who had a fish on became rough and even a little vicious. But they caught fish and they fished together without any of them becoming outright enemies.

Last summer, however, the expeditions had become more infrequent. One of Te Water's partners had left to study as a specialist anesthetist and the young man who had replaced him in the firm was too newly qualified to be able to afford expensive hobbies. The four of them had bought out the fifth share, but with reduced numbers it was proportionately more difficult to get away on fishing trips. During the winter the *Boa Esperança* had undergone another costly refit and so far this summer she had not been to sea at all.

Charles de la Porte had asked himself the uneasy question: Did the partners' apparent reluctance to go fishing have anything to do with Janice Case's illness and his handling of it? He tried to dismiss the idea as a paranoiac fancy, but it lingered.

So when Te Water had telephoned a fortnight ago to propose a trip he had gladly accepted.

"Hello, Charles," Te Water had said.

"Hello, Charles."

The shared given name and the consequent repetition of salutation had become a small joke between them. Charles te Water now gave an awkward laugh, as if he did not care to be reminded of the joke's existence.

"I had a call from Gasant this morning. He says there are tunny in the bay. Care to go down and have a look this weekend?"

"Why, sure. Sure. That's a great idea."

"It'll be just the two of us, I'm afraid," Te Water said casually. "None of the other boys can make it."

"Geoff is on hospital standby," Charles de la Porte told him.

"I know." And then, as if he feared having given away something, the other man had quickly concluded the conversation. "I'll meet you at the boat Saturday morning. I've got business in town on Friday and I'm staying the night. Try to get down as early as you can."

Charles de la Porte had looked quizzically at the telephone receiver before replacing it. Had there been a dismissive note about the farewell? Absurd to think so. The man had invited him to go fishing, hadn't he? He must rid himself of this persecution complex, for it would undermine his determination to resist.

It occurred to him to wonder whether his opponents also had absolute belief in their cause. It was not an easy decision: to ostracize one of their own. Could they possibly have come to it malevolently? Or were they crusaders in their own eyes, and therefore unerring and uncorrupt?

He had to stop thinking that way.

And yet, early on the Saturday morning, when he came to the boat lying alongside the fishing jetty, there was still a resentful feeling of being maneuvered by forces beyond his knowledge. It made his greeting less than friendly, but if Charles te Water noticed he showed no sign. Te Water was down in the boat, helping one of the Coloured crewmen load flat cardboard boxes into the hold. He wore faded jeans and an old, soft-worn suede jacket and looked the role. His expression was animated.

"Gasant says the big babies have come in. The big bluefin."

"Bluefin?" Charles de la Porte said. He laughed doubtingly. "I've heard that one before."

The Malay skipper had excited their imaginations, that first summer, with tales of the big catches of bluefin tuna made in False Bay in past years. He had described giant fish of close to half a ton. They had gone out week after week in high anticipation and on each occasion Gasant had ended up by spitting over the side and gloomily declaring that the fish were there but that the sea was wrong. Eventually they had gone back to bottom fishing or occasionally trolling for yellowfin tunny which, small as they were, were at least not fictitious.

"He swears he saw bluefin yesterday," Te Water said. "He was out from Kalk Bay and the fish took his lines twice in succession. Bam. Bam. Just like that. I reckon we should try a spot of chumming anyway."

Charles de la Porte shrugged. "As you wish." He swung himself down off the jetty. "Have we got enough pilchards?"

Te Water shoved with a foot at one of the flat boxes. "I got six boxes. That should be enough."

"What did it come to?"

"Oh, we can fix that up later. And Gasant wants to stop and pick up some mackerel on the way out."

"Okay."

There was a spluttering roar as first one, then the other motor fired. Both settled down to a quiet throbbing and Charles de la Porte could feel the deck vibrating under his feet. A stocky, dark-faced man with glossy black hair came from the wheelhouse, wiping his hands on a cotton-waste rag.

"Morning, Gasant. So you say the big ones are here?"

"Yes."

The Malay, son of a son of a son of a slave, called no white man "Master." He was taciturn to the point of brusqueness, but he was a good fisherman and an excellent boat handler.

"Is the sea all right today?" Charles de la Porte asked.

Gasant shrugged. "Sea's all right." He turned away to shout an order to the second Coloured crewman who was standing in the bows ready to slip the mooring. Charles de la Porte caught Te Water's eye. There was a queer expression, of mingled curiosity and embarrassment, on the other man's face. He turned away, too, quickly, and busied himself with his handline as Gasant, with delicate adjustments of wheel and throttle, sheered away from the jetty.

They dropped anchor close by the harbor outer wall. The sun was rising above the far mountains, across the bay. They put over the handlines, baited with strips of pilchard. There were no immediate takes and they sat waiting for the mackerel. The sea was flat, with an oily sheen. A small craft went by, its outboard motor clattering, and they rocked in the wake of its passing. There was an ocean smell.

The tall stone wall beneath which they lay was still in the shade and the sea's ripples were reflected against it. Charles de la Porte watched the dancing pinpoints of light on the mortared stone face and found them curiously troubling. They gave an illusion of motion to the motionless stone, as if its essential energy had become visible.

He wondered about the searching glance Te Water had given him. It had been the look of someone with news to deliver and assessing the recipient so as to judge whether the news would be taken well or badly.

He realized that he did not really know Charles te Water well, although they shared the same given name and their surnames were similar enough to cause occasional confusion. They shared the same kind of life, too, and as senior partners of their town's busiest medical firms, presumably income and honor and dignity as well. They had even been students at the same university, although separated by several years. They had never really been friends. Apart from the age difference there had also been a basic contrast in life-styles. He himself was the son of a man of reduced means and had been forced to live and work accordingly. Charles te Water, Sr., had been member of Parliament for a safe Northern Cape constituency and a wealthy farmer. The son had been blessed with a sports car, a winning way with women students, a head for liquor, and an apparently limitless allowance. He had failed his second year and had only been allowed back because of his father's influence.

It had been a surprise to Charles de la Porte, returning to his hometown a good ten years ago, to find the other Charles finally qualified and in practice there. The surprise was so much the greater at the discovery that the former rake had reformed and was proving to be, as were many other mediocre students, a good and conscientious doctor. He had gained the professional and personal esteem of his colleagues. He had now been chairman of the local medical association for four years in succession.

Charles de la Porte wondered apprehensively: What is the news he is planning to break to me?

He stretched his arms, aching from the strain of leaning over the cockpit coaming and shifted to a more comfortable position, and at that instant there was a vicious tug at his line. He jerked at it, but was too late. One of the Coloured men, fishing over the stern, struck, too, and brought a darting, silver-green mackerel to the surface. Within moments the mackerel were furiously on the bite. The Coloured man had caught another, and Te Water and Gasant one each, before Charles de la Porte was able to rebait.

The skipper waited until they had a dozen fish swimming in the keep net and another dozen dead in the bait box before ordering the anchor up. He worked the wheel and the boat swung away from the harbor wall in a long, curving turn, gathering speed as she went.

As the boat headed out across the bay Charles de la Porte realized that it was going to be a particularly fine day. The sun was now bright on the water and there was a breeze out of the east, enough to turn the crests of the small waves, sparkling like endless strings of diamonds on a vast velvet bed colored in violet, blue, and green. He put thought of motives and manipulations behind and gave himself to the day and the moment.

The *Boa Esperança* surged quietly ahead, her long twin wake as straight as a furrow made by a good ploughman across a heavenly field.

Gasant anchored off Fish Hoek corner, buoying the anchor cable so that it could be let go in a hurry. He came out of the wheelhouse carrying the sturdy banana-butted rod and its massive reel. He started to set up the rod in the single fighting chair aft.

Te Water looked uncertainly at Charles de la Porte.

"Go on, Charles. Your turn."

All the partners had their own tackle for conventional deep-sea fishing. But the cost of this particular combination of rod and reel had been so astronomical that they had bought it in partnership. Gasant had pointed out, when they consulted him, that in any case only one really big fish could be fought at a time.

"You take it," Charles de la Porte said. "I don't mind. Really."

He was being perfectly truthful. He did not care. And he did not really believe they would catch anything.

Te Water made conventional gestures of protest.

"No. No. It's your turn." Then, suddenly appearing to make up his mind: "Tell you what. Let's toss for it."

He had a small coin ready even as he spoke and it spun in a silvery blur. He caught it in his palm, slapped a hand down on it, and turned it over.

"Heads," Charles de la Porte said unwillingly.

Te Water lifted his hand away. Jan van Riebeeck, in profile, showed uppermost in his palm. His disappointment was so obvious that Charles de la Porte was briefly tempted to surrender his privilege. But at once he realized that Te Water could not accept with honor. With a shrug of annoyance at the complexity of human relations he clambered into the gimbaled chair and strapped its harness around his chest and shoulders.

Gasant, seemingly indifferent about which customer he was to cater for, had been rigging the heavy rod. There were seven hundred yards of 120-pound breaking strain line on the huge reel and he had doubled back and tied the last twenty feet. Now he was fastening a swivel and its length of wire trace to the doubled line. In dead seriousness, with no sign of recognition of incongruity, he produced a child's rubber balloon from a jacket pocket, puffed and blew it up, and fixed it to the top of the trace with string. He ran the trace through his fingers until he had hold of the big 11/0 hook at its end. Hook in one hand he stooped and dipped into the keep net with the other, bringing up a lively, wriggling mackerel. Swiftly, all part of the one movement, he impaled the fish and released it, with trace and line, over the stern.

The fish swam lopsidedly on the surface for a moment, then righted itself and pulled more strongly. It bored downward to where the slanting sunlight made prisms in the deep water. The slack went out of the line. A red balloon drifted on the surface.

Gasant rinsed his hands and straightened up. "Give him line," he said, without looking at Charles de la Porte in the chair. He watched as the drag was slacked off, then held up one finger. "Enough." He gave the line an experimental tug. "More drag." He tested the line again. "Okay." He went forward, passing close by the chair, and Charles de la Porte caught the smell of fish and wine which came from him.

One of the Coloured crewmen took his place in the stern. He had a body like a barrel and a nickname, "Cat," the origin of which was a mystery. His flat, almost Oriental face wore a habitually villainous expression. He had once presented Charles de la

Porte with the gift of two dozen large white mussels and had explained, on interested inquiry, his method of discovering these in their hiding places in the sand. He went methodically down the beach with a scythe, just above low-water mark, raking the sand until the blade struck a colony of mussels. Charles de la Porte had laughed to himself at the thought of the consternation among people, especially those with white skins, confronted with a burly, tough-looking Coloured, apparently gone mental and cutting up portions of beach with a scythe. The mussels had been delicious.

In fact Cat was inoffensive and anxious to please. He was also the ship's humorist. He sat down in the stern now with a bait board and a knife and opened a box of pilchards. Very rapidly and deftly he chopped up three of the fish. He dropped the bits over the side and they sank slowly in the blue water.

"*Kom, vissie,*" he said. "*Kom.*" Come, little fish. Come.

He dropped pieces of another pilchard into the sea.

"*Kom daar uit die hole uit.*" Come out of the hole.

He put the third and last pilchard overboard.

"Come and take my bait," he said in mock pleading tones. "Come and look at this nice bait. Eat it and it'll make you fat." He added, in a sinister aside: "Eat it and it'll make you dead." He chuckled.

Charles de la Porte wondered, not for the first time, how much of this byplay was intended for the customers. Te Water was leaning against the side rail, listening, too, an amused smile on his lips.

"Nothing yet," he said.

"No."

"I've got a feeling we're going to get something today."

"Hope you're right."

They watched as Cat prepared another three pilchards for chum.

"How old are you now, Charles?" Te Water asked suddenly and disconcertingly.

Charles de la Porte stared at him. "Fifty. Why?"

"Fifty, eh? Yes. I'm forty-eight. You were two years ahead of me at 'varsity, weren't you?" Te Water paused. An expression which, if it had been anyone else, Charles de la Porte would have identified as shyness came to his face. "Do you know how much I used to admire you? Hero worship, almost. To me you represented all the qualities I lacked."

"You must be joking."

"Not in the least. I remember that year you played for Western Province. What year was that?"

"My third year. Nineteen forty-seven."

"That's right. My first year. You would have played for the Springboks that year if there had been a test series."

"Well . . . possibly."

"Possibly, hell! You were the best postwar rugby center by a long way. I'll never forget the try you scored in the intervarsity that year. You got the ball from a loose scrum in the middle and ran through the whole UCT pack and dummied their left wing and then ran away from the fullback as if he was standing still."

The description sounded suspiciously well briefed and Charles de la Porte acknowledged it with no more than a smile.

"The All Blacks came out in forty-nine, didn't they? But you weren't playing rugby then."

"I was in my fifth year. I had to choose between rugby and passing my exams."

"Well, I know a lot of people were bitterly disappointed not to see you playing for the Boks."

Charles de la Porte was saved from the need for a reply by the mackerel, which had been dormant for a while, as if discouraged by its inability to escape the object which held it pinned through the back. Now, suddenly, it began to swim and tug, as if something had frightened it down in the green water. Everyone was silent, watching the line. Nothing happened. After a while the mackerel ceased its struggles and a slow curve reappeared in the line.

Te Water balanced himself against the roll of a bigger-than-usual wave.

"We doctors have had to change a great deal in the years since you and I qualified, haven't we?" he said.

Charles de la Porte did not allow himself to show surprise.

"Change? Do you think so? As far as I can see we still practice the same kind of medicine."

"I mean in the sense that a doctor these days has to regard himself more as a partner with his patient. The senior partner, perhaps; the better informed one. But still no more than a partner. Certainly not the arbiter of man's fate." Te Water smiled, to show that he did not take the phrase seriously.

Charles de la Porte saw, with chill recognition, which way the conversation was heading.

"Is an individual doctor obliged to conform to ideas he does not hold simply because they are fashionable? I like to think we are free to make our own decisions about our role in society and our duty toward our patient."

The ready smile flashed. "Of course, Charles. Free within the disciplines of the profession. For that is the concomitant, surely? If you are prepared to make use of the privileges of the profession you must abide by its rules, too, not so? The law of the land doesn't prohibit you from publicly criticizing your colleagues or from seeking undue publicity. But your peers would certainly take a dim view if you did either, even if just to proclaim your individuality."

"I don't think there is a parallel."

"Perhaps not." Te Water seemed to be contemplating the darting movements of a number of small fish which, attracted by the chum, were swimming alongside. At last he said: "This business between you and Jay. It's very sad really."

"Yes," Charles de la Porte said.

"And especially so since it could have been prevented."

"Prevented? How?"

"I understand there is an option of settling out of court? Isn't there?"

"Where did you get that information? And, with respect, what has it got to do with you?"

Te Water seemed unabashed. "Naturally all your friends are concerned. And naturally the Medical Association shares that concern."

"I don't see that it's any of their business."

"My dear Charles, family rows should be kept within the family, don't you agree? Do you realize that the press will have a field day if this thing ever goes to open court? There's your rugby career for them to gloat over. And for the extra bit of spice the fact that you were married to Antoinette Krynauw. She's still a legend among the literati. You won't find it pleasant."

"So you maintain that to keep a medical scandal out of the newspapers, I should compromise with what I believe?"

Te Water winced delicately.

"Hold on, old boy. That's not the issue. It's your position we're concerned about." He threw his hands out in a gesture of candor. "I admit that the image of the profession is tied up..."

Charles de la Porte shook his head decisively. "No, I'm sorry, but I'm seeing this thing through. If your mission has been to put some kind of pressure on me then I'm afraid you failed."

A spot of color appeared in Te Water's cheeks. "You don't have to be holier than thou with me, Charles. All I'm urging is that you reconsider before it's too late."

"There doesn't seem to be any room in your mind for the thought that I might have been right in what I did."

"Charles, they're going to crucify you. Breast cancer is a highly emotional issue and they're going to prove you made the wrong decision."

"I don't see how they could possibly do that. There were so many factors involved, and ... "

"The law doesn't like nuances. They're going to reduce the whole issue to this: You should have operated and for some reason you didn't. And how do you answer that?"

"But it was totally contraindicated."

"And if I tell you that they have found a radiologist who's prepared to say your reading of the X rays was faulty? And that there's a surgeon ready to swear that he could have saved that woman? I don't have to tell you his name. They're going to tear you apart in that court, Charles. And all for nothing. She's going to die anyway."

"Yes."

"What it comes down to is that you should have told her she had cancer. And then you should have done that operation. Why didn't you, Charles?"

110

Charles de la Porte heard his own voice. It was brittle, like dry parchment torn by clumsy fingers. It said: "I have already explained everything."

Te Water turned away with a gesture of frustration. "For God's sake." His face had taken on a pinched look. "Why don't you learn ... " He did not complete the sentence.

They watched, in angry, separate silences, as the Coloured man in the stern sliced up and dumped three more pilchards.

"Come eat my nice bait," Cat said. "Come and get a bellyache."

A vast feeling of desolation had overcome Charles de la Porte. All of this was unreal: the sea and the slow rocking of the boat floating upon it, the heavy tackle which strained his arm muscles, even the thin beading of sweat which had collected on his forehead. There was no meaning or joy in any of it. He wondered in brief panic whether he was experiencing the first symptoms of seasickness. He wished devoutly that he was somewhere else.

The wind had dropped, but it had settled in to rain. They stood for a moment, sheltering under the porte-cochere where the ambulances stopped, looking at the dismal day.

Geoff Hutton clicked his tongue in vexation.

"I forgot. Haven't got a car. My wife dropped me here this morning."

"I'll give you a lift," Charles de la Porte offered.

"I'd be grateful. She's picking me up at the surgery when I'm through."

"Right. I have to get back to the surgery, too." When Hutton moved to follow out into the rain he made a restraining gesture. "Wait. I'll collect you here. No sense in both of us getting wet."

He had carelessly left the driver's side window open at the top and rain had sifted in over his seat and its sheepskin cover. He mopped up water with a handkerchief, swearing under his breath. When he stopped for Hutton a moment later there was a depressing smell of damp sheep's wool in the car.

They traveled for a while in silence. Then, slowing down at a crossing and glancing across to check on traffic from the side, he noticed that Hutton had been surveying him surreptitiously. Charles de la Porte felt a momentary flash of annoyance. It was aggravating to find that people were awkward in his company, as if he had become an object of pity. He had felt it earlier this morning with Sister Groenewald and now Geoff, too, had seemingly succumbed.

It was perhaps this which caused him to put unnecessary bite into his tone when, continuing an earlier thought, he said: "Charles te Water has become very cool toward us, hasn't he?"

Hutton blinked and looked at him quickly. He gave a dry cough. "I suppose so." He added, elaborately casual: "Did I tell you he came to see me last week?"

Charles de la Porte said nothing for a moment.

"Must have slipped my mind." Hutton laughed somewhat artificially. "It wasn't very important anyway."

Charles de la Porte allowed himself a noncommittal "Hm."

A traffic light changed to amber and then to red as they approached. He brought the car to a slow, gliding halt, then turned to face his partner squarely.

"Am I correct in assuming that this meeting of yours concerned me?"

Again Hutton could not hide his dismay. "Well . . . yes. Yes, it did."

"I see. And am I permitted to know what was discussed? Or is that also a secret?"

112

Hutton flushed. "I don't think you need to adopt that attitude, Charles."

"I suppose he told you about our little chat on the boat the other day."

"Yes. He did."

"And did he make it clear that I regard any interference as gross impertinence?"

"Well . . . naturally he's worried. We all are."

"Much as I appreciate your concern I fear that you force me to tell you it is none of your business."

Hutton's lower lip sagged and he looked both frightened and astounded, as if he had been struck in the face. Then his jaw hardened. He sat up stiffly, staring directly ahead. He said nothing.

Stop, Charles de la Porte told himself. Stop now before you say something irrevocable. But he was driven.

"I think I, too, have reason for concern when I find my partner involved in an apparent conspiracy to put pressure on me. Or is that the real reason for your concern? Do you fear that this unsavory business might damage your reputation? Well if that is the case I am perfectly willing to dissolve the partnership."

"Those are hard words." Geoff Hutton was very angry.

"Is the truth too hard to take? Would you prefer that I pretend not to notice what's happening. Did Dr. te Water not tell you that I am utterly resolved to defend this action?"

"He did."

"And what was your response? I suppose you agreed with him that I was wrong and stupid and stubborn? I suppose you promised you would try to make me see the error of my ways?"

Hutton was silent for a moment.

Then he said: "I told him to go and get stuffed. In so many words."

The light changed. Charles de la Porte touched the accelerator and the big car responded smoothly.

They did not speak for a long time.

"Would it help if I were to apologize?" Charles de la Porte asked finally.

"There is no need. You were free to draw whatever conclusions you wished."

"But not to draw the obviously wrong ones. To assume automatically that all your friends are knaves and traitors is the reaction of either a paranoiac or a fool."

"We know that you are neither."

"That is more than I deserve," Charles de la Porte said humbly. And then: "Oh, God, Geoff. I'm tired to death."

Anger was immediately replaced by solicitude. Hutton looked at him with an anxious frown.

"I know. I wish there was something I could do. Perhaps I should take over from you for a bit. Just until it's all over anyway."

Charles de la Porte laughed tersely. "It's kind of you to offer. But I doubt if it would really help."

"I guess not." Hutton made a brushing, despairing gesture with one hand over his thin hair. "But at least understand, Charles, that I am firmly behind you in this. Never be in doubt about that."

"You make me more ashamed of myself than ever."

"You are *not* to think that way."

The unconscious echo (in tone, both chiding and fond—and almost identical in phrasing) of his wife's reprimand last night succeeded in bringing a smile to Charles de la Porte's lips.

"Thank you. I'll try to remember."

As always on a Saturday morning there was heavy traffic around the square. Saturday was the traditional shopping day for Coloured people and it had become a social event, too, as they came crowding to town to shop and talk, strolling with a proprietary air along the broad pavements or dodging in and out of the supermarkets or sitting at the side of the street and on the lawns, even on benches marked: "Whites Only."

A group of young men in jeans and T-shirts stood in a tight, closed group outside a liquor store. Their faces, as they turned toward the two white men passing in the big car, bore uniform expressions of cold menace: the disdain of two fingers in a V, flicked indifferently toward the onlooker.

"We'll probably have a couple of knifings to cope with in Casualty tonight," Hutton said.

"Are you on duty?"

"On call."

They parted at the Drostdy entrance. Hutton climbed out of the car and stood at the half-open door, stooping, looking in.

"Thanks for the lift. And remember what I've said."

"I will. Thank you. Now hurry up before you're soaked."

Hutton shook his head like a patient golden retriever coming wetly out of a pond and raindrops flew in a spray from his hair.

"When are you going down to the Cape?"

"Monday morning early."

"Then I won't see you before you go. No, wait a minute. Are you going to the Shaws tonight?"

"So my wife informs me."

"So are we. Good. I'll see you there."

Hutton was gone at a head-down run, dashing for the shelter of the Drostdy. Charles de la Porte drove his car around to the parking lot and then went in to where his patients waited.

"I'm almost ashamed to be holding you up," Frank Edelstein said. "It's not important enough to warrant dragging you away from all your sick customers. I merely wanted to go through the final pleadings with you and clarify one or two points. But I could easily have brought the papers out to Hoog-in-het-Dal."

"No trouble," Charles de la Porte said. "I was busy with my last patient when you called."

Visiting Frank's office was always a pleasure. He had decorated it himself, with the stated intention to make it appear as little as possible like a room where dull business was conducted. The effect was that of going into the drawing room of a prosperous but broad-minded Dutch merchant of the mid-eighteenth century.

Charles de la Porte sat down in front of the great table with its silk drapings and tassels which served Frank as desk. Frank had crossed to the far wall. He pushed at its paneling and a section slid aside. There was a small well-stocked bar behind it.

"I take it you are off duty in that case. I think one needs cheering up in this ghastly weather. What'll you have?"

"Thank you. A very moderate Scotch."

They raised glasses in a silent toast and sipped at their drinks with a conspiratorial air. Charles de la Porte found himself relaxing for the first time today. Tensions slipped away, as they always did in the company of this cool and elegant man. Frank Edelstein had the ability to draw from others qualities they hardly knew they possessed. His was the steel against which his friends could sharpen the foils of their wit.

Then Frank, unusually serious, said: "Going through all these documents again made me realize afresh how wasteful all this is."

"I certainly realize it."

"But you would see it more clearly. Knowing so well that life is short, you would know this, too. That's what I tried to convey to Cliff." He stopped short, with a slight suggestion of being flustered.

"Cliff McOwen?"

Frank nodded. The mocking smile was back, but he had a guarded expression.

"I didn't know you'd seen him. When was this?"

"Oh, quite a while ago. As a matter of fact he wanted me to act for him in the matter. But I refused."

"I didn't know that."

"I thought it best that you didn't. It would have been an unnecessary obscurity. And goodness knows we have enough of those."

"I suppose I should read it as a vote of confidence in my cause."

116

"I didn't know at that stage that you had a cause." Frank made a languid gesture. "Perhaps, my dear fellow, it was more like the insane impulse one has when one watches a fox hunt. To jump in there among the hounds and save the poor little fox."

They laughed.

"What were the points you wanted to clarify?"

"This operation Edwards-White carried out on Jay. A mastectomy and what was the other?"

"Oophorectomy. That means the removal of the ovaries."

"Yes. Now what was the purpose of doing this?"

"It's tied up with the hormone therapy which, you'll remember, I prescribed for her. The rationale is that, with the removal of the ovaries, you also remove the source of estrogen and progesterone. In fact castration was the original method of endocrinal treatment."

"Hormone treatment?"

"Yes."

"And how does it work?"

"The theory is that the growth of breast cancer is controlled by the same hormones as normal breast growth. Cancel out one and you cancel out the other."

"I understand. You sought to achieve this canceling out by giving her male hormones?"

"That's correct."

"But the suggestion is that you could have achieved the desired result more effectively by doing this operation in time?"

"That's a very contentious claim. You must remember that it's a crippling, mutilating operation. I don't believe it would have been worth it in this case."

"Don't you think Jay should have been consulted for her views on the subject?" Frank Edelstein asked gently.

"No. I had decided not to tell her."

"Were you afraid to tell her, Charles?"

Charles de la Porte's jaw stiffened. "What do you mean?"

"It's something that occurred to me. It's an inference the judge might draw. But forgive me if I have offended you."

"Nothing to forgive," Charles de la Porte said somewhat

117

gruffly. He pulled his thoughts together. "You must understand that telling a patient he is dying is a hell of a thing. But I wouldn't shirk it because of that. In Jay's case my reasons were quite different."

"What were they?"

"God, man, we've been through this innumerable times. The hopelessness of her condition. The fact that she wasn't in pain. The chance that hormone treatment might prolong her life."

"Was that all?"

"What else do you want? Oh, yes, there was something else. She had a revulsion against being mutilated in any way."

Frank looked suddenly intensely interested. "Really? That's something new. You haven't told us that before. When did you learn this?"

"Oh, a long time ago."

"What form did this phobia take?"

"I wouldn't say it was quite as strong as a phobia. It was just that she hated the thought of losing any part of her body. Of anything being crushed or severed."

"I see," Frank said doubtfully. "She told you this? What were the circumstances?"

"I can't quite remember. I probably gathered as much during the . . . you know, during the course of the years. When she consulted me . . . talking to her . . . that kind of thing."

"I see." Frank was toying with the silk tassels which dangled from the tablecloth fringe.

Charles de la Porte said, as if suddenly inspired: "She even wanted me to do a needle biopsy. She knew it would be inadequate, yet she disliked the thought of being cut into."

"Why didn't you tell us this before?"

"I don't know. I suppose I never thought of it."

"I see," Frank said again, and Charles de la Porte sat back in his chair, numbed by the realization that the other man had not believed him in the least.

118

It was only when he reached the torn red earth and the muddy pools that Charles de la Porte remembered his intention to complain about the state of the road. As he drove carefully over the deviation scar, avoiding the left-hand side, where the mud was slippery as grease, he thought again about the freeway. The damned thing would be a disaster and, in an era of expensive gas and reduced speed limits, an absurdity.

Anger, and a frustrated desire to strike out at something, anything, rose within him.

"We'll fight them," he said aloud.

The machines stood at the side of the road, motionless objects of steel, with the rain sifting steadily down upon them. He felt suddenly ashamed of the excess of emotion. He corrected the steering against a skid, then drove further.

What exactly are you trying to preserve? he asked himself. All these projects of loving restoration and preservation you're involved in. The campaign against the freeway. The plans to save the Drostdy. The campaign against removing the oaks on the Square. The memorial garden scheme. The time and money spent on Hoog-in-het-Dal. What's it all for?

Is your aim to safeguard a life-style which is worn out and threatened? Or is it an attempt to re-create something of youth: the experience of being young and secure in the feeling that all things were fixed, that nothing would ever change?

He remembered his thoughts in the Italian snack bar this morning, and his conclusion that security was the first of youth's illusions, and first to go. Was he trying to cling to a dead past, as his father had tried before him?

Now the familiar terraced slopes of Hoog-in-het-Dal lay

ahead of him. The green of new growth made bright patterns across the lower, nearer vineyard.

He thought of his grandfather, who had been Charles Michel de la Porte, too, and who had built up Hoog-in-het-Dal from the ruins after the ravages of phylloxera, and then of his father, proud of his name and his heritage, who in the end had been left with little except the name. He had not been a wicked man, nor a spendthrift, but somehow it had all slipped away. "Charles, always remember that there are more important things than money." Father, sitting reading the biographies of great men while the Coloured workers loafed in the lands. "Breeding always tells, Charles." Until, of the two hundred acres, only the two vineyards, one above and one below the house, were left. That was when his mother, abandoning her causes (votes for women; the spiritual uplifting of the Native races; the design of a new South African flag) had stepped in. Small, fierce, and relentlessly energetic, she had kept them all going through the lean years of the war and afterward. "Your mother is determined to see you through university, Charles. I think we must abide by her decision." Poor Father.

And yet the name De la Porte still meant something in the town and its countryside. It spoke of six generations, of two centuries of the history of this place. There had been earlier settlers, Dutch and German, but the first De la Porte on this land had been one of the Huguenots, a refugee from religious persecution who had come to alien Africa and had tried to make it, with typically French bourgeois stubbornness, a replica of what he had left. It meant something to be a De la Porte of Hoog-in-het-Dal. Perhaps, he thought, this was one of the reasons why the hunting dogs were baying at his heels.

He recognized, with a small smile, the vanity which lay behind the thought, and turned in through the stone gateposts of Hoog-in-het-Dal.

The lower driveway was blocked again, not by a barrow as it had been last night, but by a car which was strange to him, dark

120

green and low-slung like a racer. It had been carelessly parked, leaving barely enough room for him to maneuver between it and the hibiscus hedge which edged the drive. He went carefully past the sleek vehicle, noting the manufacturer's emblem, Dino-Ferrari, and the CA registration plate and wondering. Who in Cape Town did he or Gillian know who drove a car like this?

He took the wide turn to the double garage on the terrace below the house. Gillian's little red Mazda was in its usual place.

As he opened the front door he heard voices from the living room. They ceased at the sound of the door closing. He paused, considering whether to go past to the bathroom.

Gillian came to the living-room door. On her face was the familiar expression, half humorous, half rueful, with which she greeted minor disturbances such as incontinent babies or cats stuck in trees or the unannounced arrival of awkward relatives.

"Hello, darling," she greeted him overbrightly, meanwhile pulling a face at him. "Home at last. Here are two gentlemen to see you. A Mr. Bachelli and a Mr. Van Wyk."

He showed his surprise and she rolled her eyes.

"Bachelli?"

She nodded and, still with her back to the doorway, not speaking, signaled with mouth and eyes: Please! Rescue!

Frowning, he went past her into the living room. Bachelli was in the chair beside the fireplace. He wore his usual expression of bored composure, but there was an edge to it, as if of excitement only barely contained.

"Hello, Charles. Sorry to break in on you like this."

The familiarity was surprising, even faintly shocking. Charles de la Porte tried not to show it.

"Hello. Not at all."

He looked toward the other man who had been sitting in the window seat overlooking the valley and had thus, presumably, been able to watch his car coming up the drive. The stranger was stocky and his hair, like Bachelli's, gingery, with the difference that he wore it short and neat. He had a blunt, snub-nosed Afrikaner face. He rose and came forward, holding out a hand.

"Van Wyk," he said.

Charles de la Porte shook the proferred hand. He looked at Bachelli for an explanation.

"Charles, can you spare us a little time?"

"Certainly," Charles de la Porte said. "But you'll have to excuse me for a moment. I must go and tidy up. Please do sit down."

He left them and went to the bathroom at the end of the passage. Gillian followed him. He closed the door.

"What's all this about?"

"I have no idea. They arrived about fifteen minutes ago and said they had to see you urgently. At least, the one with the moustache did. The one in the suit hasn't spoken a word."

He realized that they were whispering in spite of the closed door. He raised his voice to normal. "Bachelli is the barrister who's handling the case."

"I gathered that. What on earth could he want? On a Saturday afternoon. Could something have gone wrong about the case?"

"Frank would have told me. I saw him just before I came up from town."

"Could it be something Frank doesn't know about?"

"I doubt it. Bachelli would have let him know."

"And the other one? Who's he?"

"I can't imagine."

"He looks like a policeman."

"Do you think so?"

"He's got that look about him. Sort of . . . you know . . . square. I don't mean in the slang sense."

"I know what you mean. You could be right."

"What on earth could they want with you?"

He rinsed his soapy hands under the tap, drew a comb through his hair, examined his reflection in the mirror, and said, with carefully judged cheerfulness: "I imagine they're dying to tell us. Shall we join them?"

The two men were where he had left them: Bachelli lounging in the chair at the fireplace, the other man in the middle of the room, expectantly facing the door.

He said again: "Do sit down, please." He waited until

the stranger was seated, then asked: "Can I get you a drink? Darling?"

"A gin and tonic."

He turned to Bachelli, who smiled and said with unusual warmth: "Thanks, Charles. I'll have the same."

"Mr. Van Wyk?"

The supposed policeman at first refused a drink, but was talked into having a cold beer. Charles de la Porte deliberately drew out the process of putting out glasses and pouring and serving the drinks. For an obscure reason he needed to establish that he was master of this house and they were his guests.

Only when everyone was seated and had a glass did he ask pleasantly, not addressing either of the two men in particular: "Now, then. What can I do for you?"

Bachelli leaned forward with an air of incisiveness.

"Charles, I brought Lieutenant Van Wyk here. There's something he wants to discuss with you."

"Lieutenant?"

"I'm sorry. I should have introduced you. He's from the police."

Charles de la Porte lifted his eyebrows. Full marks to Jilly.

"I see."

Again that swift, self-assured forward lunge.

"It concerns Janice Case and her husband. And it's all very delicate. And, of course, highly confidential." He looked pointedly at Gillian.

Charles de la Porte studied the young barrister for a moment, frowning slightly.

Gillian put down her glass and made to get up. "If it's about business, then perhaps I ... "

He stopped her with a glance and raised a hand. "I can't think why that should be necessary." He turned to the policeman. "No matter how delicate, if it concerns me it also concerns my wife. Is there any reason why she should not be present?"

Directly challenged and forced into the discussion, Van Wyk seemed nonplussed.

"Of course it's very confidential. But ... uh ... if she

prefers ... uh ... to stay." He spread his hands in a gesture of acceptance.

"Then that's that," Charles de la Porte said firmly. "What is it you want to say?"

The police officer looked uncertainly at Bachelli. The barrister's face had taken on an expression, relieved and superior at the same time, like that of an amateur conjurer who had completed the preparations for a trick without being detected and was about to demonstrate it, confident of being able to baffle his audience. He waved a hand.

"Lieutenant, I think you can best explain it."

Van Wyk cleared his throat. "Yes, well. As Mr. Bachelli says it concerns Mr. and Mrs. McOwen. We have reason to believe that they have been mixing with communists."

Charles de la Porte heard Gillian, at his side, draw in her breath. He said thickly, into a mist: "Oh, don't be absurd."

The policeman said doggedly: "Perhaps it's difficult for you to believe, Doctor, but we have been given certain information."

"Who are these 'we' you talk about?"

Bachelli had been examining his own fingernails in pretended boredom. The eagerness with which he interrupted now gave him away. "Perhaps you don't quite understand, Charles. Lieutenant Van Wyk is in the Security Branch. It appears that the McOwens have been under surveillance for a long time."

Charles de la Porte asked him with contempt: "And where do you fit into this?"

Bachelli shrugged. His look said: I am utterly remote from this affair. But he moistened his lips with his tongue as a man might do, watching, with vicarious excitement, another man's struggle for life. "I happened to come to hear of the lieutenant's interest in the McOwens. And as it might have some bearing on your court case, naturally I offered our cooperation."

It was the claustrophobic world of intrigue and conspiracy and lies and mean deceit. It was like living inside a cavern, deep down where it was dark and you moved by groping from place to place, always with the dread that one of the wild things which lived in the night would seize you. Charles de la Porte shook his head to dispel the suffocating tension.

Van Wyk was speaking again.

"We have been keeping an eye on everyone associated with Mr. and Mrs. McOwen."

Charles de la Porte did not miss the slight emphasis. He was sure he was intended to notice. Because of this he said with bitterness: "Do you realize Dr. Case has cancer? Is this what your so-called security consists of? The persecution of dying women?"

Van Wyk showed his teeth in a grin which was totally devoid of humor. He said nothing, but his eyes were as quick as a lizard's.

"What evidence have you got anyway?" Charles de la Porte asked. "That the McOwens have friends the government doesn't like? So have I, probably. So what?"

"We have information about attempts to set up a subversive underground newspaper."

"And am I supposed to accept your word that that's true? What do you want from me? Do you expect me to turn against my friends because you claim they are subversives?"

"Hold it, Charles," Bachelli said. "He hasn't asked you to do anything."

"Then why come to me?"

"Because I brought him, don't forget."

"Then perhaps you should explain the reasons."

"Charles, we can't afford to quibble. We've got to accept, and not ask too many questions."

"That's where you are totally wrong. This, of all times, is a time to ask questions."

"All right, but won't you please realize that we're here because we might be able to help you with your court case. If only you'd give the man a chance to speak."

There was a nervous irritability about Bachelli which alerted warning signals. If he was excited about the court case, could it mean he was worried about it? And did this in turn reveal doubts about its success which he had concealed until now?

Charles de la Porte addressed the policeman. "I suppose

you have a job to do, no matter how unpleasant. But I fail to see how I can be of any help."

Van Wyk rocked his upper body back and forth, back and forth, like an eager dog waiting for the word of command which would loose it; a small, energetic breed of dog: a terrier hunting rats in a vast, straw-filled barn. But when he spoke, his words were slow and deliberate, startling by contrast.

"Doctor, you have known Mrs. McOwen for a long time, haven't you?"

The quality of leashed tension about the man began to fill Charles de la Porte with a slow fear.

"Yes, comparatively long."

"We are looking for certain information about her past. And I think you might be able to help us."

"I doubt it."

"Doctor, I am sure you could help if you wanted to."

Gillian had been sitting on a low footstool close to her husband. She had not spoken, but she had looked alertly at the faces of each of the men in turn as they spoke. Now she put her glass down by her side.

"Charles, what is all this about? What is this man saying?"

He met her eyes, forcing himself to appear unalarmed. "My dear, I have no idea."

She turned to the policeman. "What are you trying to say? What are you insinuating?"

Van Wyk looked away.

A laugh burst from Bachelli, a wild cackle which he immediately suppressed, with obvious self-disgust. They all looked at him with curiosity.

Charles de la Porte began to wonder about the young man for the first time. Was Bachelli more than just a performer inside the ring, going through his polished routine with bored skill? Was he riding another, higher, and wilder trapeze, all alone?

"What he means is that he wants to offer you a deal, Charles."

"What kind of deal?"

"In return for this information he wants he might be able to bring certain pressure to bear. And then we'll find on Monday that the action has been withdrawn."

Morality and scruples were luxuries which could be abandoned. What mattered was to win the case. The client and his interests were of lesser importance. What mattered was to win.

"But surely that kind of thing . . . it's not possible."

Bachelli shrugged. He turned to face the big window with its view over the valley.

"It has been known to happen."

He was moving into the black world of the cave again. It was an unreality which was more tangible, more hard-edged, than reality itself. Inside the cave you either lived or died.

"What do you want to know?" Charles de la Porte asked the police officer.

Family legend held that the old vine had been planted by that first De la Porte who had come to Hoog-in-het-Dal in the 1760s. Charles de la Porte doubted the truth of the story, although he never contradicted Gillian when she told it to marveling visitors. He had seen bigger vines than this, none of them dating back more than a hundred years. Nevertheless, there was no doubt that the vine was very old. The base of its trunk was as thick as a stout young tree. Its wandering tendrils, suspended from wires between stone pillars, covered an area twenty paces square and bore, always a little late in the season, small bunches of grapes with a delicate flavor.

He walked under the shelter of the old vine now. The rain had held off for a while, but slow drops formed and fell from the tangled foliage. There were pools of water here and there on the flagstones.

At the last row of pillars he paused and stood with his hands in his trouser pockets. Before him was the driveway, empty now that the green car had gone away. Beyond was the hibiscus hedge and then a steep fall of land to the vineyards and the valley. He saw that the gray clouds above the valley were thinning and tearing. Perhaps tomorrow would be a fine day.

The vine under which he stood was ancient; had already been old before he was born and would endure long beyond his lifetime. Yet it could be destroyed by one blow.

An ax had been wielded against the branches of his own life: all that slow-growing complex of reaching and touching and finding which was the structure of existence.

He remembered the anguish in his wife's face as she asked him: "But why? Why?"

And he: "I can't answer that."

He had felt it last night, sitting alone in his consulting rooms. He had become aware of the wasteland of silence between him and those around him. Now that wasteland was populated by terrible and terrifying creatures. His flesh was soft and he had become prey to strange hunters; naked to unknown fangs.

"I don't understand it," she had said. "Janice was your patient, but that was all, wasn't it? What else could there possibly be?"

PART TWO

A time to plant ...

1

He took the correct turning at the flyover more by instinct, through having turned his car here a thousand times before, than with conscious thought. In the same preoccupied state he sat watching for a break in the traffic. It came, and he accelerated to join the swift shuttle of vehicles on the mountainside road.

But he was still thinking of other things. Principally about the hospital and the girl he had operated on this morning. Why should she have sought to end her life? And to choose caustic soda, of all ways. God. Her esophagus had been so badly burned that she could not even swallow her own saliva. The surgeons had decided that further attempts at dilatation of the stricture would be dangerous, so he had been called on to do a feeding gastrostomy.

The sight of a distant clock on a tower made him check his own watch and then start to drive faster. He was going to be late. The lift club arrangements had broken down and his wife had telephoned asking him to fetch Paul from the nursery school at noon. Only ten minutes to go.

To his annoyance the traffic was slowing down and telescoping. Brake lights were flashing redly up ahead. There was some honking of horns. He cut from the inside to the outside lane, but was soon stuck between a high-finned American car and a delivery van. Progress slowed to a crawl. He sat drumming his fingers on the steering wheel. The sky was a furious, intense blue. It was hot in the open car. He was going to be late for sure.

At least they would now be able to feed the poor wretch. And once she had fattened up a bit they would be able to do a bypass of the stricture. He hoped the prof would let him do the operation. But probably the old man would keep it for himself.

130

Would it be better to use a bit of the ascending colon or a loop of ilium?

A siren sounded in the distance. There was probably an accident up ahead. That would be the most likely explanation for a traffic jam at this hour of the day. But Paul would not understand. He would cry about having to wait after all the other children had left. He was weepy for a sturdy five-year-old. He cried easily, over small things. Almost as if he sensed that there was something wrong within his tiny world.

What could have brought her to the point of wanting to end her own life? She was pretty, probably attractive to men, healthy, young. How could someone like that decide that there was no future? A row with a boyfriend? She was a secretary; had there been trouble at work? At home?

Those burned and blistered lips could not give reasons or explanations. But even if they could, would he have understood? He accepted in theory that people could be overwhelmed by a sense of meaninglessness. He understood the need for a future goal and the shattering loss which accompanied its disappearance.

But he ran his life differently. Which was why he was engaged in the struggle for the life of a girl without a future.

The shark-fin car had moved forward while his attention had wandered. He engaged gear and went hurriedly after it. He passed a bus. The scattering of passengers were all staring ahead, watching something. They could probably see the accident scene over the roofs of the cars.

The long, graceful university buildings were on the slopes above but he did not, as he usually did, look up at them and at the mountain behind. He was watching the brake lights of the car in front, which had flickered warningly a few times.

He was puzzled to hear the sounds of voices over the noise of the traffic; sounds of shouts; voices chanting. And then the road curved toward an interchange and the brake lights under the tall fins in front glowed firmly and he could see the cause of the stoppage.

A row of young men and women, some of them in academic gowns, stood along the center of the road. They were holding posters, showing them to the occupants of the cars. "Free Our Leaders," said one, held by a lean, red-headed youth who was shouting and waving a fist at someone beyond Charles's line of sight. "Avenge Sharpeville," said another. The shootings at Sharpeville, in which black people had died under police fire, were already several years in the past, but were still a bitter memory for many and an emotional rallying cry. The traffic moved again, jerkily. Now Charles could see that the students had driven a car, a decrepit tortoise-shaped old Morris, across the central island, half blocking the road. More slogans were chalked on its rusty sides.

There were police vans on the opposite verge and a line of policemen in blue and khaki uniforms on the pavement. The students shouted at them and chanted: "Fascist pigs." The policemen watched impassively. Behind the line stood an officer speaking into a walkie-talkie. Gaping pedestrians had gathered behind the police vehicles.

Bloody kids, Charles thought. What did they think a university was for? They wanted to make it a battleground for their confrontations with authority. The other day the prof had neatly summed up the character of one of their leaders. "He's not so much a personality as a civil war within himself," the old man had said. And yet one had to concede that the cause this same young man proclaimed so passionately and recklessly was the worthy one of an end to racial discrimination, of social justice and equality. Charles searched his own conscience uneasily. Were the young people right? Was confrontation the only way open when the minds of South Africa's white rulers remained so obstinately closed?

He looked at his watch. Five past twelve. At the nursery school little boys and girls, Paul among them, would be chattering away as the supervisors helped them into their home clothes. Parents would be arriving at the front door.

The police officer was speaking into a bullhorn. The amplified voice, tinny-sounding, as if it had no connection with the person producing it, blared: "This is your final warning. This is an illegal gathering and I am giving you one minute to disperse." He raised his wrist and looked at the watch on it. "One minute from now."

The shouts of the demonstrators had faded briefly before the mechanical onslaught, but they sounded up again in the same dirge as before.

"Fas-cist-*pigs! Fas-cist-pigs! Fas-cist-pigs!*"

The uniformed policemen watched, fingering their buttoned-down revolver holsters. The officer looked at his watch. He seemed worried rather than angry.

"Fifteen seconds left."

The rhythm changed slightly.

"*Fas*-cist-pigs! *Fas*-cist-pigs! *Fas*-cist-pigs!"

The officer lowered his arm resentfully. He stared at the students. Charles, watching from his car, could see the man square his body into an attitude of decision and resoluteness. He knew at once what the policeman had decided and he felt his throat go dry with apprehension.

The officer gave a command which was drowned out by the derisive yells of the demonstrators. His men drew their batons. Opposite Charles was a tall constable whose face under his cap looked young and frightened. Beside him was a burly older man who held his baton like a hammer. His lips were drawn back from his teeth.

The line of policemen surged like a breaking wave. The men ran among the stationary vehicles, stiff within the restraint of their uniforms, all polished belts and buckles and badges. The students scattered before the swift advance. One paused to scream a final challenge and was beaten over the head and, when he covered his face with his hands, on the shoulders. A poster soared through the air. There were shouts and some screams. A group of students ran raggedly along the top of the road embankment, where yellow flowers grew. Half a dozen policemen ran after them, brandishing their batons. A young man was trapped against a diamond mesh fence while two uniformed men hit him. A police van, engine screaming, went bucking across the sidewalk. Two of the demonstrators, a boy and a girl, were bundled into the back. There was blood on the boy's face.

It was all over, reduced to scattered figures running in

the distance, to faint cries and faraway shouts. After the brief moments of tension Charles felt oddly frustrated.

Then, horrifyingly, explosively, it was upon him. A girl appeared from between the stalled cars and ran toward him, screaming. She ran and she screamed in an extremity of terror and behind her ran a man in a blue uniform, baton raised. The girl dodged this way and that, her long black hair swinging. She ran with clumsy grace like that of a young animal uncertain of its footing. The policeman ran sturdily, gaining ground rapidly. Charles recognized the young, scared-looking constable who had been in the line opposite him earlier.

The girl saw the open MG and saw Charles. She hesitated, then plunged toward him. Her eyes were huge with fear.

"Please!" she cried at him. "Please! Please!"

The policeman was close behind her.

Charles beckoned. He shouted: "Get in!"

She tumbled over the low door of the sports car and landed in the right-side bucket seat in an undignified sprawl of legs and undergarments. She lay there as the policeman reached the car. He stopped, looking down at her, breathing heavily. There was dull anger and resentment on his face.

A traffic officer in a white crash helmet had started directing cars around the obstacle. He waved the shark-fin car forward. Charles let out the clutch and shot after it. The young constable stood and watched him go.

Several policemen, assisted by a second traffic officer, were manhandling the old Morris off the road. The girl sat up, watching them. She pulled her skirt down over her knees.

"Bastards," she said, but not loudly.

They passed the Morris. Traffic was already moving more swiftly.

"They're pigs and shits," the girl said. "They would have liked to kill us."

Charles switched to the fast lane. He felt vaguely irritated. The little bitch hadn't even thought of saying thank you.

"If you want to play with the big boys you must expect to get hurt."

134

The girl moved in her seat, settling herself, pulling her clothes straight. She put her knees primly together. He was aware of her sidelong, assessing stare.

"We have a right to make our views heard, haven't we? But do people have to try to kill us because they don't agree?"

She had a throaty voice, with a vibrant quality about it now that she was no longer afraid.

"Do you seriously think your little effort today will change anything? Don't you think your time would be better spent attending classes and qualifying yourself to change things?"

She did not reply immediately. Then she asked: "You're Dr. de la Porte, aren't you?"

He turned to her, astonished. She had very dark eyes, to match that hair. The eyelids were dark, too, and she had a trick of lowering them which gave her a vaguely Oriental look.

"How on earth did you know?"

"I've seen you at the medical school. You're a registrar in the surgery department."

"Yes. What were you doing at the medical school?"

"I'm doing medicine."

"Oh." He had believed her to be an arts student, or perhaps one of the little dollies who studied drama. "This your first year?" She looked about eighteen.

"No," she said. "Fourth."

He was displeased at having to make the rapid reassessment. This, and his own ambivalent attitude toward the demonstration he had witnessed, made him speak more sharply than he had intended.

"Why aren't you at lectures? Why waste your time holding up placards with stupid slogans?"

"Because I'm concerned about the diseases of society just as much as those of people."

"That's a very glib answer. It doesn't excuse you breaking the law."

"A law which makes people voiceless because their skins are the wrong color? A law which prevents other people from

135

protesting about this? Are those the kind of laws you admire? Does it make you happy to see a bunch of police thugs chasing and beating unarmed people?"

"The police were doing their duty."

"Have you considered that you and I have an equal duty to protest about injustice?"

"A medical student's duty shouldn't extend beyond his textbooks."

"Some doctors' vision doesn't extend further than what's in their wallets."

Startled, he slowed down the car, looking at her. She glared back, unrepentant. Suddenly he grinned. "With a tongue like that, miss, you're never going to have need of a scalpel."

She did not smile back.

He took the Wynberg turnoff. "Where do you want me to drop you?"

"Anywhere on the Main Road, thank you."

There was a long period of silence. Eventually he said: "By the way, what's your name?"

She replied unwillingly: "Case. Janice Case."

"Well, let's be friends, Miss Case. If you can bring yourself to be friends with a wallet-minded elderly doctor."

She seemed about to make a sharp retort, but apparently thought better of it. She looked around. They had reached the business district, with dingy buildings and shop fronts and crowded pavements.

"You can drop me anywhere along here."

"Are you sure?"

"Quite sure. Thank you."

He pulled in behind a bus which was discharging passengers. She opened the door and got out quickly. She had a good figure, with high breasts and a trim waist. She was a very attractive girl.

"Thank you," she said, standing on the sidewalk beside the car. She gave him a grave smile. "And thank you for coming to my rescue."

"My pleasure."

"Good-bye."

She was gone in the crowd. He pulled out into the traffic. On the far side of the bus he saw her walking and raised a hand in greeting, but she did not see him. He drove on, to the nursery school and a waiting, weeping Paul. The child would be upset for the rest of the day and when Antoinette came home from the school where she taught she would ask about it. He would explain irascibly that it wasn't his fault he had been held up. Then there would be another of those strained, tortured scenes in which neither of them said very much, but both of them suffered. God, how they suffered.

He saw Janice Case again during the following week.

He was on his way to the medical ward to see a patient and was hurrying down the bleak corridor, deep in thought. He hardly paid attention to the handful of young people coming the other way. They wore short white jackets trimmed with green, but beyond registering that they were students he did not think about them.

The patient was a man of sixty-five with hematemesis. The physicians usually sat on these cases until they were exsanguinated before asking for a surgical opinion. He considered suggesting to the prof that . . .

One of the white-coated figures stopped in front of him. A shy voice said: "Hello."

For a moment he could not remember her name.

"Oh. Hello."

"I've been hunting for you. To thank you properly. You must have thought me very rude. But I was upset, if that's any excuse."

"No need to apologize. I quite understand."

"Anyway, Doctor, I wanted you to know that I really was awfully grateful."

The white jacket reduced her to the status of just another student, earnest, shy, and polite to everyone who was older and had already earned the right to be addressed as "Doctor," although prone to secret group jokes about those same elders and betters.

"Glad I was able to help you, Miss Case," he said in a kindly voice, and passed by.

That would probably have been the end of it, except that on the Friday of the same week he was invited to a party. A young doctor who worked in the pathology lab had asked him to the pub where the students went and they sat out on the terrace, drinking beer and watching the girls. (And had he perhaps, without admitting it to himself, been looking out for long dark hair which would stand out immediately among the boyish crops of blond and red and brunet? He had asked himself the question later.) They had chatted amiably, exchanging hospital gossip, laughing at small jokes. Charles looked at his watch a few times and thought about going home. But it was pleasant and relaxing here, drinking in young company, involved in uncomplex situations. Home would be different.

The young man said: "Did you hear about the guy who came to Dr. Williamson in the psychiatry clinic yesterday?"

He said: "No."

"Well, old Williamson saw him and this guy told him: 'Doctor, life isn't worth living. I wish I could die.' So Williamson asks: 'But what's the matter? Why are you so depressed?' 'Well, Doctor, the problem is I'm empty inside. I haven't got any innards.' 'What do you mean you haven't got any innards?' 'Doctor, I haven't got a heart and I haven't got lungs, and no liver and no stomach.' 'But if you haven't got those organs you can't be alive.' 'Well, Doctor, that's the other problem. I can't die.' 'Why can't you die?' 'Doctor, I haven't got lungs so I can't give my last breath.'"

They laughed and then a friend of the young doctor joined them and after a while two girls came over, both tall and leggy and blond, so alike in appearance and outlook that they could have been twins.

The four younger people seemed to know one another well. They had a private vocabulary and laughed at references Charles did not understand. He began to feel elderly and neglected. He looked at his watch again. Time to go.

One of the girls said: "We've been invited to a fabulous party. Let's all go. Who's got a car?"

"Old Charles here," the young doctor said.

She looked at Charles, teasingly provocative. "He's not old."

"Not a day over ninety-two," Charles said in a wheezing voice.

They appeared to find it very witty.

"Let me help you with your walking stick," the girl said. "Then let's go to the party."

A twinge of conscience, which he suppressed. No harm in merely giving them a lift to their party, was there? It would seem graceless and unsociable to refuse.

The blonde who had flirted with him sat beside him in the front seat while the others squeezed into the back. She had nonchalantly annexed him and gave him driving instructions in a crisp, proprietary way. He wondered, without illusion, whether his own charm or that of the sports car weighed most heavily. Buying the MG had been a whim and he was still unsure of the propriety, at the age of thirty-five, of driving a very young man's car.

He did not see her at first. The party was in full swing and there was constant movement between the portable bar, set up beside the swimming pool, and the main bar, which was in an elaborately equipped games room.

It was that kind of house, obviously the home of someone extremely wealthy, and Charles had felt an uncomfortable intruder. He had soon realized, however, that there was no need to feel concerned. He was unlikely to be noticed among the throng which moved restlessly from bar to bar or swayed on the open-air dance floor or wandered lecherously into the dark shrubbery.

He stood back, a drink in his hand, and surveyed the party. It reminded him of the parties of ten, twelve years ago when he had been a student, too. This was more luxurious: the setting more glossy and the liquor more expensive, but the aims were the same: inebriation and fornication. It was a very young kind of party and he was not sure that he still appreciated it. His and Antoinette's were more sedate, usually running to dinner with one or two other couples in a quiet restaurant, or the very occasional cocktail party at home. And even that had been curtailed after he had come back to medical school. Doing his FRCS, living in the small flat and having to study, social life was almost nonexistent. Antoinette did not seem to mind. She was always tired these days. She taught all morning and now she had taken on extra classes in the afternoons to earn more money. Their friends were all his friends, men who exchanged medical shop by the hour. Their wives talked about cooking and servants and children and schools and regarded Antoinette's reputation as an acclaimed poet forbidding. They mistook her reserve for disdain. The only friends left from her youth and from the years of her sad, despair-ridden first marriage were a couple who farmed in Natal and two young women who lived a defiantly Bohemian life in Paris. And her father, now very old, running his hotel in the small Karroo town, still unable to comprehend the dark movements, the oceanic promptings, which ruled his silent daughter.

About to put down his drink, about to go home to his wife, he saw Janice Case.

She had her back to him, but he had no doubts. She was talking to a young man who was the epitome of a languid student, all denim and hair and beard and awkward-jointed arms and legs. As he watched she turned animatedly, long hair swinging, to laugh up at the lanky youth. He was astonished to feel a momentary knife-twist of jealousy.

For God's sake, he thought. You'd better go home.

The young man said something to her and moved away. She was left standing alone. Charles's legs propelled him forward. He heard his own voice. It sounded full of warmth and confidence and false charm.

"Hello there."

She recognized him with visible surprise. "Oh. Hello. What are you doing here?" At once she looked annoyed, as if he had tricked her into asking the banal question. "I wouldn't imagine it's your kind of party."

He pretended not to notice the aggression in her voice and looked at the milling mob instead. Suddenly he felt a subtle tension, the suggestion of a challenge, about the night.

"Perhaps not." He lifted his glass. "But the whisky isn't to be despised." He noticed that her hands were empty. "May I get you a drink?"

"No, thank you. Peter ... someone is fetching me a drink."

He said, to bridge the brief awkwardness: "Taken part in any good riots lately?"

She said angrily: "I don't think that's funny at all."

He was disconcerted and also faintly irritated.

"Admittedly it wasn't very funny. But there's no need to jump down my throat."

There was a hostile silence. The bearded young man joined them, carrying two glasses of wine. He looked at Charles with curiosity.

"Here, Jay. You wanted white?"

She took the glass. "Thanks."

Mutinously, she performed introductions. The young man's name was Peter, but Charles did not catch the surname she muttered.

"Are you at the university?" he asked.

The young man laughed derisively. "Me? Good God, no. I'm a journalist."

"That must be interesting."

The young man gave him a bored look. After a moment he raised his glass to his lips and said: "Cheers."

Charles turned away. He was out of place here.

He saw that the girl was watching him. There was a curious expression, half guarded, half eager, on her face. He glared back at her. He sensed the antagonism she and the bearded boy shared toward him: the instinctive alliance of youth against age. And suddenly he was weary of young people: of their trite complexities, their repetitive reasoning, their affectations of disdain and smooth cynicism. He was bored by the awful predictability of it all.

He was about to leave them, and planning a curt greeting, when the girl said: "Dr. de la Porte saved my life from the fuzz last week."

The slant-eyed look she gave him was so brief that he decided he had imagined it. Nevertheless, he changed his mind about leaving.

The young man raised his eyebrows. "Oh?"

She ignored him and spoke to Charles. "You really did save my life, you know. I have this thing, this absolute horror, of being maimed. That pig could have smashed my face."

Did he also imagine that there was a degree of provocation about the way she held her body? Hemlines had been creeping steadily upward in the last year or so, but even so her dress, a full hand's breadth above her knees, was more daring than he was accustomed to. He shifted awkwardly, trying not to show that he was staring at her.

"Then you chose the wrong profession, I'm afraid. You're going to see a lot of mutilation, both intentional and unintentional." He was puzzled by her. "Why did you decide to take medicine?"

She tossed her hair. "It was as good an excuse as any to come to university."

He said acidly: "I would have expected a greater sense of mission from you. Are your banners and posters more important than human lives?"

Her anger flared again. "And if you really want to know, I came to 'varsity because I wanted to be involved with people who're working for social change. That's more important than what you or I can achieve individually."

"What does society amount to if it isn't the concerted efforts of a lot of individuals?"

"That's a typically capitalist-defensive kind of remark."

"When you grow up a little you'll learn that putting labels on things is symptomatic of lazy thinking."

"What has age got to do with it?" she blazed at him.

"Because of what you would call another capitalist cliché. And that is that most people of reasonable intelligence go through all these stages. First you think revolution is the panacea. Then you become cynical about human nature. And finally you end up as a reactionary."

"Like you."

"Like me. Just remember that I have more experience of being young than you have of being old."

"So you would condone everything that's happening in this country, the treason trial, bannings, Sharpeville, simply because you think opposition to it is a kind of juvenile phase everyone goes through?"

"That wasn't what I said."

The young man, Peter, had been listening to them, fidgeting and making it clear that he resented Charles's intrusion. Now he interrupted them brusquely, speaking to the girl, not even looking at Charles. "Look, if you're going to spend the evening talking politics I'm going."

Her anger transferred itself abruptly. "Well, bugger off then," she said witheringly.

Peter looked first dismayed, then offended. Finally he managed a mocking laugh. He walked off with a perceptible swagger.

It seemed a good time to change the subject.

"I'm afraid you've hurt his feelings."

"He needs putting in his place every now and then."

"Is he really a journalist?"

"So he claims."

Her indifference seemed to argue against a special relationship. Again he surprised himself by the sense of relief he experienced.

He risked saying, banteringly: "I suppose he's one of

those journalists who are more interested in other people's troubles than their own hygiene. Frankly, he smells."

For a moment he thought he had gone too far. But then she laughed.

"I could see you weren't crazy about one another." Her eyebrows lifted fractionally. "I bother about other people's troubles, too. Do I smell?"

He wrinkled his nose. "Yes. Chanel Number Five."

She laughed again, more easily than before. She asked abruptly: "Are you married?"

Denial was tempting but unwise. She was bound to discover the truth sooner or later. But should this concern him? Was there any reason to suppose that anything would come of this after tonight?

"Yes. Sort of."

"And what does that mean?"

"Let's not talk about it. If I say too much you'll think: same old story."

"That doesn't matter. But you are married?"

He grimaced. "I thought we weren't going to discuss it."

"I said it doesn't matter, not that we wouldn't talk about it."

"All right then, I'm married and I have one child. Two, actually. A son and a stepdaughter."

"What's your wife like?"

"Is that important? The fact is that I am married and I have children. I am as I am and you have to accept or reject me on that basis."

"We're not talking about accepting or rejecting. I simply want to know more about you. Do you mind?"

"Then let's stick to my professional life. I'm a surgical registrar, as you know. I did my FRCS last year and now I'm working on my Ch.M. thesis."

She was immediately interested.

"What is it about?"

"It's an idea I have to manage bleeding peptic ulcers by cooling the inside of the stomach. Topical hypothermia."

"Like using ice for a nosebleed?"

"That's it exactly. You're a smart cookie."

"Glad you think so. You may be my examiner one day. But now let me ask the questions. How would you manage this stomach cooling?"

"Intragastric cooling."

"All right. How would you go about it?"

"I don't want to bore you with it."

"I'm not bored."

She was being truthful, and he sensed it. In time he would grow accustomed to her sudden switches of direction and bursts of enthusiasm. Now, encountered for the first time, they left him with a feeling of being steamrollered.

"You probably remember that there are cells which secrete hydrochloric acid and others which secrete pepsin in the stomach wall."

"Yes."

"It's believed that ulceration of the gastric or duodenal mucosa is caused by oversecretion of this acid and enzyme. If we can dampen down the action of the glands the ulcers will heal. My idea is to do this by cooling the stomach wall down to ten degrees centigrade. That should slow down the metabolic activity."

"If you could do that you'd be a smart cookie, too."

There was a teasing tone in her voice, but he was sure, almost sure, that she was not really teasing him.

"You said a while ago that you hate the thought of mutilation. Well, it may sound funny coming from a surgeon, but so do I. I hate to cut out an organ simply because we don't understand the reason for its malfunction. It's sinful to take out three quarters of a normal stomach because we don't know the cause of the ulceration."

"You think gastric cooling will avoid this?"

"I think it's worth a try."

"It makes sense."

He said persuasively: "You should come and help me with my experimental work one evening. That would make it a collective action, and you approve of that, don't you?"

She laughed. "I'd love to."

145

There was a cathartic warmth of feeling between them, as if they had survived physical danger together and, in their relief, could share confidences. A week ago, after real danger, there had been only thin rancor and an edgy sexuality. But now the wall was breached. He found himself eager to talk, to explain. He tried to stop events in his mind and explain them to himself, but already he was being swept along.

"Let's drink to that. Can I get you some more wine?"

"I don't really drink an awful lot." But she surrendered her glass to him. "You really do believe in the work you're doing, don't you?"

"I believe it's the only thing worth doing."

"Then I can understand your being furious at me for not taking my studies seriously."

"I wasn't really furious. A bit shocked, perhaps. But perhaps I'm too conventional in my thinking."

"If you believe something you don't have to be ashamed of saying it. I must introduce you to Joel."

"Who is Joel?"

"A friend. He's a communist and he would refute every one of your arguments."

There was a perceptible hesitation about the way she had said "a friend." Did the evasiveness conceal the fact that "friend" was something more? Lover, perhaps. Jealousy was absurd, but there it was.

"Does he belong to the party?"

"Don't be silly. It's banned."

"Proclaiming yourself a communist in this country is rather risky. Your friend must be a brave man. Or very foolish."

"He's not brave. He calls himself a socialist. But he's a Marxist really."

"If he calls himself a socialist you shouldn't call him a communist. How do you know I'm not a police spy?"

"I can see. There are spies on the campus, but I know you're not one of them."

"You're very trusting."

"Spies have a look about them."

"What kind of look?"

146

"As if they're missing something and can't think what it is."

"Perhaps they miss their dark glasses."

She seized joyfully at the fantasy. "Yes. These days they have to go around in denims instead of trench coats and it makes them insecure."

Laughing, they continued to build up the notion, piling one absurdity on top of another. And as they joked there was a languorous undercurrent, a shared knowledge of awakening sensuality.

"You must be serious," she reprimanded him.

"I'm too serious. I'm always so deadly serious."

"It suits you."

"It doesn't. At times I even bore myself."

"Be serious again just for a minute. I want to know more about your experiments."

His explanation was interrupted by a couple who, moving past, called out to the girl.

"Jay! Hi there!"

She turned with a look of irritation.

"Oh. Hello."

The man and the woman came up, showing their teeth in social smiles. They had a sleek glossiness about them, like starlings on a rooftop, and quick, hard voices. The woman was younger than Charles, the man older. Both looked at him speculatively, then at the girl. They spoke to the girl about people he did not know. The man looked at the girl as if he owned her, or would like to. Charles stood by, feeling discarded and sour.

The girl turned back to him.

"Dr. de la Porte was telling me about the work he's doing and he has invited me to help him."

She looked expectant and, hesitatingly at first, he described his work in the dog lab. He explained how, by inserting a balloon into the stomach of an anesthetized dog and circulating cold water through it, he had succeeded in cooling down the stomach wall. The next step was to take samples of the gastric juices from inside the stomach during the cooling process, so that he could analyze the acid and pepsin content. Again it was as if their self-sufficiency, the interest they had in one another, was able to set up a barrier between them and others. The man and the woman listened with glassy disinterest. Eventually the man drifted away in search of a drink. After a while the woman followed him, pausing to say brightly to the girl: "Bye, Jay. Love to your mother," and to Charles, with a touch of malice: "Goodbye, Doctor. So interesting to have met you."

"They're awful bores," the girl muttered.

"Jay," he said.

She looked up expectantly.

"Jay. Is that what people call you?"

"My friends do."

"May I call you that?"

She smiled with that warmth which made her eyelids lower and gave her a look of sleepy incitement.

There was a commotion at the swimming pool and they looked in that direction. The lights around the pool had been dimmed. As they stared, puzzled, a white body arched out over the water in a raking dive. Then there were further splashes.

"Now the skinny-dipping starts," the girl said. "Ya-a-awn."

But they moved closer to the pool. Two young women and three men were in the water. He recognized one of the blondes who had brought him to the party and realized that he had forgotten their existence. People stood watching and laughing, holding their drinks. The swimmers splashed water at them. The underwater lights went on, showing the naked bodies in the sapphire-green water. There were squeals of protest. The lights went off, came on again, and then were switched off and stayed off. The spectators drifted away, losing interest.

"Come on," the girl said to Charles in a tense whisper. She had already discarded her dress. Her underclothes followed, falling in a jumble on the grass. He saw the slim shape of her, the curve of breast and hip, the darkness between her legs. She was gone as he reached for her and he heard the smack of her body against the water. He fumbled with shirt and trousers and clumsy shoes.

148

He had drunk more than usual, but the shock of the cold water closing over his head sobered him. It made him less carefree but also more calculating. He looked for the girl and saw her swimming with a dreamy breaststroke. He swam after her and caught her in the middle of the pool. Briefly, she did not resist. Their lips met in a watery kiss. His hand moved and touched the unexpected wiriness of pubic hair. She slid away from him, her body slippery and agile as a fish. She swam to the side and again he went after her, swimming powerfully, exultant in his strength. He trapped her against the side of the pool and crushed her naked body to his. Dark hair hung over her face. He felt her breasts against his body, her legs kicking.

He kissed her mouth, forcing it open.

She bit his tongue, hard.

He exclaimed in pain and anger and let her go. There was a taste of blood in his mouth.

She had backed away and was treading water, just out of reach, watching him like a cat which has clawed, alert for reprisal but with a look of cross satisfaction.

"Don't ever do that unless I let you," she said.

She swam away and he let her go. He heaved himself out of the water and went to find his clothes. His body was wet but he dressed, pulling on his shirt over a soaking back.

The girl had left the water, too. She had found a towel and wore it around her shoulders while she dried herself. She dressed with the towel draped around her and he did not look at her.

"Have you a comb?" she asked matter-of-factly, as if nothing had happened.

He gave her a comb without speaking.

She had partly dried her hair, but even when she had combed it, it clung close to her head, giving her face a thin, defenseless look. She handed him the comb.

"It's no good being angry, you know," she said in those rounded, husky tones.

"I apologize," he said sulkily.

"You don't sound very happy about it."

He shrugged.

"Perhaps we'd best talk about your work again."

"Perhaps we had better not talk at all," he said.

Her eyebrows lifted. "Perhaps we shouldn't."

And he was instantly overwhelmed by the burning possibility of loss; by the chance that in just one more moment she might step out of his life altogether and walk away with that lean, abrupt stride and that he would be left with the knowledge of his failure and his folly.

"No," he said harshly. "I'm sorry. I didn't mean that. I really am sorry."

She looked at him, her lower lip caught between her teeth. On her face was an expression of wonder and almost of dismay, as if what he had said had deeper meanings which she had immediately grasped and which had made her fearful and uncertain.

And in another moment he understood that she had, that they both had, cause for fear.

Antoinette was usually scrupulous about not entering the bathroom while he was using it. But this morning she opened the door unexpectedly and caught him standing with his bare back to the tiny shaving mirror, looking ruefully over his shoulder and dabbing at himself with iodine.

She was distracted and did not at first notice what he was doing. "I'm sorry, Charles. I have to . . . " She rummaged in the back of the rickety cupboard where towels and sheets were mixed in with drug samples and bottles of patent medicine. Blushing faintly, she pulled out a packet of sanitary pads. "Sor-

150

ry," she said again, breathlessly, as if the apology were less for the intrusion than for the inescapable facts of female physiology. Then she asked: "What are you doing?" She saw his back and gasped. "Charles! You've hurt yourself!"

He tried to laugh it away. "Just a few scratches."

"But how on earth did you manage it? It looks as if you've been dragged through a barbed-wire fence."

He had prepared an explanation in case something like this happened. He gave it now, speaking gruffly, not quite looking at her.

"Mental patient in Casualty last night. The Casualty officer needed a second opinion to commit the guy so he called me down. And the damn fool of a policeman who was supposed to be restraining him let him go. He flew at me like a wild cat, all teeth and nails. Just about tore my shirt off my back."

She made a sound of distress. "Turn around. Let me have a look."

He turned reluctantly. She drew in her breath again. "He actually cut the skin, do you know that? Were his nails dirty? I hope it doesn't go septic. Let me do it for you."

"He was none too clean," Charles said. It was all right. She believed him. He stood with his back to her while she worked with cotton wool and iodine.

"Were you only wearing a shirt?"

"I had taken off my coat. It was hot in the hospital last night."

"What did you do with it? It must be full of blood."

"Yes. And torn, too." He was uncomfortably aware of the shirt, untorn and free of blood stains, reposing in the dirty linen basket behind the door. He would have to smuggle it to the laundry. "I left it at the hospital. One of the sisters said she'd have it darned."

Surprised and a little blankly she said: "Oh?" She was hurt that he had sought others to do his mending. He caught her eye in the mirror and at that moment her face grew still. He was watching her reflection and saw the change at the very moment when another possible explanation for the scratches occurred to her.

151

She was still essentially innocent, even after two marriages and two children. She could not really understand how some women could do the things they were reputed to do. But failure to understand was not failure to perceive. These things were there, unpleasant perhaps, but as undeniable as the flow of menstrual blood. If aspects of life were sad or brutal or strange, then Antoinette had the courage and the determination to face them. But not to accept. And never to condone.

She faltered only for a moment. Then she carried on treating the last of his wounds.

"There."

She put the stopper back on the bottle and threw the stained cotton wool into the waste bin. She smiled at him briefly and left the bathroom, carrying her packet of pads.

He wriggled his smarting back, looking irresolutely at the washing basket. Even if she found the shirt and went to the trouble of counting the others in his wardrobe to check if any were missing, would it make a great deal of difference? What was in her mind was more than mere suspicion. It was absolute certainty.

He decided uneasily that it would be best to get rid of the damn shirt. Maybe he would give it away to one of the caretakers.

And, mingled with the guilt and his resentment at the loss of one of his few decent shirts and the dismaying knowledge that his wife had guessed what he had been doing, there was still a carnal twinge, an afterglow of remembered pleasure.

He had never imagined it like this: wild as a wave, joyous as the feel of a wind, calculated as the passage of a ship under sail, tense as the eye of a hurricane.

Jay overwhelmed him. He was wrecked on the ocean of her sexuality, a drowning sailor flung here and there by incalculable forces, engulfed and sucked deep, clawing his way to the gale-torn surface. And cast up finally with other flotsam onto a gray and empty beach.

Where she had learned her lovemaking skills he did not dare to ask. There was an edge of hysteria to it which he did not dare to fathom. But he was satisfied at first to accept her as he found her: vigorous and young and totally uninhibited.

There was undoubtedly a deep current of sadness about all she did but he did not, at first, love her well enough to attempt to measure it.

That came later.

It was Sunday morning and they were alone in the two-room kitchenette shower-plus-lavatory unit which her landlords, with more sportiveness than honesty, had named a twin bachelor apartment. Her roommate Vicky, wearing a white dress which showed off her long legs, had smiled her vague and beatific smile at them and gone off, swinging a tennis racket.

They had made love with fierce urgency the moment she was out of the flat. Now Jay was in the bathroom and he was lounging among the cushions she had thrown on the floor, looking with fond amusement at the room which was her home. There was little of Vicky in the flat: a photograph of her in a tutu; a wineskin souvenir from Spain. The rest was all Jay.

She had scornfully obliterated the landlords' pastel color scheme under great slashes of scarlet. Along two entire walls she had painted, with considerable skill, a mural of intertwined dragons which glowed in green and silver and gold. She had begged or stolen two hanging lanterns from the owner of a Chinese restaurant, had borrowed Oriental prints from the library on more or less permanent loan, had bought secondhand cane furniture from the widow of an ex-India civil servant. The effect was startling. But after a time the eye adapted and came to like, then even to love, the brashly and determinedly alien place.

Jay came naked from the bathroom, padding barefoot across the reed-mat floor. He got up from the cushions and reached for her, but she evaded his grasp neatly, smiling in an alert way. He recognized the signal and let her go with a shrug.

"The place is a mess," she said. "I must get it straight.

153

Can I make you some coffee?"

"No thanks. Need help?"

"Stay where you are. Or, rather, sit in that chair." When he had moved she crossed briskly to the record player. "What would you like to hear?"

"Anything."

"I've got the new Leonard Cohen. But that'll keep. Segovia?"

"Fine."

He listened to the ring of the guitar chords swooping through the room like small swift birds. He had never cared much for music and Antoinette's taste was too high-brow for him, but this music filled a space within him. He sat back in the chair and listened to it, watching the play of Jay's muscles as she moved with deliberation through the room, the swing of her breasts as she plumped cushions and straightened furniture.

Summer sunlight came like honey into the room.

And yet he was not content. There was never anything like content in her company. She was made of too quick a metal to allow the luxury of an easy mind. With her there was stimulation and bite, but also a constant need for vigilance. She flickered like a fencer's foil, both steely and pliant, always searching for the fatal gap in the guard.

The more he learned about her, the greater the mystery of the things which moved her.

Not that she was in any way secretive. She told him all he asked about. She came from a moderately wealthy family. Her father and his elder brothers owned meat-packing factories in Cape Town and Johannesburg. Her grandfather had been an Estonian Jew by the name of Kasnowitz. He had been a peddler as a young man and had traveled with a mule cart among the frontier farms, selling rolls of cotton and calico and sewing needles and buttons and mirrors to the Boers. He had obligingly changed his name to Kas because his Afrikaans-speaking customers could not get their tongues around the rest of it. They paid for his trinkets with sheep and he had drifted into speculation with livestock and then into being the owner of a number of small butcher shops. When his sons were grown and had built

154

their own edifice on these foundations they retired him to the supervisor's flat in an apartment block they had bought, and changed the family name again. Here he spent his time dreaming who-knows-what dreams and telling his rare visitors about frontier life in the old days.

He had died long before Jay was born, but her eldest brother remembered being taken to see the old man. He had told the story to Jay, as a snide comment on their father's contemptible attempts to cover up the past. But she had been serious about it; had seized on the fragments retained in her brother's memory and constructed an entire world from them.

She imagined her grandfather moving through great rooms filled with perpetual gloom. She saw the old man handling moldy materials and bits of tarnished jewelry with lingering love. Old garments fell into cobweb shreds as he lifted them. Over all was the smell of dust. She grew savage about the way her father and uncles had neglected the old man and proposed to have her name changed back to Kasnowitz. She would have done so if there had been opposition. But her father had been greatly impressed by a fire-spitting visiting Israeli general and he had no objections. She had lost interest.

Charles had seen photographs of her then, at the age of fifteen. Her hair had been short and her face more full. But there was the same ironic, questioning tilt to her eyebrows and the same enigmatic smile.

Part of him sought to solve the riddle; another part warned him to keep away. And sometimes he suspected that the riddle did not exist; that she was a sphinx without a mystery.

Crashing chords brought the record to an end. Jay moved to the player in two long strides and changed the record for another. Leonard Cohen this time, although not the new one. This was old and familiar, played many times, so that the grooves had worn and the record would stick at particular places which they both knew well enough to anticipate and so avoid by a timely jolt.

He had at first been provoked by the bitterness which lay behind the romanticism and had argued with her about it. It was all very well, he had said, for Cohen and her other heroes, Bob

155

Dylan and Joan Baez, to glorify the revolution. But what would they sing when, like him, they had to stanch the blood and stitch up the wounds after the bombs had been thrown?

Eventually he had ceased to argue and simply listened, as he was listening now.

> *I choose the rooms I live in with care.*
> *The windows are small and the walls must be bare.*
> *There's only one bed and there's only one prayer.*
> *I listen all night for your step on the stair.*

She sat on the couch, leaning back among the red and gold cushions. Their eyes met knowingly as they listened, both smiling now and then as the familiar lines struck home.

> *But I know from your eyes,*
> *and I know from your smile,*
> *that tonight will be fine,*
> *will be fine,*
> *will be fine,*
> *will be fine . . .*

then the long wait

> *. . . for a while.*

The sleeve of the record showed the interior of a room with bare white walls and shuttered windows. A girl sat typing at a table in a corner, smiling at the camera over one shoulder. Close by was a second table with ornate legs. A chessboard lay on its polished surface.

They had made a fantasy inside the room in that picture and about the view thay would see once the shutters were open. They banished the second table, the one of the chessboard, as an encumbrance. All they needed was one table and one bed and one chair. In time they settled on the view. The window would look downhill toward a white village at the edge of the sea. There would be olive trees and dusty roads but the breeze through the window would always be cool.

The room became their private place. They would live there and not need to be concerned about anyone else. When she protested that the girl in the picture was blonde and that she would have to dye her hair, he said they would change the picture. She did not know how to use a typewriter, so they would leave that out, too.

The room was their refuge.

The record came to a scratchy end and the automatic mechanism lifted the needle with a whirr and a click. She did not move to replace the record.

She asked: "How's the study coming along?"

He was nonplussed. "Study?"

She gestured impatiently. "The gastric cooling. You promised I could help with the research, but you haven't even taken me to the lab yet."

"Oh. Well, I haven't been doing much work lately. I spend most of my free time here."

She seemed determined to be businesslike and unyielding. And yet she had come from the bathroom without clothes; was now half lying on the couch in an attitude of invitation. He was faintly irritated.

Her next question did not ease his mind.

"How is Tony?"

For an obscure reason which he did not really care to unravel he had led her to understand that his wife's childhood nickname, which he himself used only when speaking to his father-in-law and which Antoinette disliked, was the name by which she was known.

"She's fine. Why?"

"I wanted to know."

"Well, she's fine."

"Are things still screwed up between you?"

He realized uncomfortably that he had exaggerated the extent of disharmony.

"We get on. But not very well."

"Has she always been like this?"

"I suppose so. She has her own vision of the world. It's a scorching vision. But at the same time it's terribly restricted. And she feels things very deeply."

As he spoke he was aware of the falseness, the distorted

157

view. But it pained him to think of Antoinette (not only because of his present situation, although there was that, too), so it came out too pat, like psychiatric analysis from a slot machine.

"I read some of her poetry the other day. She didn't come across like that."

Noncommittally: "No?"

"You make her sound bigoted. That isn't the impression her poems leave."

"I've never said she's bigoted. But she's . . . sort of narrowed down. As if there's only one thing in life and that's between her and her God."

"Oh." It was her turn to be cautious. "Is she very religious?"

"By no means. Don't forget that I said *her* God. It's not the same God as that of her fathers. But do we have to talk about her? Just take my word for it that we are bad for one another and let's leave it at that."

She was not prepared to leave it.

"Then why did you marry her?"

He spread his hands. "Why does one marry anyone? Because they're attractive to you. Because you think you share the same things. Because of sex."

"But there wasn't much of that."

He looked at her and she looked away. He took advantage of her indiscretion. "You know, I really don't want to talk about her."

"Sorry. Would you like some more music?"

"Yes. Play the new Leonard Cohen."

But inevitably his mind went back to Antoinette, to her dark closed face and the smile, uncluttered as that of a child, which infrequently lightened the darkness. He thought about the conversations they shared at times, skipping from subject to subject, delighting in their quick understanding, switching effortlessly from English to Afrikaans and back again. An advantage of being a hotelkeeper's daughter and spending vacations at the reception desk was that she could use both languages with equal skill.

He remembered the night he met her.

He was doing a locum in a town in the Karroo. The man he was relieving had talked idly about taking on a young, energetic partner and had promised that they would talk about it when he came back from his vacation. Charles was determined to impress his absentee employer and this meant involvement in the town's social life. He was in considerable demand, and not unflattered by the knowledge that all the eligible young women were being paraded for the new bachelor doctor. Except for a young teacher with whom he had a brisk, no-demands-made affair, none of them were to his taste.

He went to the party at the mayor's house expecting to find the usual lineup of plump, rather vacuous girls. He would flirt with them while having his customary two or three drinks. Never more, for, although the two-month locum was drawing to an end, there was the prospect of the partnership to stay his hand. The mayoress, inviting him by telephone, had spoken about a girl who had written a book and had come back to town after living overseas, but there had been a patient with him at the time and he had not paid attention. So he was unprepared for the somber-eyed young woman who was introduced to him as Mrs. Barris. Their conversation was halting and awkward and yet he was intrigued. There was a sense—more than that: an awareness—that they would have much to say if only they could find a common language. The dark girl had left the party early and he had cornered one of the plump brigade and drawn information from her while (he imagined) concealing his interest.

Antoinette was her name. She was the daughter of old Krynauw who owned the Royal Hotel. She was a bit funny. No, she wasn't married. Divorced. Her husband had been Dudley Barris who had been from these parts, too. He drank too much and some people said he beat Tony. They had gone to Vienna so that he could study music. People said it was with her money. She had come back alone with the child. Yes, a sweet little girl of two. Had she returned here to live? His informant was not sure. Tony had taught at a school in the Cape before her marriage; perhaps she planned to go back to teaching. And she wrote books. Poetry, or something.

The girl had given him a shrewd, humorous look and

159

said: "You're wasting your time. I'll tell you a secret. She's not interested in men." And, with a wink: "You know."

Nevertheless, he had persisted. He had persuaded her to come out with him: to the cinema, on picnics in the veld with her small daughter, once to a rugby club ball in a neighboring town. It was a delicate process and once or twice he was overhasty and she fled from him, so that the patient work had to start afresh. He never stopped to question whether it was worthwhile or even what his eventual aims were.

His locumship came to an end and there was, after all, no further talk about a partnership. He was not very surprised. He had already calculated that the practice was not big enough to support two. He found another locum job, in a town across the mountains, eighty miles away. It kept him busy but he managed to get away for an occasional weekend afternoon and was able to continue his careful courtship. Early that summer he and Antoinette and Marianne went away to the coast for a vacation together, and there one night, in a thatch-roofed rondawel within sound of the sea, she allowed him to make love to her for the first time. They were married in the new year.

"What are you thinking about?" the girl asked.

"Nothing much. Listening."

"Were you thinking about her?"

"No," he lied.

"I'm sorry."

"What for?"

"I'm sorry I said that about you. About you and her."

He laughed. "Don't be silly."

"Still. I'm sorry." She changed the record again. Back to the old Leonard Cohen. "Do you want me to make up to you?"

With affected unconcern: "If you like."

"Shall I do this?"

"Yes."

"Shall I do this for you? This?"

"Yes. Oh, God, yes."

160

And the singer sang.

Oh sometimes I see her undressing for me.
She's the soft naked lady love meant her to be.
And she's moving her body so brave and so free.
I've got to remember that's a fine memory.

It was a big house, although not ostentatiously so. The square front garden was tidily kept, with roses there, annuals over here, lawn trimmed short, and everything in its place. It was a reflection of the suburb in which it stood, which was comfortable without being careless; rich, but not very rich.

The owner of the house came to the door to meet them. He was a stout, balding man and he looked briefly and worriedly at their faces and then beyond them into the dark garden, as if someone else might be concealed there.

"Hello, Jay," he said unhappily. "And is this Charles?"

"Yes."

"Hello, Charles. I'm Dennis. Come in."

The hallway had the make-believe look which indicated a professional decorator, with hunting bows and copper lamps and animal prints on the walls. The man named Dennis led them into the living room beyond, a large room with drawn curtains along one entire wall. People were sitting on the three sides of a hollow square of interchangeable chairs. Their animated conversation ceased abruptly with the entry of newcomers.

It took a while to notice individual faces: a fat African man with an overdressed African woman by his side, a lean Coloured man with a little beard, another with the face and build

161

of a prizefighter. He singled out the black people first and only then the others: a fierce-looking little woman who reminded him of his mother; two nondescript young men; a very plain girl with her hair in a bun; a bearded man in jeans and a leather jacket (he lifted his eyebrows as he recognized the journalist, Peter somebody, who had snubbed him at the swimming pool party); another quite pretty girl with glasses; a middle-aged man with a dog collar and an ascetic face.

He was introduced. They were Joan and Bob and Liz and Robert. Surnames did not seem to exist here and he wondered whether they used a form of noms de guerre. But everyone called Jay by her name, so perhaps he was unduly suspicious. The African was Thomas and the woman Caroline. The big Coloured man was Michael, and Joel was the thin man with the beard.

She had told him this, but there was still a slight shock about meeting Jay's "friend" Joel, the communist, and finding that he was not white.

Jay had proposed this excursion into a world which was strange to him and had secured the invitation. Some friends of hers, she said, held discussion groups at one another's houses to which black intellectuals were invited. It was not precisely against the law but there was an element of risk. The Special Branch would probably like to know what happened at these meetings. And some of the black leaders said very forthright things. For this reason the people who organized the discussions had to be careful about whom they asked. But she would vouch for him. He had at first been reluctant, until she had asked scornfully whether he was by any chance scared of losing an argument with Joel.

Now, looking at the man, shaking his hand in greeting and receiving a stiff acknowledgment from the weary-looking face, he wondered again about his friendship with Jay. Joel did not seem particularly interested in either of them. After a few formal words he resumed his interrupted conversation with the clergyman.

Drinks were brought and distributed. People stood talking in small groups. The conversation was no longer general.

162

Conscious of the fact that his presence was an intrusion, Charles stood on the fringe of one group, listening to what the others were saying. It was not very much. Diffident criticism of the pass laws, a half-humorous attack on the Immorality Act, a doubtful thesis on the Afrikaner's tendency to equate sex and sedition. He had heard more powerful politics and more violent views in the hospital tearoom.

He intercepted a sideways glance from one of the young men (was it Bob or John? He could not remember) and was at once angry. The hell with them, he thought. Bunch of parlor liberals making a song and dance about having a few people of color sitting in their armchairs and drinking their whiskey.

"I'll never understand it," the other young man was saying earnestly. "If you ask me, the Afrikaners are obsessed with sex."

A dry voice spoke at Charles's shoulder. "It boils down to that old election-winning slogan: 'Do you want your daughter to sleep with a kaffir?'" Joel stood smiling at the young man.

There was an instant of shocked silence. Then the African laughed heartily and the others laughed, too, with the restraint of having recognized themselves.

Joel turned to Charles. "Don't you agree? In the crazy logic of a racial society nothing is more logical than to outlaw love."

For a moment Charles believed that the Coloured man was mocking him, that he was flaunting a relationship with Jay, confirming suspicion and flinging the confirmation down like a gauntlet. But he checked himself. Joel's expression held only friendship.

"I do agree," Charles said. "Provided that one remembers concern about sex stems from other forms of race prejudice. I don't believe it's basic."

It was as if Joel's deliberate stratagem to draw Charles into the conversation had been the stamp of approval they had awaited. The young man began to argue with almost hysterical gaiety.

"You're wrong. Sex lies at the root of it. It all comes from whites who hate to think what the blacks might be capable of

163

doing with their great big *things*." He smirked at the girl with the glasses. "Sorry, darling." She shrugged to show her lack of concern.

"Charles is on the right track," Joel said. "The point about apartheid is its totality within the social structure."

They wrangled on, while Joel's hand rested trustingly on Charles's shoulder. He had the slender bones of a child and the skin was stretched tightly over them. He argued with an air of tired patience.

Charles wondered uneasily about the man's obvious efforts to be agreeable. Did they stem from more deep-hidden motives than friendship with Jay?

" . . . will lead to the eventual collapse of the system," the young man was saying. "You can control everything about a man except his appetite. And once you start making allowances for that you have to grant concessions in every . . . "

The sound Joel uttered was short and husky, more like a cough than a laugh.

"Never," he said. "Never ever. And I'll tell you why. It's not a problem of sex or separation or anything else. It's a question of numbers. We outnumber you, so you dare not make concessions. And that means we'll have to take what we want."

Faces were alert and intent on what he was saying. It was almost as if a shudder of delicious horror had gone down half a dozen white-skinned backs at the contemplation of their predicted doom.

Michael had joined the group and now he and Joel began to describe a plan of operation for the disruption and eventual paralysis of a large city by means of industrial sabotage. The others listened to the coldly horrifying scheme without interruption, and with every indication of approval.

But as the two Coloured men unfolded their plot Charles grew more and more suspicious. It seemed to him almost as if the whole affair had been elaborately stage-managed. Not for the benefit of the spectators but for the actors themselves. He became convinced that this was a game Joel and Michael had devised and played, with appropriate variations, at many similar

164

gatherings. One expected, almost, that at the end of it they would unmask themselves and reveal that they had been playing in blackface; that deep down they were as white as anyone else here.

Vicky was singularly obtuse tonight. Usually, when Charles called at the flat and she happened to be at home, she would remain in their company long enough only to maintain the fiction that he was a mere visitor before retreating to the tiny bedroom and leaving them the freedom of the living room.

Neither of the young women had ever appeared much concerned about the situation. Nevertheless, he was always embarrassingly aware of Vicky as an invisible spectator and had tried to persuade Jay to give up her share of the flat and move to a place of her own. He hinted delicately that he would contribute to the cost. She refused even to consider the idea.

"Why not?" he had asked in exasperation.

"It suits me here."

"Yes, but ... "

"And besides," she had added with a wicked grin, "I feel safe with Vicky around."

This evening the unwelcome third-party presence had been particularly irksome. He only had an hour; he had to be home by nine o'clock, but Vicky had shown no sign of leaving them. She had got up twice, but then only for a visit to the bathroom and later to bring washing from the balcony, a bundle of stockings and underclothes which she dumped unceremoniously in a spare chair. At another time this sign of his acceptance in their close feminine world might have charmed him, but tonight it irritated. Adding to his annoyance was Jay's apparent unawareness that he was annoyed.

She jumped up herself now and said brightly: "Coffee, everyone?"

He looked pointedly at his watch before nodding. He watched her clean, swinging movements as she went through to the kitchenette and thought of following her there. But that would be too obvious. He decided that he would leave after they had finished their coffee. The hell with her. He might not even come back again. He knew that it was unfair to blame her but, perversely, could not desist.

"Charles," Vicky said. Her voice was low, hardly above a whisper.

He turned to her, puzzled. She had moved to the balcony door. She beckoned.

"Hm?"

She beckoned again and he crossed the room unwillingly.

"What is it?"

Softly: "I must speak to you about Jay."

Now what? A lecture on morality? A warning about the evils of adultery, about trifling with a young girl's affections?

He kept his own voice low. "What about her?"

"She's mixed up in something. I don't know . . . I don't like it. Someone should speak to her."

He still felt guilty, ludicrous as it was. Defensively, he said: "What do you mean? What about?"

"Here." She was groping inside an empty flower vase on a bookcase by the door. She pulled out a sheet of paper and unfolded it. Her young and pretty face, usually bemused as if the affairs of the world passed her by, was troubled. "Read this."

He glanced at the paper. It was a crudely printed form. He scanned it quickly. From the kitchenette came the bubbling roar of water boiling in an electric kettle. He began to read.

There was a heading: "A Call from our Leader." Then:

"The Communist Party considers that the slogan of non-violence is harmful to the cause of the national democratic revolution in the new phase of the struggle, disarming the people in

166

the face of the savage assaults of the oppressor, dampening their militancy, undermining their confidence in their leaders. At the same time the party opposes undisciplined acts of individual terror. It rejects theories that all nonviolent methods of struggle are useless or impossible and will continue to advocate and work for the use of all forms of struggle by the people, including noncollaboration, strikes, boycotts, and demonstrations. The party does not dismiss all prospects of nonviolent transition to democratic revolution. This prospect will be enhanced by the development of revolutionary and militant people's forces. The illusion that the white minority can rule forever over a disarmed majority will crumble before the reality of an armed and determined people."

Another heading: "The Oath." And below it:

"We are soldiers of Umkhonto We Sizwe, the Spear of the Nation. We are scouts in the people's army. We promise to obey without question. As soldiers we promise to serve our people and our country with our lives, to uphold the policies of the national liberation movement led by the African National Congress, and to safeguard the rights and the dignity of the people from all attacks."

He frowned, holding the sheet of paper.

"Where did you get this?"

The girl looked uncomfortable. "In Jay's wardrobe. I didn't mean to ... I was looking for a pair of my earrings and then I found this and I couldn't help reading it."

"Have you spoken to her about it?"

"No. I didn't want her to think I was scratching in her things."

He tried to make his voice light. "I wouldn't worry too much. It's probably one of those things people hand out at a 'varsity. Probably she kept it out of curiosity."

"You think so?" Vicky sounded relieved.

Jay's voice came from the kitchenette. "Hey! What are the two of you whispering about?"

He thrust the pamphlet hastily at Vicky. "Here. Put it back."

When Jay came into the room they were standing apart

167

like strangers thrown together and unable to find a basis for conversation. She scowled at them in make-believe suspicion.

"Are you getting up to something behind my back? Vicky, I'll scratch your eyes out."

The kettle boiled and the awkward moment was passed by with the business of setting out cups and pouring and drinking. Charles put down his cup and looked at his watch again.

"I must be going." He looked at Jay. "Coming down to the car?"

It was chilly for a summer's evening. She had pulled a sweater around her shoulders, letting the sleeves hang. He had taken the usual precaution of parking his car at the end of the block, around a corner. (There was always a curious guilty elation about the need to be circumspect, to park the car inconspicuously, to choose restaurant tables in dark corners, to avoid crowded places.) A streetlight shone distantly through the trees but here, where they walked, they were in shadow. Their footsteps echoed.

"Have you seen Joel again?" he asked abruptly.

She looked at him. "Why?"

"I want to know. Have you seen him?"

"Once or twice."

He sensed the evasion. "I would prefer it if you didn't."

She blazed up, as he might have expected.

"I don't see what the hell it's got to do with you."

"No?"

"No."

"If I were to tell you he is dangerous company?"

"Because of his color, I suppose. You disapprove because I have a Coloured man for a friend. Isn't that a typical bigoted, narrow-minded—"

He interrupted determinedly. "His color has nothing to do with it. But you must be able to see for yourself that he's dangerous. He doesn't trouble to hide his political views, does he? So it's more than likely that the police have an eye on him."

Sulkily: "I'm not scared."

"Courage doesn't enter into it. It's a question of being sensible."

168

She did not reply. They walked for a while in silence.
He decided to try again.

"What is the Spear of the Nation?"

She stopped and gave him a startled look.

Finally: "I don't know."

"Now you're lying. Umkhonto We Sizwe. Is it a revolutionary group?"

"I don't know what you're talking about."

"Is that what you'd say if the police were to question you? And do you think they'd accept your answer?"

She shrugged, but her voice was uncertain. "The police have no reason to ask me anything."

He knew that he had an advantage, but was uncertain how to use it.

"It's a wing of the ANC, isn't it? Or of the Communist party. Which?"

"How should I know?"

"An extremist wing? Militants? Are they the people responsible for those sabotage attempts? Who blew up those power pylons?"

She said angrily: "You sound like a police interrogator yourself. What are you? A spy for them, maybe?"

"Don't be childish. Do you think I like doing this? It's for your own good. Has Joel got ties with this organization?"

"My own good, my own good," she mimicked him viciously. "What would you know about what's good for me? And what's it got to do with you anyway? Why don't you go back to your wife?"

It stung like a slap in the face. And mingled with the hurt was the miserable knowledge that there was right on her side. What business of his was it? He had no claims on her. Why did he not return to his wife?

"Can't you understand that ... " He shook his head, unable to complete the question. The point was that she did not understand. Was there an equal lack on his part? Should he sympathize more readily with youthful idealism and concern for freedom, although it at times displayed itself in foolishly deluded ways? Should he look benignly at youth while it ranted about freedom to love and use drugs and secure political aims and to proclaim the philosophy of to-hell-with-everything-else? Or should he persist, boringly and infuriatingly, in pointing out that freedom had a reverse side, which was responsibility for individual acts?

"All right. It hasn't anything to do with me. But nevertheless I'm interested and concerned. I'd hate to see you get yourself into a situation you can't handle."

"I can look after myself." But less vehemently.

"I am sure you can." Careful now. "Even so there are times one needs advice. You know you can trust me, don't you?"

No reply.

"Don't you?"

Unwillingly: "I suppose so."

First obstacle cleared. Go cautiously.

"I have a feeling you're worried about something. Do you feel like telling me about it?"

She was silent again.

"You can confide in me, you know. That's what I'm here for."

They came to the end of the block. The MG stood a short distance down the next street.

"Do you want to sit in the car for a moment?"

She pulled the sweater closer around her shoulder. They went to the car in silence.

"Cigarette?"

"Thanks."

The tiny flame from the lighter shone on her dark hair and her brooding face.

Gently: "Do you want to tell me?"

She drew on the cigarette.

At last: "They want me to go to Johannesburg."

"Who?"

"Doesn't matter."

"What are you supposed to do there?"

"They're expecting a consignment."

"Of what?"

"Explosives."

Despite his good intentions he said: "My God!"

"What did you expect?" she asked angrily. "Toilet rolls?"

"No. Go ahead."

"Michael is going as well. He'll be the courier."

"The big guy who was with Joel that evening?"

"Yes."

"Then why do they want to involve you? What are you supposed to do?"

"Make the pickup."

He passed over the gangland slang without comment. "Where?"

"The ... parcel will come to my hotel. Michael can't collect it because he's Coloured. Besides, no one will suspect a white woman."

"I hope that's more than a theory," he said. "Do you know what kind of explosives you're supposed to be collecting?"

"The plastic stuff. Gelignite. And detonators and fuses."

It was difficult to stay calm. "Good Lord, child. Do you realize how dangerous this is? What happens if the stuff goes off?"

She said contemptuously: "If you believe in something you must be prepared to take risks."

Nevertheless, he sensed her nervousness. Don't argue, he cautioned himself.

Slowly, by patient questioning, he drew the story from her. It was a melodrama of intrigue and assignation and passwords. He thought he could detect Joel's touch. The date had not yet been arranged. They would be told later. On that day she and Michael would travel to Johannesburg by air, but on separate aircraft. She would book into the hotel. She would receive a telephone call that night. The recognition signal would be: "The goods for Mr. Cohen are ready." Delivery would be made the following morning and then she was to buy a suitcase of a particular make and color at a shop in Eloff Street. Michael would already have made an identical purchase. They would contrive to exchange suitcases at Jan Smuts Airport and the case with the explosives would be booked as Michael's luggage. When she arrived in Cape Town she was to leave the airport imme-

171

diately, carrying only her hand luggage. Joel would be waiting and he and Michael would recover the suitcases.

She did not know for what purpose the explosives would be used and she had not wanted to ask too many questions, for fear of seeming naïve. Or perhaps she had not really wanted to know.

What else but for booby-trap bombs, left to explode in crowded shops, on station concourses, in amusement parks, to kill and maim the innocent and unsuspecting. Not, perhaps, a prospect she could contemplate without a degree of inner doubt.

Charles listened with horror, but also with a mounting sense of absurdity. After a while her stubborn look, her reluctant confession, struck him as comic as much as startling. A child was owning up. She and other children (boys and girls together!) had been playing at secret societies, making hideouts and devising initiations and code words and secret writing, making war raids with cap pistols. Now one of them had become afraid of the dark and, given a sympathetic grown-up ear, was blurting out all the secrets.

He had to force himself to remember that the game was in deadly earnest, that the guns would be loaded with real bullets, and that the explosives were more than fireworks to celebrate Guy Fawkes Day. He was overwhelmed by the responsibility he felt toward her and the need to dissuade her. But he hardly knew where to start.

"I imagine you realize I think this escapade is silly and futile," he said. "I won't even mention the appalling risk you'd be taking. But have you considered what would happen if the police step in? They'll charge you under the Sabotage Act, and you could get a death sentence." He saw her in profile, the stubborn look, the set of her jaw, and he sighed. "All right. We won't argue about that now. Just promise me one thing. Think about it again. No matter what you say, I know that you have your doubts. So think about whether it's worth it. And promise that you'll speak to me again before you decide. Promise?"

She stubbed out her second cigarette.

"All right."

His relief was profound.

"Good. I'll drop you at the flat."

Joel, he thought, as he started the car. I must find that corrupt, scheming bastard before he destroys her.

Antoinette left nothing: no note, no message, no last-minute telephone call.

When he reached home the following evening there was nothing to show that she had gone. Yet there was: a sound of emptiness about the flat which made him call her name out loud.

No one answered.

He walked down the short passage to their bedroom. It was empty. So was Marianne's room. He went back to the lounge, looking at objects with more attention. Their few pictures were there; so were other things, bric-a-brac, the clutter of possessions they had managed to accumulate in spite of the self-proclaimed poverty which was intended to rule his study years. Nothing seemed to be missing.

Their bedroom again. On the small bed in the curtained alcove where Paul slept was a battered yellow tin lorry, his favorite toy. Somehow it had been left behind when he had been taken for a visit to his grandparents at Hoog-in-het-Dal a week ago. Charles turned it over in his hands and into his mind came a picture of his small son: sturdy legs and arms, a rebellious ruff of light hair, the promise of a good-looking face under the softness of babyhood. He put the toy down on the bed. Paul would miss it. He went everywhere on the farm with his grandfather, playing on the ground at the old man's feet.

He looked at the telephone beside their bed, and then at his watch. Twenty past six. Too late for her to be away on a last-

173

minute dash to the shops. Perhaps she had run out of cigarettes and had gone to the delicatessen down the road.

Her car would be here. Of course.

With a sense of buoyancy he went clattering down the stairs to the basement parking garage. Down here it was always chilly, even in summer. The pressing weight of concern returned the moment he saw that the Volkswagen was missing from its usual bay.

Slowly and thoughtfully back up the stairs. Could she have gone visiting? But at this time of the evening, taking Marianne out when there was school homework to be done, a meal to be prepared and eaten, baths and teeth-cleaning and the other routines of evening?

Try the kitchen.

Inside the refrigerator were two lamb chops and a small bowl of potato salad. There was nothing to show they were there for any special purpose.

He took out a can of beer. The rip-off top made a sharp, explosive sound. Carrying the can, he walked slowly back to the bedroom.

Was it possible to start afresh? Could you discard the things which held you shackled to the past?

He had the wish, perhaps even the compulsion, to do so: to scrap everything which had gone into making him: memories of childhood, parents, Hoog-in-het-Dal, profession, obligations and commitments as well as the promise of joy and success; all the possessions which littered his life in the way ashtrays and ebony figurines had come to fill these few rooms and had made them (and his life, too) a compromise with the beauty of barrenness. Now he wanted to be rid of it.

To go with his new young mistress in search of that room which was the center of their playful dream?

But as he thought of it he knew that he would never go. The room belonged where it was, which was in a dream. For no amount of wishing could eradicate the reminders of the past.

Thought of Jay brought to mind the problem of what to do about her absurd involvement with half-baked terrorists. The obvious course was to go straight to the police, but he cringed

174

away from the prospect. Apart from the reluctance to play informer and the certainty that she would be in serious trouble, there would be all the explanations and uneasy confessions. How would he explain his own involvement? He imagined knowing looks and ill-disguised prurience. He could not face that.

Tomorrow he would make a determined effort to find Joel. He had thought about it today but he hardly knew where to start. He knew very little about the man and trying to trace him through Jay, no matter how subtly, would alarm her.

Had she mentioned once that he was a teacher? It might be a lead worth following. He would try tomorrow.

Where the hell was Antoinette?

He began to telephone, dialing all the acquaintances he could think of, asking the circumspect question and then evading the instant curiosity. No one had seen her.

Ten past seven. He lit a cigarette, made another circuit of the bedroom. Where the hell could she be? He opened doors at random.

One of the suitcases was missing.

Until now he had not thought of looking in the wardrobes, but when he did he missed the suitcase at once. It was the black one with one broken clasp. Her dresses hung in their places. She did not have many clothes and he went slowly through them. Was the dark blue dress gone? And a pair of orange slacks and an orange top she liked particularly? And surely she had more underwear than these few flimsy bits and pieces?

He made up his mind abruptly, rang the exchange, and booked a trunk call to his father-in-law.

The call took a long time coming through. He thought about frying the lamb chops and eating them and the potato salad. But he found he was not hungry. He opened another can of beer instead.

He heard footsteps on the stairs a few times and got up hopefully, but they passed on down the passage. By the time he spoke to his father-in-law it was already nine o'clock. Old Krynauw was mystified and then worried. He had last heard from Tony about two weeks ago. Her letter had sounded quite cheerful. Why, what was wrong? No, she had said nothing about coming home for a visit. What was wrong?

The old man was not to be persuaded that there was no reason for concern. Charles hung up, swearing and feeling guilty. He tried to obliterate the guilt with anger. Really, it was too bad of her to go off like this, without saying anything to anyone.

But then memory was jolted with the force of a real blow and he remembered, feeling sick, an occasion a few weeks ago when he had tried to persuade Antoinette to duplicate a sexual trick Jay performed with casual skill. The experiment had ended in disaster, with Antoinette in tears and he feeling both resentful and guilty, as now.

He found a fresh packet of cigarettes in the bookcase, ripped open the cellophane with unnecessary vigor, and lit yet another cigarette. Should he phone the ambulance service and the police to ask about accidents? The thought was terrifying.

On the bookcase lay a small pile of books with the identical dove-gray, unglossy dust cover. It was her new volume, out last month. He picked up the top copy and looked at the jacket. There was a strangeness about seeing the familiar name on it. He turned the pages. No inscriptions or autograph. The few copies she had presented to people (the girls in Paris: "Helga and Jane, from their loving friend Antoinette"; and her father: "Dear Papa, from your loving daughter Tony") had all been meticulously parceled and mailed. These were left over and would in time be given away to visitors able to speak about her work without embarrassing her into shyness.

He looked at some of the poems, without reading them. He had read them before and thought they were very good, especially the title poem. He felt a marveling sense of mystery about his wife and her talent. What part of her mind did she use when she wrote these poems?

He put the book down on the bedside table and then lay on the bed, fully dressed. He was weary and did not know what to think or do.

The telephone woke him from phantom-ridden sleep and he groped for it, recalling instantly what had happened. Nevertheless, he did not at first recognize the thick, distorted voice at the other end for that of his father-in-law. It needed, too, several repetitions before the sense of the message that agonized voice was conveying could penetrate his mind.

A commercial traveler, coming over the mountain pass in the late afternoon, had spotted the marks on the road. He had stopped and seen the car far down below. The police had, with considerable difficulty, recovered the bodies. Both Antoinette and Marianne had probably been killed instantly.

Once he understood that he understood everything. He ended the conversation by saying the right things, using the custom-worn phrases of participants in disaster. Yes, it was terrible. Terrible. No, Paul was all right, thank God; he was with his Granny de la Porte. Mr. Krynauw must get some rest; it would be a good idea to get Dr. Louw to come and have a look at him and perhaps give him something to make him sleep. He would phone Dr. Louw himself. He had to make a few arrangements at the hospital and he would be on his way immediately that was done. If all went well he would arrive early in the morning. He would see to everything when he came.

Even as he spoke the questions were crowding into his mind like maggots inside a festering wound. They crawled and squirmed and nothing, not even the searing pain of grief, could destroy them.

An accident? It had to be an accident. The road over the pass was notoriously treacherous, steep and untarred with a multitude of hairpin bends. But it shortened the journey to her hometown by almost fifty miles and that, presumably, was why Antoinette had chosen it. Of course it was an accident.

He would never be utterly convinced.

She had decided unexpectedly to take Paul to visit his grandparents. They had not discussed it and he had been a little surprised. But of course such visits were not unusual for it was only a couple of hours to the farm and the old people, particularly Charles's father, adored their only grandchild.

And yet. Had she started planning then, a week ago?

She had known some things. Had she guessed at others? Overheard? Been told?

177

Had she suffered?

It had to be an accident; could be nothing else.

He pictured it as, hastily, he threw clothes into a suit-case; the other, the brown one. He knew the road well for he, too, preferred its dangers to the dullness of the safe extra fifty miles around the mountain. It could have happened at any one of a dozen spots. He imagined her approaching the corner, driving a little too fast perhaps, anxious to get home. In her impatience she might have cut the corner. The rear wheels would have spun on the loose gravel and the car would have started to drift. Perhaps she had overcorrected. A skid had developed the other way; in terror she had wrenched at the wheel again. And the car, lurching out of control, went with slow inevitability over the edge and into its head-over-heel tumble.

He found himself standing motionless by the suitcase, a shirt in his hands, his facial muscles stiffened into a mask by the awful reality of the vision. He grimaced, threw the shirt on top of the rest of the clothing, and slammed the suitcase lid.

That was most probably how it had happened.

Side by side with this picture, however, was another. It was almost a duplicate, but with subtle shadings which made it quite different and compared to which the scene of hell he had imagined was utter serenity.

He saw her reach that bend in the road. And then, instead of taking the corner, her hands froze on the wheel. She held it rigidly and, as Marianne in the seat beside her began to scream, looked calmly out through the windshield at the face of nothing.

Did she decide to do it then, at the instant before she came to the bend, moved by sudden impulse? Or had she planned it a week ago and moved toward it steadily, day by day and eventually mile by mile?

Impossible. It was an accident.

But he would never know.

The patient was not breathing normally, so he had decided to escort the stretcher to the intensive-care unit, pausing only to shed gown and mask outside the operating room. He was still wearing a cotton singlet, ill-fitting white pants, and rubber boots when he went out to meet the young man who was waiting for him.

Peter was standing in the corridor between the two surgical wards. Perhaps he felt out of his element, for his face had been arranged to show detachment from the alien bustle around him. But his eyes, quickly taking in Charles's functional dress, admitted that he felt himself overdressed and therefore an intruder. Charles, in turn, was surprised by the young man's gray suit and quiet tie. Presumably his newspaper disapproved of denims. His hair and beard were as tangled as ever.

The journalist tried to cover up for unfamiliarity by feigning a knowing manner.

"Morning. Sorry to trouble you. Very busy in theater?"

Charles greeted him curtly. "I must get back. The next patient is already under anesthetic. What's the problem?"

Peter looked discomfited. "I'm sorry, Dr. de la Porte. I wouldn't have come if . . . But it's urgent. It's about Jay."

The first twinge of alarm.

"What about her?"

"Have you seen her lately?"

"What's that got to do with you?"

Peter made a placatory gesture. "Please. I'm not prying. But it's important."

"Well, I haven't." Why should he feel guilty? "I've had a . . . uh . . . personal matter to settle and I've been very busy."

"Of course." The journalist hesitated, searching Charles's face. "I was very sorry to hear about your wife."

Charles looked at him, frowning. "How did you know about it?"

Peter's expression showed innocence. "We carried the story. I mean, my paper did. About the accident. I recognized the name." But was there also an element of sharp observation, as if mention of Antoinette's death had been a kind of test.

"I see. What did you want to tell me about Jay?"

Peter looked around. "Can't we go somewhere a little more private? I can't talk here."

Charles considered for a moment. "All right. This way." He led the way to the closetlike room near the lifts where the surgeons hung their coats. At this time of the morning it would be deserted. He closed the door. "Now, then."

The journalist had lost something of his furtive manner. He took a squashed packet of cigarettes from his pocket, shook one halfway out, and offered it.

"No thanks."

Peter lit the cigarette without asking leave. Then he asked: "Do you know anything about her planning a trip to Johannesburg?"

He had half-expected this, but nevertheless the shock was numbing.

"No," he said quickly. "As I told you, I haven't seen her for quite ... "

"I happen to know she is going there."

"She's free to go where she wants to, isn't she?"

"Sure. Sure. But there's something I want her to do for me."

"Then why don't you ask her?"

"Because she might refuse. But she won't refuse you."

"I don't understand."

Peter gave him a look: sharp, knowing, indulgent, the coded glance of conspiracy. It said: I know all about you. You can't fool me.

"I hope you'll use your influence with her," he said.

"Can you give me any reason why I should do that?"

Peter drew on his cigarette.

"Do you remember Joel Paulse?"

He had to gain time. "Paulse? Paulse?"

"Yes. Thin Coloured guy. You met him with Jay at Dennis Goldsmith's place. I was there too, remember?"

"I remember vaguely."

"Jay is going to Jo'burg to do a job for Paulse. I need her cooperation to do something for me, too. Something quite small."

"Where do you fit into this?"

"That really doesn't matter at present, Doctor."

"Are you one of them, too?"

Peter dribbled smoke through nicotine-stained teeth. But his look was alert and wary. "One of whom?"

Charles knew that he had stumbled. "This . . . this bunch of whatever they are."

The young man smiled disarmingly. Suddenly Charles wondered how old he really was. The unkempt look had something of the theatrical about it, as if it was fancy dress donned for the occasion.

"No, you're not, are you?" he said with sudden understanding. "You work for the other side, don't you?"

Peter continued to smile. "You could put it that way."

Close to panic, but he had to, positively had to, control his feelings. "Why come to me? Why not approach Jay herself?"

The smile became thinner and more cryptic. "Let's say that it doesn't suit me to show my hand just at present. Besides, you would stand a better chance of persuading her than I would."

"And if I refuse?"

The smile vanished. "You're free to refuse, of course. But that might lead to certain . . . difficulties for Jay."

"That sounds like blackmail."

Peter shrugged.

"Have you any official standing? Are you from the police? Or are you just a spy?"

"That's immaterial. I have approached you. That's all you need to know."

181

"What do you want me to do?"

"Tell her you've been approached. Warn her there's danger. Suggest that she should cooperate."

"All this is very vague. What danger? How should she cooperate?"

"She'll be told when the time comes. I don't want to alarm her unnecessarily."

"And you think this ... this mystery won't alarm her? Naturally she'll want to know more. Then what do I tell her?"

"Whatever you like."

"Can I mention your name?"

Swiftly: "No." Then, obviously dissembling: "Best not to."

A slight point gained. He pressed it home. "That's going to be difficult. How else can I explain having inside information?"

Peter was not easily drawn. "You have no information," he said, as if pointing out the obvious. "You've been approached and that's all you tell her, without naming names. If she asks for names you simply say you don't know any."

"Your name particularly, I suppose." Charles put a sarcastic note into his voice. "You don't want to ... what's the phrase? ... blow your cover."

Peter was unruffled. "My name is the only one you know. So you're right, I don't particularly want you to give it to her."

"But you've come to me."

"I believe I can rely on your discretion."

"Look, I'm sorry. I can't do anything unless you confide in me. As far as I'm concerned this is all playacting. Naturally I don't want Jay mixed up in some childish nonsense. But you'll have to tell me a great deal more before I decide whether I'm prepared to help you. I don't even know whether or not to believe you. Have you got a police identity card?"

Peter said quietly: "It may seem like playacting to you, Doctor, but I can assure you it's very serious. I assume you wouldn't like to see Miss Case arrested."

The sudden formality was more convincing than the words. Again Charles felt that chillness, like the thought of snow falling far out at sea.

He said stubbornly: "At least tell me what form of cooperation you require. I must be sure it holds no danger."

Peter hesitated, cigarette at his lips. "Something will be delivered at her hotel in Johannesburg. All we want is access to that object, for a couple of minutes. That's all. And after that she'll be perfectly safe."

"This . . . object. What is it?"

"It's best that you don't know."

"It wouldn't be a consignment of explosives, would it?"

He had calculated the risk, but still he wondered if he had been too reckless. There was a long silence.

At length the other man said: "I can see you are better informed than I had believed, Doctor."

"You'll have to trust me," Charles told him. "I'm in it now, whether I like it or not."

The seemingly candid smile had returned. "Yes, you're in it. Like it or not.

Vicky's welcome was cool. She stood at the flat door and clearly was not going to invite him inside.

"I don't know where she's gone, Charles. She may be staying with friends."

"Surely she would have told you?"

"Well, she didn't. The last couple of weeks she's been out quite a lot." Her voice was full of reproach. She intended him to understand that he had failed Jay.

"Perhaps she's gone to her parents," he suggested.

"Her parents," Vicky said derisively.

He prepared to leave. "Will you give her an urgent message? When you see her please ask her to ring me."

"If I see her."

The door was closed before he had reached the stairs.

There was an ominous edge to Peter's voice which had not been there before.

"You didn't quite level with me yesterday, did you, Doctor?"

His grip tightened on the telephone receiver.

"What do you mean?"

"You told me you didn't know when she was leaving for Johannesburg."

"Well, I didn't. I told you I hadn't seen her for at least a fortnight. Since before my wife was killed. I tried to reach her last night, but . . . "

"Would it surprise you to learn she was on this morning's flight?"

"Oh, my God. I didn't know . . . I didn't think . . . "

"You say you haven't spoken to her?"

"No. I told you. I tried to see her, but she was out."

"I see." A thoughtful silence. "That rather complicates matters." Another pause. "We'll have to think of something else."

"At least speak to her. Give her a warning. For God's sake, you can at least do that."

"I don't know. It might complicate things even further."

"You're going to let her walk into this with her eyes shut, aren't you?" Charles said bitterly.

The voice became brisk and detached. "On the contrary. I'd say that she walked into it with her eyes wide open, wouldn't you?"

He continued to hold the receiver after the connection was cut, listening to the dial tone.

"We'll allow them to bring the stuff to the Cape," Peter had told him yesterday. "We want it here."

"Why?"

"We have our reasons."

"You'll allow a suitcase full of gelignite and detonators to travel on a commercial plane full of passengers? Then you're as callous about human life as they are. You call them fanatics, but so are you."

Peter had smiled. "Oh, no. We're not as careless as that. It won't even get near the aircraft. That's why we need Jay's help. When she goes back to her room with the parcel someone will be waiting for her. She'll go to the airport with the suitcase all right, but it won't hold anything more lethal than a brick or two. By that time the parcel should already be on its way to Cape Town on a military aircraft. We'll do another switch here and when Joel goes to claim his suitcase it'll be waiting for him, snug as bait for a tiger."

Charles left the doctors' common room where he had taken the telephone call and wandered irresolutely down the corridor. He felt sick with worry, but at the same time there was a growing sense of grievance. Everyone seemed determined that he should be responsible for Jay; first Vicky, then Peter with his schemes, and even Jay herself. Why should he? Why couldn't they leave him alone?

He realized that he should have asked the journalist, or policeman, or agent provocateur, or whatever he was, for the name of her hotel in Johannesburg. But probably he would have refused to give it. Was there any sense in telephoning all the hotels in the book? Chances were that she would register under a false name. This possibility somehow completed the sense of vacant absurdity, as if he was watching a detective farce and waiting for the villain to remove his false nose and moustache.

He went back to the ward to seek out the senior surgeon and arrange for a day's leave. He felt even more guilty and aggrieved when his request was granted immediately. It was understood, without words being needed, that the leave was compassionate. Everyone had been very kind and gentle since Antoinette's death.

She was on the early afternoon flight, one of the first passengers through the gate. Her expression, when she saw him waiting,

185

changed rapidly from delight to uncertainty. She faltered and looked around her.

He gave her no time to ask questions.

"You haven't any luggage, have you? Only this?" He took her cabin bag. "Let's go." He made his way rapidly through the crowd and she followed, still bewildered, half a pace behind. Joel was nowhere in sight and he did not stop to look.

It was only in the MG, as he pulled away, that she was able to ask breathlessly: "How on earth did you know I'd be on that plane?"

He had already decided how to answer that one. "Vicky told me you were away. I guessed where you'd gone."

"But this particular flight. How did you know?"

"I've been watching them all."

"For two days? My poor Charles. But why?"

He bypassed that, too. "Did anyone ... uh ... try to reach you while you were in Johannesburg?"

The guarded way in which he framed the question caused her to misunderstand. "Yes. The message came. But it's all off."

"All off?" Relief, but doubt as well.

"They didn't deliver the goods. I waited half the morning but it didn't come." Her relief was obvious, too, and it made her communicative. "It was pretty awful. I didn't know what to do. I hadn't bought the suitcase yet, you see, and time was running out. Eventually I simply had to give it up. I missed the airport bus and I had to take a taxi."

The police had not been to her. So much for Peter. Was that good or bad? He did not know.

"Was there a procedure to follow? To abort the mission, so to speak."

"Yes. If it didn't come I was to fly straight back. Michael wasn't at the airport either. So I caught the plane."

"They can't possibly ask you to go through it again."

To his surprise she agreed. "I wouldn't like to do it again." She gave a little shudder. "Now that it's over I can tell you how I hated it. I kept thinking about the possibility of an

186

accident and that stuff exploding. Not so much that I'd be killed but that I might have an arm or a leg blown off." She attempted a smile. "My old phobia about being mutilated."

"Why did you do it? I thought you'd promised you would speak to me first."

She looked at the road ahead.

"I couldn't. Not after . . . not with all your troubles. And you hadn't been to see me. So I decided I had to make my own decisions, carry my own responsibility."

And the shadow of Antoinette, unobtrusive and remote as ever, came to sit gently but immovably between them.

His telephone rang twice during the early hours of the morning, but when he answered there was only a listening silence. The second time he sat up in bed, staring at the phone, mystified. It did not ring again until much later, when he had only just managed to fall asleep again.

He rolled over, snatched up the receiver, and said fiercely: "Stop playing the bloody fool, whoever you are!"

There was a series of clicks and then her voice said gently: "Charles."

He said: "Yes. Who . . . ? Oh. Jay." He squinted at his watch. Twenty to three. "What's wrong?"

"Charles, I need help. May I come around?"

"What? Now?"

"Yes."

"All right. If it's really urgent."

"Yes."

"All right then. Where are you calling from?"

She had already hung up. He put down the receiver with a muttered "Hell!" and looked at his watch again. It had sounded as if she was speaking from a pay phone so there was no telling how long she would be. He pulled on a dressing gown. He'd make coffee meanwhile. He had an uneasy feeling that something was seriously wrong, without being able to determine exactly what. There was the same restlessness he at times felt after an operation, when he simply *knew* there were going to be postoperative problems.

He stumbled through to the kitchen. Soiled dishes from several meals were piled in the sink. He contemplated washing them before she came, then compromised by filling the sink with hot water.

He put the kettle on to boil. What the hell could have happened? She was clear of Joel and Michael and Peter and the whole damn bunch of them, wasn't she?

He tried to analyze his feelings toward her. He had loved her. Did he still? Everything was in a mess.

Jay had obviously used a telephone from close by for it was barely ten minutes before there was a hesitant knock on the door. Perhaps she hadn't noticed the bell. Or was she reluctant to make too much noise? He went to the door.

She was wearing a dark blue anorak over a dark track suit. The anorak hood covered her hair. She was alone. She looked at him anxiously.

"Charles."

"Hello. Come in."

"Is anyone else here?"

"Of course not."

She went to the top of the stairs and called in a muffled voice. The person who had been waiting on the half-landing below came into sight and started slowly up the stairs. He paused halfway, a hand on the concrete banister, and looked up. The dim wall light shone on Joel's face, dividing it into planes of differing darkness. He looked expressionlessly at Charles and then continued upward.

188

"What the hell is he doing here?" Charles asked the girl roughly.

"He's been hurt," she said. "Can you help us?"

Joel wore a khaki greatcoat which was too heavy for the warm night. He held his right shoulder curiously, hunched up as if in pain.

"Why don't you take him to hospital?"

Jay looked at him wordlessly. Her face was deathly white under the anorak hood.

"Let me see."

The Coloured man pulled away, as if resisting any move which could cause him further pain. There was sweat on his forehead and his skin was a sickly color. He was obviously in shock.

"Bring him inside," Charles said grudgingly. "I'll see what I can do. But then he must leave."

Joel accepted his aid in removing the coat. He was not wearing a jacket under it, only a white shirt of which one sleeve had been ripped off and used as a makeshift bandage for the right upper arm and shoulder. The rag was soaked in blood.

"It's started bleeding again," the girl said.

"Yes."

Joel winced as he unwound the bandage, but made no sound. He was swaying.

"Come here to the light."

Joel shuffled across, supporting the injured arm with the other. But as he reached the standard lamp he lurched forward. Charles caught him as he fell. The inert body was curiously weightless.

"Help me," he said breathlessly. "He's lost too much blood. I must get him to hospital, Jay. What a bloody mess this is."

She had started to weep, without making a sound.

He lowered the unconscious man to the floor and knelt next to him. Already there was blood on the carpet. Joel's skin was cold and clammy. He felt for the pulse. It was hardly palpable and very rapid.

"He must get blood," he said, more to himself than to the girl. "Else he's going to die right here. I don't think he'll even stand up to being moved to hospital."

Forget everything else. Forget that Joel was an unwelcome interloper. Forget that he would probably bring trouble. Forget his revolutionary aims. Forget that the police were watching him. He was a patient. That was enough.

He went quickly to the bathroom, found bandages and a freshly laundered towel. On the way back to the living room he stopped to rip a blanket off the spare-room bed. Jay was kneeling beside Joel, feeling his pulse.

"We must stop that bleeding," he said. "Tourniquet. Wait. I'll do it. You make a pad for the wound out of that towel."

Hurriedly they dressed the injured arm. Then he covered Joel with the blanket.

"I'm going to the hospital," he told the girl. "I'll have to get some things there. You stay and watch him. Okay?"

She had stopped crying. She nodded. She needed encouragement. He patted her on the shoulder.

"Good girl. Loosen the tourniquet if I'm not back in twenty minutes."

There was hardly any traffic on the dark streets and he drove recklessly, cornering at speed, jumping red lights. He was thinking ahead, making a mental list of what he needed. There was no room for any other thought.

A hospital orderly watched with sleepy eyes as he ran past the front desk. Doctors in a hurry were commonplace in his life. His sleep-numbed mind apparently did not register that this doctor had on pajamas under his coat or that he wore shoes without socks.

By good luck there was no emergency in the operating block and the corridors were empty. The sisters would be in the tea room, busy with their knitting. He collected a number of disposable drip sets, some needles, and two vacoliters of 5 percent dextrose in saline, wrapping it all in a surgical gown.

Carrying the green bundle under his arm, he hurried down to the blood bank. The attendant here was more wide awake and examined his dress with pointed interest.

"Emergency in Casualty," he mumbled.

He collected two pints of Group O negative blood, giving the name of a patient he had discharged in the afternoon. At the central sterilization station he signed for a stitch tray with the same excuse. More curious glances. Should he delay and try to draw morphine or some other pain-killing drug? It would present problems, and there was no time. He would have to make do with what he had.

He was halfway back to the flat when he realized he had forgotten to bring sterile dressings and more bandages. No time to go back.

Little had changed. Joel was still unconscious on the floor. Jay was taking his pulse again. She answered Charles's unspoken question with a shake of the head. "He's deteriorated. I can hardly feel a pulse. And he's developed a sighing respiration."

There were probably only minutes left before the failing heart stopped altogether. Charles stooped over the dying man.

"We'll get the blood going. Right arm. Compress the upper arm so I can find a vein."

She obeyed at once. In this sort of situation they spoke the same language.

He unfolded his parcel on the floor. Drip set. Number 12 needle. Bottle of dextrose and saline. He ripped off the bottle top and connected the drip, then looked round for somewhere to hang it. He saw the lamp standard and dragged it closer. He fitted and flushed the needle. Nothing with which to clean the skin. No time to hunt for antiseptic. Wait. Liquor in the wall cabinet behind him. There was a half bottle of brandy at the front. He unscrewed the cap and poured brandy over Joel's arm. He pulled his head back from the fumes.

Difficult to find a vein because of the state of extreme collapse. Finally he slipped in the needle.

"Let the drip run as fast as it'll go."

Jay let go the arm and opened the stopper.

"Now hold the needle in place so I can get the blood going."

He exchanged the saline for a bottle of blood and turned

191

the plastic stop cock wide open.

"He could probably use about six pints. But I couldn't take more than two without someone getting suspicious. Any change in the pulse?"

Jay was still holding the needle. She reached out with her free hand and felt the radial pulse.

"Yes. It's stronger already."

"I must look at that wound before the blood pressure comes up too much. Else we'll lose the blood as fast as we put it in."

He found Elastoplast in the bathroom and cut off a strip to tape the needle in place. Then he rolled up his pajama sleeves and scrubbed his hands.

Jay had unwrapped the stitch tray. Joel was stirring and occasionally he groaned. His breathing was quieter.

"Take off the bandage."

He took the sterile towel off the tray and unfolded it.

"Pour some brandy into this dish and hold his arm up."

He cleaned the skin around the wound with brandy, then placed the towel on the floor.

"Okay. Rest the arm on it."

Using a sterile swab, he wiped away the congealed blood. He examined Joel's shoulder. There was a small wound at the back near the base of the neck and another, almost big enough to put his fist into, at the midpoint of the front of the shoulder girdle.

"This is a gunshot wound," he said accusingly to the girl.

She said nothing.

The bullet had entered from the back and would probably have gone through the muscle without doing much damage, except that it had hit the clavicle and exploded, causing the nasty-looking exit wound. Most of the damage would be in front.

He wiped away more clotted blood. There was fresh bleeding below it. Now he could clearly determine the extent of the injury. Fortunately the track of the bullet had been a little high. It had missed the subclavian vessels and the brachial plexus, but had severed a large branch from the subclavian artery. He could see one end starting to spurt again. He searched in the tray with his left hand, not taking his eyes off the bleeding vessel. He found a pair of forceps and, swabbing away more blood, clipped them over the artery. He watched for a moment.

"I think I've stopped the bleeding. Put up the second bottle and let it run at about fifty drops a minute."

He found the distal end of the severed vessel and closed this off with a second pair of forceps. There was catgut on the tray and he tied the two ends, then released the forceps. He hunted and found further small bleeding points which he also tied off. He could do nothing about the smashed clavicle and the large wound in front; too much tissue had been lost. He poured brandy into the wound and covered it with gauze. He found a sheet which Jay tore into strips and with these he tightly bandaged the wound. Joel opened his eyes and mumbled something indistinguishable.

"You'll be all right," Charles told him.

Joel closed his eyes again.

The doorbell rang.

Their heads swung around in unison and then they sat motionless, like contorted figures in a frieze which the artist had tried to represent as the moment of fear before flight. Joel tried to sit up and groaned and flopped back again.

Charles wet his lips with his tongue. His heart was hammering. Jesus, how could he have forgotten? Peter. The police. Peter would know. He would tell them where to look.

Think. Think quickly, despite the stranglehold of fear.

He whispered: "Get him to the bedroom." He reached up quickly and unhooked the bottle of blood from the lamp. Then, to Joel: "Listen. We'll help you up. But I've got to carry this bottle. Only one hand for you. Help as much as you can. Got it?"

Joel nodded. His face was gray.

"Okay. Let's go."

His arm was around Joel's shoulders and he felt the man's thin muscles tighten and strain. Joel whimpered with effort but he could not lift his body. No good.

There was a second ring on the doorbell, longer this time.

Be quick. Be quick.

"Jay, hold the bottle."

He reached down and lifted Joel with one heave. Jay, taking small, nervous steps and holding the bottle and its coiled tube high in the air, followed as he carried the dead weight through the bedroom door. He lowered his burden to the floor.

"Hurry. Hang the bottle there. From that key in the wardrobe."

No time to make sure the blood was still flowing. Close the bedroom door behind him. A rapid scrutiny of the lounge. Dressings and surgical instruments lay scattered on the floor. He bundled them into the gown and shoved the untidy parcel behind an armchair. Suspicious stains on the floor. Spread the blanket over them.

"Lie down," he whispered to the girl. "Pretend we were sleeping here."

He walked to the door. A last check. Nothing obviously out of place. If there was it was too late.

He put on the aggrieved look of someone newly roused from sleep and opened the door a crack. A khaki uniform stood beyond. He saw polished buttons, then a black face.

Harshly, he asked: "What do you want?"

The familiar voice of the nightwatchman, puzzled, obsequious: "Sorry, Doctor."

His knees were trembly. He leaned against the doorpost. "What is it?"

The black man in his frayed, much-patched uniform tunic stood looking at him diffidently.

"Sorry, Doctor. Your car. The lights, they are burning."

"My car lights?"

"Yes, Doctor. They are burning."

"Why didn't you switch them off? The car's not locked."

"Sorry, Doctor. I don't look."

"Okay, George. Just switch them off for me, will you?"

"Yes, Doctor."

"Thank you, George."

Stand at the closed door again. Think. Had he forgotten the lights? It was possible. Had the African seemed eager to see inside the room? Nonsense. Don't start suspecting everyone and everything.

But he could not dispel his fears so easily. Now, with the medical emergency partially behind him, he was more than ever aware of the dangers all around. He was a blindfolded man in a dark room strewn with traps, where one blundering misstep might cause the steel jaws to snap and close.

Jay was sitting up on the blanket. He passed her without a word. In the bedroom, incredibly, Joel was fast asleep. Pain and shock and tension had finally forced the body to seek its own protection and overcome the mind's resistance.

The second bottle of blood was almost drained so he changed back to dextrose and saline. He checked the flow, made sure that the needle was still secure. The thin limbs lay sprawled on the floor. Should he move Joel to the bed? Best leave him as he was. He closed the door softly. Joel slept on.

Jay stood in the middle of the lounge, in an attitude suggesting imminent flight. Sensibility warned him to go easy with her, but he could not keep the reproach from his voice.

"This is a nice mess. What happened to him?"

Her voice had the same wariness as her body. "He was shot."

"That's obvious enough. By whom?"

"The police."

"Good God! What happened?"

"They were following him and he spotted them. He got away but they shot him."

"Why were they following him?"

"He had explosives in his car. They knew. Someone must have told them."

He said heatedly: "Well, I didn't, if that's what you're thinking."

"I don't know what to think."

"Believe me, I did not." Even as he made the denial he thought guiltily about Peter. "How would I have known any-

195

way?" How much should he tell her? How long would it take Peter to add up a wounded Joel and a sympathetic doctor and make the calculation which would bring a police raiding party to the flat?

"You knew I was in Johannesburg."

"I guessed."

"And you knew why I had gone."

"Do you really believe I would have betrayed you to the police?"

She hesitated. "No."

He felt like a prisoner reprieved, but he forced himself to be stern.

"I thought you were going to steer clear of these people in the future. How did Joel get you entangled again?"

She said defensively: "I couldn't just desert him, could I? He might have died."

"How did you come to know about it?"

"He phoned me from Langa. He said he was hurt and told me where to find him."

"Do you mean to tell me you went into the black township at that time of night, all alone?"

"I was in my car."

"You're quite crazy. Do you realize what . . . " He shook his head. It was no use talking to her about risks. A thought occurred. "Where's your car now?"

"Around the block."

"Is there blood on the seats?"

"I don't know. I didn't notice."

"There must be." He looked with distaste at the blanket which covered the stained carpet. "He was bleeding like a stuck pig. Look, you had better go home now. I'll attend to him. And you'd better try to clean your car. And skip classes today. Give yourself time to recover."

"All right. I don't think I could face people today."

The confession of weakness was unusual and a further reminder of his responsibilities. Was there anything else left undone?

"These explosives. What happened to them?"

"The police must have got them."

"Is there any way in which they could be linked to you?"

"Not that I know of."

"How did he get hold of explosives? I thought you said the whole thing was off?"

"I think Michael brought them. At least, that's what I understood. Joel was too weak really to tell me much. And I was too busy trying to patch up the wound."

"Do you realize how serious this is? If the police get hold of Joel and that Michael they'll put them in a cell and throw away the key. And the same applies to anyone connected with them." He remembered, ominously, the telephone ringing and the silence which had greeted him when he answered. "Did you try to ring me earlier tonight?"

"No. Why?"

"It doesn't matter."

Peter? Ensuring that he was home?

He said, suddenly vehement: "We've got to get this man away from here. He'll bring the whole hornet's nest down on us."

"You can't move him now."

"He'll be fit enough by tomorrow."

"Where would he go? They'll be watching for him."

"That's his lookout. I can't have you dragged into this."

"If Joel is arrested I'll be dragged in anyway."

Too late, now, to tell her of Peter and his promises of immunity.

"Well, hell, he can't stay here forever."

"Only till arrangements can be made."

"Who's going to make them?"

"There are . . . people," she said with deliberate vagueness. "But don't you see that until then this is by far the safest place? No one would associate you with him."

Too late, also, to tell her of Peter and his knowledge.

"God, it's a mess," he said.

He tried to tell himself that his scruples were purely practical: with each hour that Joel remained hidden the risk of discovery grew greater.

But secretly he knew that his reasons were different. Apart from the danger he had no particular moral scruples about hiding a fugitive from the police and this alone came to him almost as a surprise. He wondered: Had he been influenced by Jay and her political beliefs into accepting her view that every policeman was a natural enemy?

What he really resented most was the physical intrusion into the privacy he had created. He had turned the flat into a cocoon. It protected him from the brutality of existence, from that killing ground into which he was forced to go each morning.

He had been coming home at night and sinking into the bachelor sloppiness as if into the warmth of an unmade, recently vacated bed. He bought food only for the day: a T-bone steak from the butcher when he remembered, a ready-roast chicken from the delicatessen when he did not. He wore his oldest, most comfortable clothes: a disreputable track suit, knitted slippers with a hole in one toe. He sat reading while he ate, or listened to innocuous plays on the radio. Sometimes he bought chilled cheap wine and drank himself into oblivion.

Last Sunday he had driven to Hoog-in-het-Dal, but apart from the excellent lunch it had not been a success. His father had been ill again with the long-standing cardiac problem and his mother was worried and distracted. She had hinted broadly that it was time he took Paul away from the farm but he had been deliberately noncommittal. He was still not ready for the discipline the child would impose. He knew that eventually Paul would have to return to live with him, just as he knew that he would have to resume work on the thesis someday. But not yet; not now.

Living as he did he was already able to forget—sometimes for an hour or two or three, occasionally for as long as a day—that Antoinette was dead.

He came home that evening and it was only as he pushed his key into the lock that he was again fully aware of the alien presence behind the door. He had lived with dread all morning, expecting at any minute to be called to the telephone for the message that Joel had been detected. Or worse, to be summoned into a passage and to be faced with two or three burly, anonymous-faced men. But the relative crises of the day had gradually dulled apprehension about personal problems.

The outpatients session had been long and tedious. It had ended with the usual puzzle: how to fit too many patients who needed admission into too few beds. But pleading and threatening, he had wangled most of them into other wards, but even so five had to be sent home. He had cursed the idiocy of an apartheid rule which dictated that half a dozen beds on the white side should remain empty while five black patients went back to their hovels. Then there had been a patient with a strangulated hernia and a young boy with acute osteitis requiring surgery. He was late in getting away from the hospital and gravel-eyed from lack of sleep.

Now, in the act of opening the door to what should have been refuge, the impossible problem of Joel returned. He was reminded of the need for caution, so he closed the latch very carefully and quietly.

Joel was not in the lounge. Nor, as he found on going through to what had been Marianne's room, was the Coloured man in the bedroom assigned to him.

With enormous relief Charles returned to the lounge. Joel had gone. Obviously he had calculated the dangers and decided to take his chance outside. Privacy was restored. He began to think about what he should prepare for supper; what he should do with his freedom.

From his bedroom came the sound of a drawer being opened and closed.

He was down the passage in a couple of strides. The door was ajar. Joel was standing at the wardrobe which had been Antoinette's. The top drawer, in which she had kept her underclothes, stood open and he was rummaging in it. He looked back over his shoulder, startled. He was wearing the pajamas Charles had given him this morning, one sleeve hanging loose over his bandaged arm.

"What the hell do you think you're doing?" Charles

199

yelled furiously.

Joel seemed embarrassed. But the familiar look of weary disdain reappeared. He held up a cigarette between the fingers of his sound hand. "I was looking for matches. I've run out."

"There are matches in the bloody kitchen."

"There are not. I've looked."

Charles felt impatiently for the lighter in his jacket pocket. "Here."

Joel lowered his head toward the flame. He inhaled deeply. "Thanks."

"And stay out of my room in the future, do you hear?"

"Yes, Master," Joel said mockingly. "I know my place, Master."

"And you can shut up with that, too. If I felt any race prejudice toward you you wouldn't even be here."

But a sneaking doubt made itself felt. Was there in his antipathy an element so crude as aversion toward a person of color?

Joel gave him a contemptuous smile and went past to the door.

"It's okay, Charles. You don't have to pretend. You don't like me. That's okay with me."

Charles asked uncomfortably: "How's the arm?"

"Hurts like hell."

"You shouldn't have got up. Go back to bed and I'll examine it."

The wound was raw and ugly, as was to be expected. But there was no infection and no fresh bleeding. He renewed the dressing in silence. Then he asked: "How did it happen?"

"They shot me," Joel said. His calm vanished, making way for a look of terrible rage and frustration. "Those white bastards shot me."

"You were lucky they didn't kill you. A fraction lower and the bullet would have severed the subclavian vessel. You would have bled to death long before you reached help."

"That would have made them very happy."

"It was the police, was it? Why did they shoot?"

200

"How should I know? They're white and I'm not. That's reason enough, isn't it?"

"Don't talk crap. Was it because you had a load of explosives in your car?"

Joel's face became still and watchful.

"What do you know about that?"

"What do you think? Jay told me, of course."

The hard-edged lines of last night, when Joel had been in pain, had returned. "She had no right to do that."

"What the hell did you expect her to do? And don't talk to me about rights. What right did you have to drag her into this mess?"

"Perhaps you should respect her for having the courage of her convictions."

"I don't respect you for forcing her into an exercise in futility."

"Futility depends on your point of view. From where I sit it doesn't look that way."

"No? On the run from the police? Wounded and dependent? You're a bloody fine revolutionary."

There was a hostile silence. "Someone gave us away," Joel said finally.

"Well, I didn't and Jay didn't," Charles said. "Look among yourselves."

"I intend to."

Under the circumstances the threat was ridiculous, but there was enough menace in the man's voice to make Charles wish to change the subject.

"How did it happen? Were you trying to blow up something? Is that how they caught you?"

"No. They knew I had the stuff. They were tailing me. I'm telling you, someone betrayed us."

"Why did they have to trail you in that case? If they knew you had it they would have arrested you without further ado."

"I was sharing it out among the action leaders and they wanted to see where I was going."

"Among the what?"

"It doesn't matter."

"Action leaders. What are those? Sabotage groups?"

"You're too inquisitive."

"All right. Leave it. What happened to make them start shooting?"

"I only spotted them when I saw this car behind me, coming into Langa. As soon as I tried to shake them off they closed in. They rammed me from behind and I broadsided. But I got out on the other side and ran. I was in among all those shanties and they couldn't use the car to chase me. I would have got away, but one of them saw me as I was going over a fence. And he shot me." He grimaced, holding the bandaged arm close to his body. "God, it was like being hit by a train. But I kept going. Finally I crawled into an old lavatory. They hunted around for a while with flashlights but they didn't come in there. Didn't care for the smell, I suppose. It didn't bother me. I stayed there till they went away."

"Didn't you stop to think before you phoned Jay? Didn't you realize you were endangering her?"

Joel shrugged.

"I needed her."

Charles stared at him and for a moment he felt ill, as if the shock of recognition had been an electrical jolt. He had listened to Joel at their first meeting with considerable skepticism. Joel, he had decided then, liked the sound of his own voice and the visible fear his wild threats inspired.

Later, when he had first heard about the sabotage plot, he had tended to dismiss it, and Joel's part in it, as a childish game. He had recognized that there was nothing childish about bullets and bombs, but he still believed Joel was too intelligent to be really dangerous.

But that had been too quick a diagnosis. The truth was more frightening and he was only starting to discern its outline. Joel was a pathological revolutionary. Revolution was his excitement and his sickness. And for its sake he would use and destroy others without a qualm.

But then a habit of reasonableness, a persistence in seeing the other point of view, reasserted itself. No matter what he proclaimed, Joel could not be totally cold, totally ruthless. What were his reasons for appearing so? Was his dedication not equal to that of the black-man-hating policeman who had shot him? He and others like him had a hard edge to their minds. They were intelligent and yet they were prepared to sacrifice the comforts of life, its honors, its rewards for compliance. Although they were constantly in danger, or perhaps because of this, their senses were never dulled. They were alive.

No. He could not believe that Joel was totally cold.

For in Joel's eyes he saw a reflection of himself.

There was a brief, noncommittal story in the following morning's newspaper. Four people had been detained for questioning in terms of the Sabotage Act. The police declined to release their names. A quantity of explosives had been seized. Further arrests were expected.

The story was repeated, with minor embellishments, in the afternoon paper. Joel studied it in thoughtful silence. Finally he put it aside. He seemed depressed this evening.

"They'll talk," he said.

"Who?"

"Michael and those others. They'll be forced to talk."

"I suppose so."

"But at least they don't know where I am."

"No."

Charles rang the newspaper office in the morning. Peter was not at work. He was believed to be ill. He had been away from work for the past four days.

The third and the fourth days came and went. There was still fear, but it had diminished, perhaps because of familiarity. He and Joel had worked out an uneasy relationship. Joel did not become visible in the morning until Charles had left for the hospital. What he did during the day was a mystery.

When Charles came home they would have one drink, then eat whatever ready-prepared food he had brought. They did the dishes on alternate nights. They talked, desultorily, about books and music. Joel went to his room soon after they had eaten, leaving Charles in possession of the lounge.

Jay had not been to the flat again. It was safer that she didn't come. She telephoned once, in the evening, when she knew Charles would be there to answer. She had no news, but she expected to hear something within a day or two.

The fifth day came.

That evening Charles felt unaccountably lighthearted. He thought that he had finally learned to live with fear. He slept dreamlessly and, in the daytime, seldom thought about what might be happening at home. He was no longer anxious when his name came sighing over the hospital broadcast system. He was reassured, although still puzzled, by the absence of any word from Peter.

It had been a good day at the hospital, too. Two complicated bits of surgery had gone beautifully and the patients had responded well. The old man had been pleased and the junior registrar who had assisted was respectful. Perhaps the schizophrenic interlude had been of some benefit after all. It had compelled him to shake off lethargy and think systematically. It was time he returned to life.

For a change, he had bought a take-out Chinese dinner. They ate prawns in batter and soy-soaked bits of chicken. Joel greedily filled his plate with extra helpings of rice.

"I love Chinese food," he said.

Charles grunted a response. He found the fried stuff greasy and after a few bites had eaten no more. He poured wine into his glass. He had finished off most of the bottle. Joel had declined more than one glass for, he said, he did not really care for wine.

"Unusual," Charles had said idly, and then wished he had not.

"Unusual for a Coloured," Joel had completed the unspoken thought with bitterness. "Okay. I know Coloureds are all supposed to be wine flies, but I'm not. Okay?"

"That wasn't in my mind," Charles had lied uncomfortably.

Now he asked, curious for the first time: "Where do you come from, Joel?"

"Do you mean where was I born? Here. In Cape Town. In District Six."

"You're a teacher, aren't you?"

"What else is there?" Joel asked with a vestige of the bitter hurt of earlier. "For a bloody Coloured there's nothing else." He retreated from hurt into sarcasm. "The bright boys become teachers and the bright girls nurses. Only trouble is there aren't enough schools and hospitals for us all. That's why you find a B.A. working a gas pump."

"What do you really want? Wealth? Big houses? Have you thought about your real objectives?"

"Charles, reality is not things or possessions. The reality is man."

"That sounds very imposing. But it's only words, isn't it?"

"Then let me put it into different words and perhaps you'll understand. The system in this bloody country is going to be changed and the only way to change it is by revolution. Is that clear enough?"

"How can you countenance the thought of bloody strife among your fellowmen? How can you urge them to revolution when you know very well they'll end up dead or worse off than when they started?"

"The system must be destroyed before we can build something new."

"And you're quite prepared to destroy a lot of your people along with the system? That seems to me the paradox in your way of thinking. You claim to be idealistic about the future and yet you use the people around you, who are surely more important than the unborn, with utter disregard."

Joel gave him a chilly smile. "Do you want my answer as a revolutionary? That's easy. People who are content don't make revolutions."

"I'd prefer your answer as a man."

"That's much more difficult. For you to understand it you would have to come and inhabit my skin for a while."

"That may be so. But then why is it that all political changes add up to the same thing eventually? Power remains in the hands of the elect few. And all you've achieved is an exchange of dictatorships."

"There have to be leaders."

"Is that the core of the matter? You want things switched about so that you, personally, can get to the sources of power?"

"You don't know what you're talking about. Have you ever been on my side of the fence? Have you ever been choked with anger but helpless to do anything about it?"

"Civilized people learn to contain their feelings. It's part of a process known as growing up."

"Civilized people don't have to contend with being shoved around as if they're less than human."

"So what's your answer? Burn, destroy, pillage, rape. I insist. That's the answer of a child who can't get his way."

They sat glaring at one another. Joel got up stiffly. He worked at the dressing Charles had renewed earlier as if it was a leash which restrained him.

The telephone rang.

Both of them were startled. They looked toward the door with something like panic. In the silence the telephone continued to ring insistently.

Charles went to his bedroom to answer it.

Jay's voice, hushed and cautious. "Charles? Is Joel there?"

He said impatiently: "Of course."

"May I speak to him?"

He put the receiver down without replying. He went to the door. Joel was standing in the middle of the lounge floor.

"For you," Charles said. Maliciously, he did not give the name of the caller.

Joel brushed past him. Charles, in cold deliberation, did not move away. Joel picked up the instrument and spoke hesitantly.

"Hello?"

He listened with total concentration. His side of the conversation was limited to monosyllables: "Yes." "Where?" "Yes." "Right."

He replaced the receiver. There was a strange, strained expression on his face.

"It's tonight," he said.

Charles said: "Huh?"

"Tonight. I'm leaving tonight."

"Oh. How?"

"They're coming in an hour. I don't know anything else."

"I see. Okay."

Joel's expression did not change.

"Michael's dead," he said.

"What?"

"I was right. He was one of the four they arrested that first night. And then he fell or jumped. Or they pushed him."

"What are you talking about?"

"They were interrogating him and he fell from a window on the fourth floor. They pushed him."

"Or he jumped. You said it yourself."

"They pushed him," Joel said with utter conviction.

"Why should they do that?"

"They don't have to have reasons for anything they do. They're above reasons. I wonder if he told them anything before it happened."

"About Jay?"

"Yes."

"I hope we never find out."

"No."

PART THREE

And a time
 to pluck up
that which
 is planted.

1

The girl called joyously: "Service!" And on the far side of the net the tousle-haired young man shook his head ruefully as he walked back to pick up the tennis ball which had gone slashing past him. The girl lifted another ball deftly between foot and racket and bounced it toward the base line. "Nice shot, partner," she said. "Thirty–five."

Charles de la Porte changed sides with her. He could feel the not unpleasant dampness of sweat down the back of his cotton shirt. He wiped his forehead with the back of his hand. It had been a hard game. Mike Smith was playing well above form today.

There had been a spattering of ironic applause from the bougainvillaea-draped tea shelter after his serve and he looked in this direction, smiling, then flicked the sweat from his hand in an exaggerated gesture of weariness. It was greeted with a small laugh and one of the spectators called out: "Remember your age, Charles! Don't strain yourself."

Charles de la Porte grinned at the thrust, one which Bob French was permitted, for they had discovered only recently that they were almost exactly the same age: Bob was his junior by only one day.

He prepared to serve to his wife. Gillian stood back from the far base line, crouching and holding her racket protectively across her body. He knew of the tension which ruled that slim body but believed that he was alone in his knowledge for she had managed, with almost fanatical determination, to conceal from their guests that anything was amiss.

He served to her, more gently, and she returned with a sturdy backhand. He played across court for the near side-line and Mike only just reached it. Charles de la Porte smashed the weak return midway between his opponents.

"Nice shot," his partner said again. Her name was Penelope and officially she was Mike's girl. Collectively she belonged to them all. She was young and a little wild, blond like Gillian, with a skin like dark honey. Today she wore a white halter top over skimpy shorts. The combined display of legs and bosom and bare midriff was fairly startling and she had received a few queer glances from the older wives. None of the men seemed distressed.

Charles de la Porte picked up another ball. Across the net Mike was bouncing apprehensively on his toes.

"Match point!" Penny called to him and stuck out her tongue.

The first service was marginally out. Mike hit the second back hard and low. Charles de la Porte caught it on his forehand and played a half volley to Gillian. Mike scrambled for the net. He was out of position for Charles de la Porte's return and got an edge to the ball, so that it popped up. Penny, nimble as a golden cat, was at the net, too, and tapped the ball neatly out of his reach.

They came off the court laughing and breathless.

Mike stood aside at the gate. "Thanks, Charles. Great game. You're still pretty good."

Charles de la Porte waited for the women, then good-naturedly preceded the young man. "Thank you. I have mental reservations about that 'still,' but thanks anyway."

Another foursome had taken their place on the court. They stood at the fence for a moment, watching. A tall red-headed man was taking first service. He was a fast but erratic player. They watched him serve a double fault.

"Donald would be twice as good if tried half as hard," Charles de la Porte said.

"He likes to think that he's Speedy Gonzales," Mike Smith said.

"He should take lessons from you, partner," the girl said to Charles de la Porte. She linked arms with him. "Fast but cool."

They all laughed and he thought it quite likely that only

211

he was aware of the edge to his wife's laughter.

"Charles the Cool," Gillian said, as if approvingly.

He gave Penny the playful hug which was expected of him and would extricate him from the situation. He allowed his arm to linger around her pliant waist, then removed it with pretended reluctance.

· "Cool it, Charles," he reproved himself aloud.

Penny always flirted with him. The movements were as formal as those of a masque and restricted to words and glances. Occasionally, as now, she would touch him, but then always as a rough, sisterly contact. The flirtation had become almost a convention, although he had at times wondered uneasily about it. He knew that his habitual appearance of composure and tolerance was a disguise. He knew (and what man could know better?) that he was not immune. Corn-golden, corn-ripe Penny could be shucked of her outer garb as smoothly as any corn cob. And then? And then? Meanwhile he restrained himself diligently, was flattered by her attentions, and took care to treat her with amiable vagueness.

Under present circumstances, however, even the usual harmless game was unwise. He had read, even if no one else had, the warning signs in his wife's still voice. He alone, probably, had noticed the tilt of her chin as she had faced him across the tennis net a moment before. Things were complicated enough without seeking further complications.

So he released himself lightly but firmly and then left the group with the excuse that he had to see to the fires for the barbecue which, like tennis, was part of the Sunday ritual. Gillian had an artist's ability with food and their friends paid her just tribute for her *braaivleis* with its accompaniments of deviled mushrooms and cream-filled baked potatoes and other trimmings.

He found that prelunch drinks were being set up on a side table under the old grapevine. Martin, self-proclaimed farm foreman, was fitted out for this occasion in a white waiter's jacket, none too clean. He was wiping glasses and arguing loudly with his wife. Charles de la Porte could guess at the reason. Plump, reliable Dora was the only servant allowed access to the liquor cabinet key and almost certainly she had resisted her husband's wheedling appeals that she should sneak an extra bottle out to him. She glanced up now and looked startled at the sight of her employer coming soundlessly across the lawn on rubber-shod feet. She muttered something to Martin and he was silent at once, industriously polishing glasses with his back turned.

Charles de la Porte asked the woman pleasantly: "Everything all right?"

She lowered her eyes to the ice bucket she had been filling. "Everything's all right, Doctor."

Martin swung around in pretended astonishment. His voice was jovial. "Morning, Doctor."

"Morning, Martin."

Charles de la Porte noted the Coloured man's expression: slightly popeyed, excessively dignified, like a prelate in a procession. There was a faint, lingering wine smell. Martin's white jacket showed he had taken it on himself to serve drinks this morning. Martin would have to be discouraged.

"How are the fires coming along?"

"Fine, Doctor. The fires will be ready soon."

"Don't you think you should be looking after them?"

"I left Jan to watch them."

"Nevertheless, I want you there to get the coals ready for the meat," Charles de la Porte said firmly. "The people can help themselves to drinks."

He remained in the shade under the vine as the two of them went into the house, Martin looking glum and deprived and Dora obviously relieved. It was cool here after the baking heat down at the tennis court. His guests were there. But he was inclined to linger.

He checked the array of bottles Dora had put out on the linen-covered table. Brandy, gin, Scotch, vodka, cane spirits, vermouth. There were bottles of white wine on ice in a tin bath, as well as an assortment of beer in cans, mixers, and soft drinks. He was thirsty and contemplated drinking a beer, but rejected it for Gillian's homemade lemonade in a tall glass with ice.

He wandered to the end of the vine-roofed walk and leaned against a pillar, sipping his drink. The flat sounds of ball against racket came up from the court, invisible from here. He looked out over the valley. It lay bright and beautiful in the sunlight, serene after yesterday's storm.

What did Martin and Dora really think about this place? Martin had lived here all his life, and Dora for at least thirty years. What did Hoog-in-het-Dal mean in their lives? Did Martin think of it in the same terms as he did himself: that it was birthplace and home place and therefore refuge in any storm? How could he? Was it not a universal experience to return home and find that home had vanished; that the mansion was rubble and that the tenement had made way for towers of glass and steel? How could Martin hold this place as his own, knowing that his tenure was in the mind, no more secure than an illusion, and always dependent on the whim of his employer? Would he go, if told to, with regret at the loss of part of his childhood? Or was this merely another place where people lived, easily exchanged?

Were Martin's and his own feelings really very different? Sixteen years ago (the recollection came to him coldly, like a small cloud drawing across the sun) he had been able to consider sacrificing it all, farm, family, and honor, for a dark-haired young woman and a phantom room by the sea.

And the irony, recognized in full, was that the same woman, no longer quite as young, might unwillingly and unwittingly accomplish in dying what she had failed to do in life.

And if this happened, if he lost the day in court and was finally compelled to give up Hoog-in-het-Dal, what then of Martin and Dora? He recognized, with wry self-knowledge, that they were surrogates for Charles and Gillian, whose probable fate he did not care to contemplate. But the question remained: What would happen to them?

There was the sound of cheerful voices and he turned to find several of his guests approaching, Bob French in the lead.

"Ha! Secret drinker!" Bob's big face was perspiring after the climb up from the court. Not a very good sign. Bob played tennis with more enthusiasm than skill once a week, but that was his only exercise. He ate and drank a little too well. He needed a word of advice. But not now.

214

Charles de la Porte held up his glass. "Perfectly innocent. It's lemonade. What'll you have?"

"Something a bit stronger than that. Don't bother. I'll get it."

Drinks were poured and served as more of the players came up from the courts. Mike Smith joined him at the end of the terrace. The young man was gulping thirstily from a can of beer.

"I need this after that game. And after the party."

"Rough night, was it?"

"You must have left early. I didn't see much of you."

"We slipped away. Gillian wasn't feeling too well."

"I thought she was looking a bit off color. I guess it's the flu."

So, in spite of Gillian's resolve, it still showed.

"Probably," Charles de la Porte said.

He turned to find that his wife was supervising the arrangement of the trays of cutlery and crockery she and Dora had brought from the house. He said quickly: "Wine, darling?"

She answered on precisely the same note, so that her voice seemed a momentary echo of his, or a deliberate imitation: "Thank you, darling." He noticed Mike look at her with sharpened interest and felt briefly aggrieved. She could try harder. But at once he recognized the unfairness of the thought. Gillian had been trying very hard. She could not be blamed, after the strain of making social conversation last night and through most of the morning, if her control had worn a little ragged at the edges. He handed her a glass.

"Everything all right?"

"Everything's fine."

There was a mechanical tone to her voice which conveyed the meaning behind the words as clearly as if the thought had been spoken: "And if everything isn't fine, what else did you expect?"

Gillian, grant her this, was not usually given to the use of a private language. She was frank about her grievances, and their relationship had always been untroubled enough to make circumlocution needless. His mother had been the expert at that.

215

"Where is your father?" "Walking in the garden." She would jump up at once. "I'll go and see to him. What if he should have a fall?" And the unsaid reproof rang out clear as a bell: ungrateful son, so to neglect your father; if he comes to grief you will never forgive yourself. That had been during the period when he and his mother had been locked in a struggle of wills over her determination that he should live at Hoog-in-het-Dal and open practice in town and his equally obstinate decision to leave South Africa altogether. "Your father would dearly love to see you settled." That meant: If he dies it will be your fault. She had a characteristic way of delivering these pronouncements: eyes rolling slightly, head making an involuntary jerking movement. "Your father thought the Harrison girl very charming." And his father, gray-faced and breathless from the congestive heart failure which would bring about his end, continued to read his books, unhearing and unnoticing.

Gillian and Mike were making casual conversation and he moved the few paces away which served to bring about exclusion from their company. He was unsure of his own motives in doing this. But he had achieved solitude a little while ago and had been faintly irritated when people had found him again.

His father had liked Gillian. Perhaps at first only because of the good name she bore and the beautiful way in which she spoke. One had to face facts: The old man had been a snob. But he believed that eventually there had been genuine fondness. In his last months his father had become increasingly withdrawn and irascible, but he had never said a cross word to the girl who was his son's fiancée and finally, only a week before his death, his new daughter-in-law.

His mother was different. Even now her feelings were hard to determine. Certainly she was happy to have had things her own way and doughtily determined that life would endure. She had found another chatelaine and Hoog-in-het-Dal was safe. But at times he had suspected his mother of resenting his new wife, much as she had labored to bring about the marriage.

The thought was unpleasant. It was time he went to inspect the fires. He crossed the terrace to where a door in a wall opened onto a courtyard.

The fires, inside two halves of an oil drum mounted on metal stands, were almost burned down. Jan, the other farm laborer, was raking the glowing mass of coals with the back of a spade. Martin stood to one side, watching.

"Ready?" Charles de la Porte asked him.

"Almost ready, Doctor."

"Did you burn the old fat off the grills?"

"Yes, Doctor." Martin made clear by his manner that the question was superfluous. He was still sulking. Charles de la Porte felt a spurt of anger. And yet there was an ambivalence.

Here I stand drinking in front of him, he thought. And then I still regard myself as having a moral obligation to keep him away from the wine. Hardly logical or fair. But the fact remains that if he has more than one drink he becomes utterly useless.

"I'll get you some wine when you've finished doing the meat."

Martin looked immediately more cheerful. "Thank you, Doctor." He spoke loudly to Jan, who grinned and stirred the coals with vigor.

There it stays, Charles de la Porte thought. Moral conflict unresolved. But at least all three of us feel better.

He stood beside the one drum, staring thoughtfully at the slow pulse of heat which spread and contracted through the bed of coals as if in its heart was a creature which lived and breathed. Jan, shielding his face from the heat with a raised forearm, flattened the coals and retreated. A finger of flame rose and flickered and died.

It had been a long time since he had thought absolutely impersonally about his wife as an individual. What did she think about this? What did she ever think about things, apart from the conventional ideas and momentary visions which married people shared?

Gillian was . . . how could he phrase it to himself without hyperbole? . . . superb to live with, to love and be married to. Superb was as close as he could get, conveying as it did to him an image of racehorse trimness, of total grace and economy. And there was the added relish, by the removal of a letter, of dis-

217

covering a modern and slangy description which also suited her well. Super in bed and out of it. A delight to watch and talk to. An efficient manager and a charming hostess. If she could have had children of her own she would have been a very good mother. As it was, in her early twenties and faced with a suspicious and uncommunicative eleven-year-old, she had gained first respect and then adoration. She was his love. She was loving and loyal and faithful.

But what was she thinking?

He remembered the shift in attitude he had noticed in her yesterday, from the wry good humor with which she had told him of the arrival of Bachelli and the policeman to her absolute and uncomprehending fury after the two men had left. He had seen her anew at that moment, and had also realized that he could not predict or fathom the processes of her mind.

For some reason her greatest wrath had been directed not at him but at Lieutenant Van Wyck, who wanted him to betray a dying woman. He had tried to reassure her that Janice was as safe from bygone recrimination as she was from future hope. Gillian would have none of it. His betrayal would be the greater because it was of no consequence. He did not have to do it.

He wondered: Was there another basis for what seemed sheer feminine contrariness? Was she substituting one act of treachery for another which she only feared? What did she suspect; what did she believe?

He shook his head angrily. There could be nothing.

He tried to hold on to this thought, but it was like a chip of soap slipping from wet fingers to vanish under the gray suds of other, engulfing thoughts. His mind was drowned in a sloshing turmoil of things and people: Jay, Cliff, his wife, his son, the practice, the court case, money, the farm, the future, everything. It was the same suffocating dread which had come to him yesterday during the interview with the police officer.

And he remembered it, too, from sixteen years before, when he and Jay Case had conspired to hide a fugitive.

Gillian said: "Charles."

He turned, startled. She looked agitated. He realized he had been unforgivably negligent about his guests. How long had he been standing here? There was a grayness of ash over the coals.

"Sorry, darling. I'll be with you in a moment. I think we're ready to start grilling." He spoke to the two Coloured men. "Please fetch the meat from the kitchen."

Gillian made a dismissive wave toward the fires.

"Charles, Cliff McOwen is here."

He said, very softly: "Cliff?"

"Yes. He wants to see you."

"I see." He looked at her. "All right. Where is he?"

"I took him to your study. And Charles . . . "

"Yes?"

"I suspect there's something very wrong. He looks . . . well . . . wild."

"In what way?"

"He simply burst in. You know. No one saw him arrive. The next moment he was right there in the middle of everything, waving his arms about and shouting: 'Where's Charles? Where's Charles?'"

"He called me Charles?"

"As far as I remember."

"That's something at least. And then?"

"He saw me and came charging over. I got him out of there as fast as I could, but I'm afraid the party's ruined. Or perhaps it's made the party, I don't know. Everyone's obviously wondering whether Cliff has come here to beat you up. They'll have plenty to talk about at any rate."

"Does he appear to be violent?"

"Wild, yes. But not violent. Not angry at all. More . . . what's the word I want? . . . distracted."

He twisted his lip, looking at her. At least there was the consolation that she seemed, even if only temporarily, his friend and ally again.

"Sounds delightful. I suppose I'd better see what he wants."

219

It was possible to reach the study through the kitchen. But he decided that perhaps this was an occasion for a minor demonstration. He went out through the courtyard door and onto the terrace. People turned expectantly at the sight of him. He left the door open deliberately so that the fires beyond it could be seen. There was nothing as normal as the sight of a meal being prepared.

He went to the drinks table, leisurely poured a fresh gin and tonic, and then, still without any appearance of haste, turned to go inside the house.

Clifford McOwen was standing at the front window of the study, looking down at the view which invariably drew the gaze of all visitors to this room. At the sound of footsteps he swung on his heel and his jaw set aggressively.

He was a short man and slenderly built. Nevertheless, he gave off an astonishing sense of vitality and forcefulness. Now there was a dull look on his normally alert face. He was wearing denim slacks and a shirt which, half-buttoned, hinted at haste or carelessness.

Charles de la Porte paused at the door and raised his eyebrows inquiringly. This was the first time they had been face to face since the start of the lawsuit. He did not know how to handle the situation.

"Hello, Cliff," he ventured after a moment.

The other man nodded what was obviously intended to be a brusque greeting. But at the same time his face changed. Charles de la Porte had a repelling impression of a wax mask to which heat had been applied, so that its chiseled features softened and melted and ran together.

"Oh, God, Charles," Cliff McOwen cried out. "Jay's dying."

Charles de la Porte deliberately withheld any sign of surprise at this sudden display of anguish about a situation which was, after all, hardly new. He pushed a chair forward. McOwen sank into it. He put his hands over his face and drew a long, shuddering breath.

"Can I get you a drink?"

McOwen, face still buried in his hands, shook his head

violently. He said in a muffled voice: "Oh, God, no. Not at a time like this."

"I think it would be a good idea," Charles de la Porte said calmly. "Stay where you are."

He was relieved to find that the liquor cabinet in the living room had not been depleted by the needs of the party outside. Suddenly he felt shy of fetching the drink where everyone would be watching, as if McOwen's moment of weakness reflected shame on himself, as pain in one part of the body was sometimes referred to another part. He carried a glass with a stiff tot of whisky back into the study. McOwen was in the same attitude, slumped shoulders down in the chair, his face hidden. For an instant he had the alarming suspicion that the man was acting and that the pretense might conceal some tortuous motive. But he reassured himself with the thought that Cliff's nature had always been mercurial.

"Here. Drink this."

McOwen accepted the glass from him reluctantly, but then took a long swallow of the almost neat liquor. He grimaced and wiped his mouth with the back of his hand.

"Okay?"

"Yes."

"All right. Now, do you want to tell me about your problem?"

"I want to apologize, Charles. For the harm I've done you. And please, you've got to help me. Help us."

Charles de la Porte could not keep a momentary expression of distaste from his face. He tried to hide it. As always, he was embarrassed by excess of emotion. Did the man really imagine, like a child, that all you needed to do to atone for past wrongs was to sob and to say you were sorry?

"Cliff, you must pull yourself together. If we could do anything for Jay we would. But we cannot. It's beyond anyone's capability, Cliff. You must understand and accept that."

He was surprised to see a movement like a contrary ripple pass over the other man's face and to realize that it was annoyance.

"No." McOwen spoke very distinctly, angered by the

lack of comprehension. "You don't understand. She tried to kill herself this morning. She tried to commit suicide."

It was the ward sister who found Janice McOwen.

She had gone into the patient's private ward with her stretcher and basin and the other bothersome paraphernalia of the morning washing routine. She had wheeled the stretcher to the middle of the room, crossed to pull open the curtains, pausing briefly to admire the day, and then had called cheerfully: "Good morning! Not awake yet? It's a lovely morning, Doctor."

There had not been the usual slow murmur of response and she had turned to the bed in surprise. The gaunt women lay on it without moving.

"Doctor? It's time to wake up."

Still the woman did not move. Her black hair had been cut short and clung in lusterless strands to her narrow head. Her face was drained of blood and she did not appear to be breathing.

The nurse was an experienced woman, accustomed to crisis and no stranger to death. But she made a small sound, as if of pain and pity. She caught hold of a thin wrist and felt for the threadlike artery. Only a flutter, but thank God at least there was a pulse. She pinched the skin of the upper arm, gently at first, then more sharply. But the woman on the bed was beyond the point where pain could register. She lifted back both eyelids. The pupils were not fully dilated. She was uncertain whether there was any response to the light. The lips were blue.

As she leaned across the bedside table to reach the emergency bell she saw the bottle, lying on its side next to a water carafe. A pharmacist's label was pasted to it. On the label, neatly typewritten: "Dr. Case. Sodium Amytal. Grains 3." And in a corner, in red capitals: "POISON, Schedule 6." The bottle was empty.

"She must have made her decision before she went to hospital," McOwen said. "She took the stuff from home. Took it with her in her suitcase. It shows what she was thinking, doesn't it?"

"When did she go back to hospital?"

"Friday afternoon. Edwards-White wanted to do more tests. And he spoke about another operation, to remove her adrenal glands. She simply couldn't face any more of it." He gave Charles de la Porte a haggard look. "You can't imagine what she's been through the last couple of months. She's been in agony. She has to have drugs every few hours and even that . . . She's become an old woman. She's a stranger to us and to herself. She didn't deserve it, Charles."

Charles de la Porte felt his face contract in sympathy. He said: "But Edwards-White has managed to resuscitate her?"

"He's a callous bastard. All he's interested in is his own glory. They called me, you know. Told me she had collapsed. Only when I got to the hospital did I find out what had happened. And I found him there at her bed. He was squeezing a balloon thing with a tube up her nose."

"It's an ambu bag. What did he tell you?"

"Well, he told me what she had tried to do. And then he said they had called him just in time. She had been on the point of respiratory failure but he had everything under control and he had managed to save her life. I couldn't believe he meant what he was saying. Then a nurse brought in this breathing apparatus."

"A respirator?"

"Yes. He connected Jay to the machine. I asked him to leave her alone but he said if I interfered he would have me thrown out of the ward. He said he was saving her life."

"I suppose that was true."

"Charles, you know and I know that the things which Jay would call being alive have stopped for her, long ago. Her heart may be beating and they may have got a machine to breathe for her, but that doesn't mean she's alive. Do you understand me?"

Charles de la Porte knew that assent would be unwise, opening onto doors and darknesses best left undiscovered. He said nothing.

McOwen watched him for a moment, then turned his head.

"She almost beat them," he said bitterly. Then, sensing the unspoken question, he explained: "They hooked her up to a cardiac monitor. And then they did a stomach washout. But she must have been very close to the end when this was going on because the heartbeat got slower and slower and finally it stopped altogether. Charles, I'm not a religious man, but at that moment I thanked God for his mercy."

Charles de la Porte shifted uncomfortably.

"But Edwards-White got the heart started again?"

"He wouldn't leave her alone. It was as if it was a personal thing with him, a kind of vendetta. He was going to keep her alive at all costs. He jumped onto the bed and started to push down on her chest with both hands."

"He was only doing that to keep the circulation to the brain going. It could have been irreparably damaged."

"To keep the brain alive? Why? So that it could start registering pain again?"

There was no answer he could give.

"The cardiac massage worked?"

"He gave her a number of injections, too. One of them directly into the heart. And finally there was a very rapid pattern on the screen."

"Ventricular fibrillation."

"That's what he said. Then they wheeled in a thing with two paddles and they shocked her with this. And finally the heartbeat went back to normal. And Edwards-White seemed to think he had won a great victory."

"Perhaps he had."

"Yes. A victory for himself. But not for Jay."

Once again there was nothing to be said. However, silence might be construed as agreement.

"Cliff, why have you come to me? It has nothing to do with me. Edwards-White is your doctor, whether or not you like what he has done."

McOwen's eyes moved, searching, but there was a still and watchful expression on his face.

"You're the only one I can trust, Charles. I'm asking you. Begging you. Switch the damn thing off. Let her die with dignity. Switch the thing off, Charles."

Although he had expected them and had in fact anticipated a complete phrase— "switch the damn thing off"—saying it in his head as it was uttered, the words came to him chill and hard, each an entity with its own weight, and yet only menacing in combination. He thought of the sound of rain on a tin roof changing, with an ominous roar, to hail.

It seemed that even McOwen was startled and briefly checked by the unpredictable force of what he had said. His eyes clouded, looking inward, and he repeated softly: "Let her die."

Charles de la Porte was moved to speak.

"Cliff, you don't know what you're saying."

But the weak protest appeared to strengthen McOwen's determination. He got up from his chair and took one, two vigorous steps forward. "Am I asking too much?" He almost shouted: "Am I? Am I?" His voice softened. "Charles, you loved her. Now have pity on her."

Charles de la Porte tried to disguise his astonished start by bringing his drink to his lips, but the other man's eyes were shrewd. He did not miss the fumbled gesture with the empty glass.

"Do you think I didn't know? I'm not blind, man!"

"I think you are overwrought," Charles de la Porte said swiftly. "Under the circumstances you might say things you will later regret."

"Charles, I know what I'm saying. For pity's sake. Help her."

"Wait. There's too much emotion about this. It doesn't help. One has to try to be cold and scientific."

"I've seen a cold scientist at work. Please spare me that."

"It's the only way. I must consider it from a purely medical point of view."

"But you will consider it?" McOwen asked eagerly.

"For God's sake, Cliff, stand off! Don't you understand that you're putting too much strain on me?" Seeing the other's crestfallen look he added more gently: "I've told you. I can only look at it as a doctor."

"But you happen to be more than a doctor. Why deny it to yourself?"

"My only role in this is as your former medical adviser."

"I know what your role was. You were lovers, weren't you? Perhaps you would be still, if Jay hadn't become ill."

Charles de la Porte felt his throat go dry. He had to speak, had to make denials. Opposite him Cliff McOwen stood in a fencer's attitude, feet apart, chest averted, right forefinger pointed like a saber en garde. His thin smile was like a sword slash.

"Cliff, you're trying to destroy yourself," he heard his own voice say. He listened to it wonderingly, admiring its timbre, its apparent earnestness. "Your accusations are fantastic. They can only hurt you yourself. And I don't believe them to have any bearing on the subject."

McOwen's expression changed once more, to one of remorse.

"I'm sorry, Charles. I know it's hell on you, as it is on me. But together we must try to help Jay. She can't do anything more."

"Cliff, stop it. Please stop. This is getting us nowhere. You can't hope to persuade me to do this."

McOwen's eyes fell. He began abstractedly to do up the top buttons of his shirt, as if suddenly aware and ashamed of his appearance.

"I'm sorry. Perhaps I have been carried away. But won't you do just one thing for me? Won't you go and see Jay? Just see her. That's all I'm asking."

"Don't you understand? It wouldn't make any difference. And anyway I can't do it. It would be unethical. She's under Edwards-White's care and I can't barge in without him asking me for a second opinion."

McOwen looked astonished. "But you've always been our family doctor. You're the only person who knows Jay."

"You made your choice. You'll have to stick with it."

But the stilted rejection was a self-betrayal. Even as he made it, Charles de la Porte wondered: Is that all there is to it? Is your refusal based on hurt pride and vengeance? Will you abandon Jay because you refuse to forgive her?

McOwen's words were an echo of his own thoughts.

"Don't hold past events against us, Charles. This is something between us. It's always been between us and everything else was only an unfortunate intermission." He said, with an appearance of great sincerity: "We made a mistake and did you an injustice. But I allowed Edwards-White to influence me. Perhaps it was revenge, I don't know. All I know is that it seems very petty now, at this moment. And Charles, I know that you were right not to tell her she had cancer. She's strong in some ways but not in others. And I've seen her go to pieces ever since she's known there was no hope. You were right, and I respect and admire you for it."

"You showed your admiration in a strange way," Charles de la Porte said. A part of his mind was still resisting; told him that if he inflicted hurt it would cause his own hurt to diminish.

But McOwen seemed surprised rather than resentful.

"Blame it on frustration," he said. "There was nothing I could do and I wanted to hit out. And Edwards-White conveniently provided the weapon. Now you say I have to go back to him? I can't. Surely as Jay's husband I have a right to call in any doctor I wish to?"

"It doesn't work that way. There are rules I have to obey. Before I could take over the case he would have to give his consent."

"But if I insist that I want a second opinion and I want you called in to give it? Surely he can't refuse?"

"You appear to forget," Charles de la Porte said stiffly, "that there is a pending legal action in which, I am told, Mr. Edwards-White is a principal witness for the plaintiff. We would both be placed in a most embarrassingly—"

"Good Lord! You're not concerned about the bloody court case, are you? I'm scrapping all that. It's of no importance now. God, man, I don't want your money."

Charles de la Porte said with intended sarcasm: "Thank you!" But he was ashamed to note his immediate overwhelming relief, the weak-kneed gratitude toward the wealthy man who

227

held him to ransom and now, so lightly, offered reprieve.

McOwen said, as if he had not noticed: "If that's the reason, then I'll withdraw the action right now. I'll put it in writing if you like. I was going to do it anyway."

Charles de la Porte tried to regain lost dignity and also (although he was not yet certain how it had come about and what direction it would take from here) a lost advantage. "There's no need to do that."

But McOwen had already stormed to the desk and snatched up a pen. He was searching through shelves and drawers. "I'm serious, Charles," he said without looking around. "I've never been so serious." He found a headed prescription pad. "This will do. There isn't much to say."

Charles de la Porte felt the need to stay the rush of events. "I must tell you that this will not change my decision."

"Of course not. The hell with that anyway." McOwen read out aloud as he wrote: "I . . . the undersigned . . . Clifford Ross McOwen . . . hereby irrevocably and unreservedly withdraw the action . . . instituted in my name for and on behalf of . . . "

Charles de la Porte made a final protest. "Cliff, this will not change my attitude."

McOwen's hand ceased in its swift flow over the paper. He sat for a moment, pen in hand, then turned slowly.

"At least promise me one thing," he said. "If Edwards-White will allow it, at least promise me that you will have a look at her."

For once there was no cajolery or forceful persuasion. He spoke quietly, with the air not of prosecutor or advocate but rather of judge: reasonable, dispassionate, and determined to see justice done.

Charles de la Porte hesitated.

"I suppose I can hardly do less."

Cliff McOwen resumed writing.

"I knew you would not fail her."

2

Perhaps it was luck more than anything else. He could remember very few occasions when he had been tempted to play the part of the black angel. And even then it was in terms of technical detail, for the mind tended to erase the fear and the vomit and the agony and the stink which were attributes of the business of dying, replacing them in time by the absolution of scientific nomenclature and figures on the records.

He had been taught, and believed he had practiced, a single-minded kind of medicine: Death was the enemy.

And yet, sitting in Cliff McOwen's luxurious car, being transported to an uncertain destiny, he felt himself beset by doubt. Part of it, he recognized, was apprehension. Leicester Edwards-White, telephoned at his home earlier, had suspiciously (but his intense curiosity was also very evident) agreed to a meeting in his rooms at the Drostdy. The interview would not be pleasant.

But this was not the sole cause of the oppressive feeling, as if he was suffocating within a windowless chamber.

Strange that he had never given the concept of euthanasia much thought. He had encountered the problem from time to time, especially when he had worked in the neurosurgery department, and had dealt with it according to circumstances. He had never approached a patient with the conscious intention to kill, but there were occasions he remembered with horror. Like the old man, a farmer from the Karroo, who had a rodent ulcer of the cheek which had been grossly neglected. Untreated for years, it had eaten away the flesh so that the bones of the upper and lower jaws were bared to view. There was secondary infection, too. In his ignorance the old man had allowed himself to be treated with manure poultices which were supposed to draw out

229

the roots of the cancer. The smelly mess made the stomach turn. Mercy demanded an overdose of morphine. An animal would have been accorded this mercy; the human was denied it.

Surely a subject as large as death and its administration should be the source of a belief, a philosophy, or at least a personal point of view. He should have thought about it before; have discussed it with his colleagues. But, as sex had been once, the subject of death was still taboo.

He tried to think what were the teachings of his profession, as if the phrases which had guided his student beliefs were touchstones. "Reverence for life." "The absolute good of the patient." "At least, do no harm." But he found, when he held them in his hands, that they were smooth-worn pebbles, clichés which held no answers.

Define: the good of the patient. Impossible. Was it good for an accident victim to survive with his skull crushed and half his brain useless? Was it good for a child to survive an operation like total pelvic exenteration and come off the table missing half a dozen of the organs which made for a full life?

Should he seek refuge in that attitude, sympathetic but impersonal, which served him well in his daily practice of medicine? It was easy to adopt: the habit of years had taught him to do it with the same unthinking ease as slipping on his symbolic white coat.

He remembered, uneasily, Frank Edelstein's criticism. Why did Frank believe that modern medicine was too remote? Had he himself been the unwitting cause? What real or imaginary act might have caused Frank to think, during that time when he was being treated for his heart attack, that his doctor regarded him as just another body in a bed? He knew that his friend was too perceptive to have held that opinion for more than a moment. But had a flavor of it lingered in his subconscious, afterward to taint his opinion?

If there was truth in the belief that society's faith in doctors had eroded, was it not foolhardy for a doctor to be involved in any situation which might be interpreted as dealing in death? A cornerstone of that faith was the understanding that patient and doctor were allies in a battle. And if the patient were

230

to suspect that his ally might at any time betray him and let the enemy into the citadel?

"Jay would want you to do it," Cliff McOwen had said to him as they left Hoog-in-het-Dal in the publisher's sleek Mercedes. "If she could speak to you now she would say: 'Please, Charles. Do it.'"

Charles de la Porte had remained silent. McOwen had looked at him, taking his eyes off the road. "You don't believe me, do you?"

"I think it would be difficult to determine what her wishes really are."

"Don't you believe her own action is sufficient indication? It is to me. She wanted to end it. But now she's being forced back and what awaits her is the fate she tried to escape. A slow and ugly death. Did you know that she had a terrible fear of ever being mutilated or left helpless?"

"I did know that, yes."

"It wasn't death so much as the indignities of dying. She felt it in others and she loathed the idea in herself."

"I know."

"Did you know about it?"

"I knew ... " He noticed for the first time that they had been talking about Jay in the past tense and corrected himself. "... I know what her feelings are about suffering."

McOwen had not seemed to notice the slip or its correction. He went on, speaking with odd enthusiasm, as if re-creating Jay's image in fact and not only in imagination. "She always had this warmth about her. An identification with people who were sick and suffering."

Charles de la Porte glanced at the other man. McOwen was sitting erect behind the wheel. His lips were turning in the beginnings of a smile, as of happiness at the contemplation of his wife's humanity.

"That's the one thing I can't forgive Edwards-White," McOwen said. "He talked false hope into her. He virtually made her believe the operation was going to cure her."

"She wouldn't have needed much persuasion. There's often a resurgence of hope in terminal patients."

231

"Yes, but when it proved to be false she was terribly depressed. That's one of the reasons she agreed to the court case. It was as if she was grasping around her for all kinds of proof that she was still alive. And that was not a fitting end for her. She gave so much loving kindness in her life that there should not have been ugliness at the end. And I can't forgive that man for persuading us."

McOwen seemed quite unaware of an innate contradiction in what he was saying. This was what he thought today and to the devil with what he had thought yesterday. What was vice then was virtue now; friend was enemy and enemy was friend. Charles de la Porte wondered briefly about the state of the mind which was able to adapt itself to such swift and radical changes.

He had tried, since yesterday, to persuade himself that Lieutenant Van Wyk's charges against McOwen were fantastic. The man had wealth, influence, a position in society. Did it make sense that he should be involved in a trivial conspiracy to undermine that society?

But doubt was not so easily expunged. He had learned something new about Clifford McOwen and, whether it was fact or fiction, it had already changed his view of the man. Only dull minds relied on proverbs to do their thinking for them: Where there's smoke…Intelligence immediately rebelled against the simplicity of the judgment. And yet.

He had thought at times about Cliff and Jay. They had seemed to him ill-matched. Now he wondered: Had that judgment been wrong, too? Was it perhaps founded on an emotion he did not even want to admit to himself: a degree of simple jealousy? Was this new-disclosed facet of Cliff—the secret destroyer, the Samson within the temple of his own people—what Jay had sought all her life, and had found? Was he the kind of man she was fated to follow? Was he a white Joel?

He shook his head dismissively. After enduring so much intensity of emotion it would be a relief to deal with Edwards-White. He might be, probably would be, hostile, but at least the atmosphere would be one of detached scientific inquiry.

"Where on earth did you get the impression that she was dying?" Leicester Edwards-White asked with well-acted incredulity.

"Her husband thought so," Charles de la Porte said.

The surgeon's expression made it clear what he thought of doctors who placed reliance on the diagnosis of a layman. He gestured languidly and Charles de la Porte added with a spurt of anger: "I assume Dr. Case must have believed this, too. I hardly expect she would have tried to take her own life while she believed herself to be getting well."

Edwards-White's lips tightened. "Probably only a brief period of depression. She'll soon snap out of it. We haven't given up yet."

"By which you mean that you haven't given up."

"It isn't a doctor's job to give up, is it?"

"But it is a doctor's job to use his judgment."

There was a brief silence while they sat assessing one another. Like gladiators, they were trapped within the confined space of the arena and they knew that it was their common fate to do battle on its hot sands under a hot sun.

"It would have been stupid to let her die," Edwards-White said.

"What is stupid about dying?"

"Nothing. Except that, given a modern hospital with modern technology, I would be ashamed to stand aside and not make use of it when a patient's life is at stake."

"You remind me of a story I once read. About one of those hospitals you mention, with all the modern equipment but with no soul. An old man was admitted with incipient left heart failure, a small bowel obstruction, an enlarged prostate, and severe arthritis. He knew that he had come to the end of the road

233

and was happy to accept it. But the doctors were determined to use their skill and equipment to keep him going. That was why they were there."

Edwards-White began to tap his fingers irritably on his desk top but Charles de la Porte pretended not to notice.

He said: "When a doctor came along to pass a gastric tube to decompress the distended bowel the old man protested. He did not want his children to see him with tubes sticking out all over. He wanted them to remember him the way he had lived, with dignity. But he was not given the choice and in the end he had a gastric tube down, a catheter in his bladder, and he was on an intravenous drip. Modern medicine was doing its best for him. During the night, however, the patient pulled out the drip needle and tried to remove the other tubes, too. They found him dead. And at his bedside there was a scrawled note. It read: 'Death is not the enemy. Inhumanity is.'"

Edwards-White gestured impatiently. "I've heard that story, too, Doctor. It's one of the set pieces of the people who propagate euthanasia, isn't it?"

"That doesn't alter its basic truth."

"Well, allow me to tell you another story. This is not something I read about. It happened to me. I was a houseman in London after I qualified and while I was working in the gyne ward we admitted a young woman with menorrhagia and excruciating backache. She was about thirty-five and divorced. Her husband had left her with three young children. She was all that those children had in the world. Well, we found she had a carcinoma of the cervix which had spread and was involving the pelvic nerves. You'll remember that we used to treat these patients with radium pellets implanted around the lesion. This was done, but she was in agony day and night. She used to lie there screaming: 'Kill me. Kill me.'"

Charles de la Porte winced.

Edwards-White caught the gesture and nodded. "Yes. I couldn't take it either. So one night I stole four grains of morphine from the drug cupboard. I pulled it up into a syringe and went to this woman's bed. I thought it was my duty. But when I got to her bed she was asleep. My courage failed me. That's probably how you would describe it. Anyway, I decided to be a coward. I didn't kill her. A couple of days later she began responding to treatment. She was discharged after a month."

The surgeon was silent for a moment.

"This story doesn't have a happy ending," he said then. "She died of cancer six weeks later. But if I had used that morphine that night those children would have been deprived of their mother six weeks too early."

Charles de la Porte hesitated. He looked around him at Edwards-White's consulting room. It had been through the hands of an interior decorator since last he had been here. The walls were painted an aseptic, operating-room white and there were large expanses of tiles around the built-in washbasin unit. The desk was set mathematically in the center of the room. It was a cubist creation of steel and glass. Elsewhere in the room, too, was an abundance of glass and transparent plastic and chrome. The effect was starkly modern. He wondered whether Frank Edelstein had ever seen what Edwards-White had made of his rooms inside the ancient walls of the Drostdy.

The implications were not lost on him, however. Edwards-White believed in modern artifacts, in modern ideas, and therefore in modern medicine. And inherent in the concept was the principle that you stopped at nothing to accomplish your aims. Science was forever coming up with newer and better tools. You were a failure as a technician if you did not use them.

"I assume you know Mr. McOwen's views on the fact that his wife is being kept alive on a respirator?" he asked the surgeon.

"I do," Edwards-White said crisply. "He created an unpleasant scene at the hospital this morning."

"I gather he requested that she should be taken off the machine?"

"That is correct. And, in case you are interested in my reply, I told him that I would under no circumstances do it myself or allow it to be done."

The arena doors were closed. The trumpets clamored. And the gladiators advanced alone across the ring of sand.

"I see."

235

"Now he has asked me to call on you for a second opinion. I must tell you frankly that I have grave doubts about your ethical standing in this case. Under all the circumstances ... " Edwards-White broke off to ask in a puzzled voice: "Where is Mr. McOwen, incidentally? I was under the impression he would be present here."

"I left him to wait in my rooms. He is in a . . . in a rather emotional state and I thought it best that we meet alone."

"That was probably wise. I assume, however, that he went to you with the same request as he put to me."

"Yes, he came to me," Charles de la Porte said.

"Then perhaps I should withdraw my remark about ethical considerations," Edwards-White said bitingly. "For it's quite clear that professional etiquette must mean very little to you in comparison with the enormity of the act you are contemplating."

"I am not contemplating anything," Charles de la Porte said. "I have been asked to take over the treatment of a patient and I am here to learn what you think of her present condition. That's all."

"I have resuscitated her and I am determined to do my best to keep her alive."

"Why?"

"I propose to undertake certain further investigations with a view to embarking on a different form of treatment for the cancer," Edwards-White said haughtily. Then, more sharply: "I don't plan to throw up my arms and say: 'This is the end.'"

"It seems to me you resent the fact that life has an end. Perhaps you would prefer all your patients to live forever? But it's precisely because life is finite that it also has purpose."

"No doubt you're right. But I wonder whether metaphysical considerations have any place in this discussion."

"They do when it comes to defining the meaning of being alive. We have probably both seen life become intolerable before a heart has stopped beating."

"Yes. And we've also seen an intolerable life become tolerable again." Edwards-White leaned across his desk in an attitude of candor. "Dr. de la Porte, I am not going to deny that Janice McOwen is a very ill woman. She may well die soon. But

I would expect any doctor to carry on treating her with all the means at his disposal. I don't believe we have as yet exhausted all the possibilities."

"Such as what?"

"Like removing her adrenal glands."

"And then the pituitary, I suppose?"

"If I think that would help, yes."

"It's small wonder some people think that medical technology has outstripped the quality of the medical conscience which guides it."

Edwards-White looked indignant, but Charles de la Porte did not give him the opportunity to interrupt.

He said: "I want to ask you something, Mr. Edwards-White. Have you considered the possibility that your attitude is based largely on pride?"

"What has that got to do with it?"

"Perhaps more than you care to admit. How can the great surgeon lose a patient? Do you feel a sense of failure when one of your patients dies?"

"Of course."

"And are you perhaps tempted to let the personal failure weight more heavily than the loss of a life?"

"You may be right. But I'm not ashamed to admit it. The reasons I do my best for a patient are not important. All that matters is that I *should* do my best."

"Provided that what you do does not prolong the suffering of your patients. Which brings us back to the present problem. Dr. Case's brain has suffered a period of anoxia. Have you managed to assess the damage?"

"I can't tell at this stage. We have to wait and see how much recovery there will be."

"She's not breathing on her own at all?"

"No. Her pupils are semidilated but I think there is still reaction to light. I have started treatment to prevent cerebral edema. I have given her steroids and mannitol as well."

"And what are your findings as far as the cancer is concerned?"

"I fear there has been some progression. She has collapsed one of her lumbar vertebrae and now shows evidence of spinal compression. She has no control over her rectum or her bladder."

"Yet you still believe there is hope?"

"I do."

"Mr. Edwards-White, medicine has managed to rephrase the old adage that where there's life there's hope. Often there is life without hope."

"All right. You have asked me a question and given your own answer. Now I'm going to ask you a question in return."

"Please do."

"Do you propose to switch off that respirator?"

"I have not made any decision. It will depend on what I find when I examine her."

"I must warn you that the consequences will be very serious indeed. And I would not put any trust in McOwen's support. The man is quite unbalanced. A week ago he wanted me to fly with his wife to some cancer quack in Finland he's heard about. Today he wants us to pull the plug on her. Look, Charles . . . may I call you that?"

"If you wish."

"Charles, you must not even think of doing it. McOwen doesn't realize what he's asking from you. I am a doctor and I do. As if it isn't bad enough to have this court case hanging over you, he wants to add another intolerable burden. I would sincerely regret having to cause you more trouble, but you must understand that my conscience would compel me to."

"Mr. McOwen has withdrawn the court action," Charles de la Porte said shortly.

Edwards-White looked startled. "Withdrawn?" Then he began to nod his head slowly and his lip curled. "I see. That certainly puts a different complexion on things."

Charles de la Porte shifted in his seat. The surgeon's instant assumption that he had allowed himself to be bribed angered but at the same time unsettled him. He knew it was not the truth. It was not true, was it?

"She's Jewish," Edwards-White said. "Did you know that?"

238

"I am aware of that."

"Does it mean anything to you?"

"Should it?"

"Have you forgotten that the so-called mercy killing you appear to advocate was once associated with wholesale slaughter?"

Charles de la Porte understood the contemptuous insinuation and made the deduction he was intended to make: that his attitude was that of those who had supervised the Holocaust. He said angrily: "Now wait . . . "

Edwards-White ignored him. "And have you forgotten that among those who took part in the slaughter were doctors. Doctors, whose most solemn vows had been the sanctity and the preservation of human life." He said bitterly: "It's no accident that the words 'hypocrite' and 'Hippocratic' are so similar."

With a curt rejoinder ready on his lips, Charles de la Porte found himself silent.

The young man had said: "I am a doctor." And, saying that, rejected the thought that doctors had not always been revered, that their art might have been suspect, their skills despised. "I am a doctor." And it was inconceivable that a doctor could be a liar, a cheat, a thief. "I am a doctor." But no doctor could be a murderer or a torturer or a sadist.

He was in his early to middle thirties. It would be knowledge he could have picked up by hearsay alone, by means of articles in magazines and pictures in history books: that there had been a time when doctors were all those things. It was necessary to set that foul-smelling reality beside his shining vision. And still he rejected it. So he would labor to prove it wrong. He would be a doctor and a hero, too. Life was his creed and the safeguarding of it his determination.

And also, Charles de la Porte recognized with regret, his illusion.

Edwards-White was speaking again, his dour, official manner now restored.

"Dr. de la Porte, I want to make something quite clear."

Charles de la Porte waited.

"I am not the guardian of your conscience," Edwards-

239

White said. "Obviously you are free to make up your own mind. But I must tell you that I believe there is a chance that Mrs. McOwen will recover. And I would regard any interference with her as being tantamount to murder. To put it to you bluntly: If you tamper with that respirator I will see to it that you are reported to the Medical Council and to the police and to whoever else might be interested. Have I made myself clear?"

"You have."

"Good. Because, God help me, I mean every word. If you touch that woman, Doctor, I'm going to have your scalp."

The intensive-care unit was housed in a small room beyond the women's general medical ward. As he walked down the wide aisle between the double row of beds, Charles de la Porte remembered with grim amusement that the establishment of the unit had been one of the few issues about which he and Edwards-White had ever agreed.

The surgeon had started agitating for it soon after opening practice. How could anyone practice modern medicine without adequate facilities? he had asked. The scornful implication that they were behind times had not been lost on the town's doctors. Edwards-White had warned that the hospital could be sued for negligence if a court found that a patient had died because of the lack of intensive observation. Cost was a minor consideration compared with a human life. But the hospital board, surprised perhaps that for once its thrift was encouraged by the medical committee, had refused to spend the money. Edwards-White had taken his case straight to the authorities and there had been a political rumpus. The board and the committee had dug in their heels. But Charles de la Porte, rational and unemotional, had argued convincingly. The board and the doctors had thought again. The unit had come into being.

Even then it had been a mixed triumph for Edwards-White. He had himself visited the manufacturers of various makes of monitoring equipment and respirators. Most of his recommendations were ignored. Gases were piped to the unit but there was no wall suction. He had to be satisfied with a portable suction machine.

Charles de la Porte heard his name called.

"It's Dr. de la Porte. Doctor. Doctor."

He turned patiently to where a frail, white-haired little woman was having her pillows rearranged by a nurse.

"Good evening, Mrs. Rosenthal. I didn't know you were back in hospital. How are you?"

"I'm fine, Doctor. Dr. Hutton wanted me back for some tests. Everyone is so kind. Thank you, Sister. Help me up a bit so I can speak to Dr. de la Porte.

The nurse's aide, who was not nearly entitled to be addressed as "Sister," obeyed with a pleased smile. It was part of Mrs. Rosenthal's fine-honed technique of flattery to elevate all ranks and one of the secrets of how she went so easily through life. She was notorious for parking her mini-car in forbidden places but she seldom had to call on her nephew, Frank Edelstein, for assistance in evading the resultant traffic fine. Even the toughest-minded cop found it difficult to resist the pleasure of being called "Captain" by a little old lady who was obviously so sincere in her confusion.

Through force of habit Charles de la Porte picked up the clipboard at the foot of her bed.

"Just some tests, eh?"

A persistent and puzzling anemia. At first they had ascribed it to bleeding hemorrhoids, but these had been removed without bringing about improvement. It was definitely an iron deficiency anemia and her occult blood test in the stool was always positive. Geoff had ordered repeated gastrointestinal studies but the source of the bleeding had so far escaped detection.

241

"I hope I won't have to stay here too long. My grandson has his Bar Mitzvah next week."

He smiled and replaced her chart.

"I see Dr. Hutton has already requested the new tests. You'll be out of hospital in a few days."

"Thank you, Doctor."

"Good-bye, Mrs. Rosenthal."

"Good-bye, Doctor. Thank you so much, Doctor."

At times he wondered if it was not better to be like Mrs. Rosenthal, undemanding and uncritical of whatever life brought, asking only that everyone should be nice, everything should be simple.

He pushed open the first of the double swing doors, picked a paper mask out of a supply in a box on the wall, hooked its elastic loops around his ears, adjusted the mask, and went through to the room beyond.

The ward he had left was unmistakably part of a hospital. But the necessary order of its arrangement and the discipline of routine could never disguise the fact that human beings lived and moved there.

The room he now entered was different. It was occupied by people, true. True also that their human needs were catered for with even greater speed and efficiency than outside. But there the stark reality of disease and its treatment was softened by human things like a bowl of roses by a bedside. Here flowers would have been incongruous, as well as being a potential hindrance among the coiled tubes and the cables and the silent but ceaseless machinery. Here people were patients first and last: bodies which had to be kept alive; collections of organs which were pumped or primed or shocked into continued performance of their functions. Here was medicine at its most impersonal.

A slim dark-haired woman turned to look at him inquiringly. She stood by the bed closest to the door.

"Good evening, Doctor."

"Good evening, Sister." He could not remember her name. "I've come to have a look at Dr. Case."

"Yes, Doctor." She nodded toward the second bed.

He looked, almost reluctantly.

242

Jay lay there, unmoving.

He looked away from her, at the machines.

The respirator stood on the stand beside the bed, a complex of dials and levers and switches which, with its trailing tubes of clear plastic, reminded him of a milking machine rather than a device designed to take the place of the human lungs.

"Is this new, Sister? I haven't seen it before."

"Yes, Doctor." She came up to stand beside him. "It's a volume respirator. Mr. Edwards-White has it on trial. It's the latest Bennett model. The M.A. 1."

Twin inlet valves in the wall above the bed brought oxygen and air to a mixture regulator. Here were two dials, one to regulate the flow and the other the pressure. A corrugated tube with a one-way valve delivered the air-oxygen mixture to the patient. Exhalations bubbled through a water trap, then to push steadily and repeatedly at a bellows within a drum of clear Perspex. The water provided expiratory back pressure and the drum was designed to measure the precise volume of every breath.

A needle on a dial moved backward and forward. The bellows lifted and fell within their transparent prison. And Jay lived, unconscious but breathing.

On the wall was a cardiac monitor. The dancing lightning-flash on its screen measured her heartbeat by way of electrodes fastened to her body. He studied the ECG for a moment. It was slow and the pattern it repeated was regular.

The nurse had moved away, back to the other bed. She spoke now, slowly and deliberately. "Mr. Matthews. I'm going to put your supper in your tube. All right?"

Charles de la Porte glanced around. The figure on the other bed made a scarcely perceptible movement with one hand, which the nurse appeared to take as assent for she started to pour liquid into a funnel at the end of the tube which ran into the nose. The man on the bed did not stir again. He was being fed directly into the stomach. The quality and taste of the food was immaterial. His eyes were closed and his face had a tight, secret look, Myasthenia gravis, probably. The nurse had the air of someone attending to a large but docile domestic animal. She would deal with Jay in exactly the same way. Probably she had never even considered the odd fact that two people of different sexes who were not married should share one room. The usual conventions of hospital nursing ended outside this door. In the community of the dying sexual differences were of no account.

He remembered her name suddenly. Sister Roos.

He turned resolutely back to Jay and now, for the first time, was able to look at her fully and frankly.

He knew the woman on the bed. He knew her name and something of her nature. He had loved her, had made love to her, had shared thoughts and action, laughter and fear. And yet this weak creature with its skull-like face and exhausted mouth was a total stranger to him. It had endured suffering which had finally extinguished the spark within it. Even courage had become immaterial, as had strength and determination and the will to survive. This creature merely continued to exist. Jay had already vanished.

There was no mercy in continuing treatment which kept the body which had been Jay's hovering in a gray place between life and death.

He examined the respirator again. The breathing tube was linked to another slender tube fastened above the lip with sticking plaster and running to the trachea by way of the nostrils. The machine pumped and the gaunt chest rose and fell obediently, although the mind had sent the lungs no command. It would continue like this, mechanically, in, out, in, out, expanding and contracting so many times a minute, so many times an hour.

The nurse was at his side again.

"Her husband was here earlier, Doctor. He left a message for you."

"Oh?"

"He said to tell you he had been to see her. And that you must please help his wife. He leaves her in your hands."

"In my hands?"

The girl pulled up her shoulders. "That was what he said. I couldn't understand what he was getting at. He was ... " She paused delicately. " ... a bit upset."

244

"I see. Thank you, Sister."

It was typical of McOwen, he thought angrily. Typically indiscreet.

After the meeting with Edwards-White he had gone back to his rooms, but had found them empty. On his desk was a note.

"Charles, I must get out of here. I hope you don't think I'm running away but I can't take any more of it. I'm leaving you my car. The key is in the ignition. I'll walk round the block and pick up one of the editorial cars. I would rather not see you. I don't want to know what you've decided."

He remembered what Edwards-White had said contemptuously about the publisher: that he would make a dangerous friend. Resentfully, he acknowledged that the surgeon had been right. McOwen could not be trusted and the demands he made were insufferable.

But did that make any real difference? Did the responsibility not rest where it had always rested: squarely on his own shoulders?

He had no doubt at all that Edwards-White would make good his threat. And he knew what action the Medical Council would take. There had been an example, a year or so ago, of a doctor who had given a fatal dose of pentathol to his father, dying of a carcinoma. The law courts had showed mercy; the council had not. The doctor had been struck off the roll.

You felt sympathy for the victim and understanding of the terrible humanness of his plight. And yet you saw the cold logic of the equation. Life was placed in trust. Trust could not be broken.

Would it go as far as the Medical Council? It did not depend entirely on Edwards-White or on the extent of his enmity. Perhaps calling it enmity was unfair. It was an element, but no more than that. He realized with surprise that he now accepted the surgeon's basic honesty. He believed that he understood, too, Edwards-White's insistent conduct of the campaign against him. That anyone should, by silence, appear to connive at death was unthinkable and blasphemous. Jay had lost time, and time was what life was all about.

He knew that many doctors believed this; that the aim of their endeavors was to gain a day, a month, a year.

Certainly, he thought, it's the least complicated attitude to adopt. Because it keeps you so busy that you never have time to stop to consider the morality of what you're doing. You present a picture of the busy and dedicated doctor who spares no one, least of all the patient. You cut into him and hook him onto machines and stick needles into him and put fluids in or take them out and measure this and that and remove some bits and put other bits back or replace them with steel and plastic. Everybody is so busy and having such a gay time that no one thinks of asking the question: Are you doing any good?

Amos, Frank Edelstein's servant, was obstinately reluctant to call his employer to the telephone.

"The master, he's very busy," he announced.

"What is he doing?"

"I don't know. He's working in the study."

"Tell him Dr. de la Porte is calling."

"I don't know," the Coloured man mumbled. "He says he's very busy."

"All right. Then ask him to call me at the hospital."

There was a muffled reply and then a clatter, followed a moment later by Frank's voice.

"Amos wasn't very keen to call you."

Frank laughed. "He's had a chip on his shoulder all day. I suspect he lost on the races yesterday afternoon."

"Frank, I need some advice."

"Sure."

"Here's a hypothetical case. I have an unconscious patient who's been in an accident and he has irreversible brain damage. He's being kept alive artificially on a respirator. Now at what stage would the courts authorize me to switch off that respirator?"

"It sounds rather like the case of that young woman in America a while back."

"Exactly. It's exactly similar. And the American courts sanctioned it, didn't they?"

"You must remember that it's a different legal system. And if I recall rightly in that case the parents requested a court order."

"Let's say that in my case we have a wife who is willing to give consent."

"That would alter the picture. But it's difficult to predict to what extent. There's no precedent in South African law. Whatever judgment was given would probably go on appeal."

"But what if it had to be decided within a matter of days? What if the condition of the patient demanded it?"

He could almost sense Frank, on the other end, shaking his head disapprovingly. "There are some processes of law which cannot be rushed. I doubt whether any judge would want to rule decisively on an issue as far-reaching as this."

Bleakly: "Oh."

"Was there any particular reason you wanted to know?"

Careful. There might be legal pitfalls he had to avoid.

"No. As I say, it's purely hypothetical."

"I see." A long, speculative pause. "It wouldn't have anything to do with the McOwens' action against you?"

He remembered that Frank would not know about the withdrawal of the case. He considered explaining, but it would take too long and be too involved. He would have to take the bit of paper on which Cliff McOwen had declared his intention to Frank for an opinion on its legal validity. But not now.

"I have something to tell you about that, but it'll keep. Thanks for your advice anyway."

He hung up thoughtfully. Again he felt enmeshed in the laborious web of the law. The slow procedure of entering pleas and presenting evidence would take weeks. And by the time it was over Jay would have recovered from the paralyzing effect of the overdose of the drug with which she had tried to commit suicide and would again be able to breathe on her own.

247

Yet he had to admit that he had never really expected anything else. Should one not honor the law's determination to do the wrong thing for the right reason? Remembering, especially, one's own dilemma, now again restored to its former dimensions.

5

He could not rest. After speaking to Frank Edelstein he had returned to the intensive-care unit. Another nurse had joined Sister Roos and he had spoken to them briefly, then carried out a token examination of Jay. There was no particular purpose to it, but the sisters knew he had accepted responsibility so he had to put up a show.

The heart was beating but there was no spontaneous effort at breathing when the respirator was disconnected. She was deeply unconscious but he thought the pupils still reacted to light. He tapped and prodded the wasted body for a little longer. The lungs sounded wet so he ordered half-hourly suction. He reduced the quantity of intravenous fluids. There was no need for sedation. The damage to the brain had destroyed its ability to respond to pain.

In the big outer ward patients were being settled for the night and nurses moved busily between the beds. He saw Mrs. Rosenthal look up at him expectantly but he pretended not to notice and went by hurriedly, his stethoscope dangling.

It was already dark outside. He had not realized it was so late. He climbed in behind the wheel of McOwen's car and struggled to fit the key into the unfamiliar ignition. But he did not turn the key. Instead he sat in the darkness inside the car looking at the lights of the building he had just left. Those lights to the right were from the surgical wards. As he watched, they grew dimmer. Soon the individual bed lights would go off, too, as, one by one, patients prepared to go to sleep. Then only a few passage lights would be left to burn through the night.

In the center of the building was the bulky blackness of the administration block, its shadowy outline marred by a single square of light from a window. A clerk working industriously after hours on a Sunday night? Unlikely. More probably an office light left carelessly switched on.

On the left was the entrance to the Casualty section. Lights glowed above its glass door and in all its windows. Casualty was never still, especially not on weekends. All night long the thin stream of patients with cuts and wounds and ruptures would arrive and depart.

This building was as familiar to him as his own home. He came to it every day, walked the treadmill of its accustomed rooms, sought to the best of his ability to heal the ailing strangers who inhabited them. He knew the pattern followed within this building almost as intimately as the pattern of his own life. But did he know anything of either?

He sat inside the dark car and looked at the brightly lit building and asked himself: Can any event ever be complete? Is every action not the accumulative result of small events in the past?

Suddenly he was overcome by self-doubt so intense that it was like a low blow in the pit of the stomach, catching him unprepared and leaving him sweating and sick and helpless.

What has happened to you? What secret germ of corruption from long ago has turned you into what you are? There was a time when you had ideals and the courage to do something about your beliefs. Why has that courage eroded? Comfort? Security? Wealth? You pride yourself that you hunt alone. And yet your weaknesses are the collective weaknesses of the pack.

Jay has not changed. Her central vision has remained: pity for others. Yes, there is fear for herself, for the softness of her human body. But pity for others above all else, even to the

249

point of transcending her fear. So perhaps, like that other time long ago and far away, you did not give her enough credit for courage, too.

He remembered his decision not to tell her about her cancer. It had been the day the second pathological report had come. Until then he had wavered. Perhaps it would be more fair to tell her. He did not know all the intricacies of her life. Perhaps she needed to make arrangements and preparations.

He had weighed it all. There was his own reluctance to cause her pain. The horror of the thought that it should be he, particularly, who had been chosen to bring her the fatal message. His knowledge of her character; her repugnance toward physical mutilation. Balanced against this was the slender hope of a cure. It might be possible, with radical surgery and drastic treatment, to keep her alive beyond the probable term of her life. But looking beyond that, to where she should be considered not as patient but as person?

Still he had wavered. He had walked beside her in the grounds of her hospital and she had seemed to him young and beautiful and vitally alive. And in his mind the words of doom had churned like sour curds.

But he had not told her.

Now, caught in the spasm of doubt, he wondered: Was I right or wrong?

Edwards-White had never doubted. Then, as now, he had believed: She is sick and I shall save her.

And what was your belief? Charles de la Porte asked himself. She is dying; let her die.

Where was the judge who could say without hesitation who had been right and who had been wrong? The choice was clear-cut: two simple decisions based on the same set of facts.

But not made for the same reasons.

Again it was like a blow, and in the anguish of the moment he gripped the steering wheel spasmodically and closed his eyes as if he feared he might glimpse the dreadful inner convolutions of his own mind.

For he knew that he had been silent about Jay's fate because he wished her evil as well as good. He had loved her, but his love had not run unmingled. It contained jealousy and resentment of the fact that she had always been able to elude him. He had tried to shackle her and she had slipped away, mocking him by the assertion of her own freedom. Then, in one stroke, he had been handed not only her freedom but her life. He had attained power and final ascendancy. And the longer the secret was his alone, the more fearful and potent it became.

He was reminded of those days when he and Antoinette had waded in the coastal lagoon and watched hermit crabs scuffling and clawing in the quick-turning little waves at the water's edge, dragging their appropriated shells behind them. Over the years his mind, like the soft body of a crab, had needed a series of shells to house and protect itself. He had lived inside them fairly contentedly, daring to go into the sea only when it was necessary to scuttle from one shell to another. But for once he had been unready. He had miscalculated and blundered during the changeover. An unexpected swirl of the current had swept away all the empty shells and he had been caught naked in the stream.

This was the price of self-knowledge: Once you had been granted it, you could never return to the security of the shallows. There were no more shells; no more illusions. You could never escape the burden of guilt and responsibility which, alone, set men above the crabs.

She had been invited to a meeting of the Medical Committee that night, although she was not a member. The Elizabeth M. McOwen Memorial Hospital had been nearing completion at the time and there were joint problems to discuss. Perhaps there was resentment from the all-male committee toward this young woman doctor who had the presumption to build hospitals with her husband's money, but if so it had vanished by the end of the meeting. Dr. Case was totally charming. She agreed with their likes, politely discounted their prejudices, flattered their vanities, and got her own way.

Charles de la Porte, watching the performance without

251

contribuing more than he was obliged to, was quietly amused. He saw her deal with old Tim Maberley, who had been medical superintendent then and was a notorious and self-proclaimed misogynist. By the end of the evening Dr. Maberley had been lighting her cigarette for her and if there was one thing he loathed more than women it was a woman smoking.

The meeting had ended with mutual expressions of esteem and promises of cooperation. Afterwards he had congratulated her.

"Thank you, Charles," she had said, not seeming to notice his irony. Then, dark eyes meeting his: "Would you like to offer me a lift home?"

In the car they had not spoken for a time. Finally he said: "Your hospital will fill a great need. As old Maberley said, we could fill our own beds twice over with the chronically sick aged."

"Yes." She ignored the rest of the overture. "You've been avoiding me."

He muttered lamely that he had not wished to reopen old wounds.

She was scornful. "Nonsense, Charles. There never were wounds. Were there?"

He was stung to protest. "You should know." Somehow the suggestion that he had loved without loving was crippling to his self-esteem.

"I did know. I was never under any illusion. At least, I hope not. If I was I would blame it on my age."

After a while he said: "You've changed."

She said: "Not really."

He said: "No. Perhaps you haven't."

She threw a cigarette out of the window. He looked into the mirror and saw the quick splash of sparks on the road behind.

He said: "You smoke too much."

She laughed. "Dear Charles. Always the moralist."

He said nothing and she asked: "How has it been for you these past two years?"

He said cautiously: "I've been all right. Why?"

She pretended astonishment. "Two whole years? Living in the same town and having to pretend that we hardly knew one another?"

He threw caution to the winds. "It's been hell."

"It has, hasn't it?"

"For you, too?"

"What do you think?"

The conversation was taking odd twists and for a moment he wanted to wriggle out of it.

"You've been very busy. Getting your hospital built."

She lit another cigarette.

"Yes." And then: "I've seen your wife. She's very beautiful."

"She is."

"You haven't any children?"

We have been here before, he thought. He said: "No."

She looked at the road ahead. "Left at the next crossing."

"I know where you live."

She turned to look at him and he saw her face by the light of a streetlamp. She still wore her hair long, but now this had become the fashion. He thought it was like her to have anticipated fashion.

"You do, don't you?"

He weighed the enigmatic phrase. Then he asked, feigning carelessness: "How is Cliff?"

"Cliff's fine." A pause. "He's away."

"Oh." He paused, too. "Are you often left alone like this?"

"At times."

He made the left-hand turn and took the long uphill run which led to the brand-new suburb which had once been a wine farm. The McOwens lived in the big double-story house at the top of the hill. Its driveway had an arch which was overhung by a creeper with large white blossoms. He stopped the car under the arch. He could smell the fragrance of the flowers in the night.

"Shall I come in?"

She opened the door on her side. She looked at him. Her

voice was low. "No. No, I don't think so."

And she was gone.

So McOwen had been wrong in his suspicion. They had not become lovers then, or later. Never again. But they could have been lovers and both of them knew it. And he knew now that, in spite of appearances, it had been Jay who had wavered at the last moment. He had been the reluctant one, excited by the signs of her excitement, her rising estral rage, but fearful at the same time. He had been there before and he was older, more conventional, more cautious. So, sensing his doubt, she had said no, and let him go.

But, sitting in another car, her husband's, he wondered: What would have happened if he had taken courage and they had gone to their fated appointment? Would they have met in joy and tenderness? Or would he have fallen on her like an animal and in his frenzy finally have exorcised the memory of his dead wife?

He realized why thoughts of Antoinette had kept returning to him tonight.

Antoinette had died and in an obscure and obstinate corner of his mind he had held Jay responsible for her death. But the blame had always been his alone.

And, with this admitted, he now had to start to pay the price.

Sister Roos was obviously surprised. "Oh, Doctor. You're back."

"I'm back," he agreed.

"She has been twitching a little on the left side. Otherwise her condition is unchanged. I've sucked her every half hour and her lungs are much more clear now."

"She's been twitching? Are you sure?"

"It seemed like it to me, Doctor."

He looked down at the weary face on the pillow. Was the brain starting to respond? Were messages of life traveling to the motor area? They were signs of recovery. He had to act.

"Has she made any effort to breathe?"

"No, Doctor. And when I disconnected the ventilator to suction her the heartbeat slowed down immediately."

"I see."

The nurse sighed. "It's cruel. She was such a pretty woman."

He grunted agreement. He looked away from the body and at the machine. The bellows inside the Perspex drum moved rhythmically: up—down—up—down.

Sister Roos sighed again. She was a pretty woman herself. Perhaps that was in her thoughts. She said meaninglessly: "Oh, well," and turned to tend to the myasthenia gravis patient.

He looked at Jay then. A drum was beating inside his head. He wanted to cry out to her: "Not like this. I never wanted it like this." He stood there, a big and broad man, his capable-looking hands resting on the bedcover beside the patient. He looked the epitome of what a doctor should be: attentive, watchful, kind, and reassuring. And a thin voice, shrill as a piper's call, wailed within him: "I cannot. Not like this."

The respirator made no sound. There was only the faint bubbling of the exhalations in the water filter.

His mind was a jumble of thoughts, of images, of flashing visions and half-forgotten phrases. He thought of his wife and of his son. He thought of a bird flying out of a hedge and of the cool, sticky hands of a little girl who had been playing in seawater. He thought of a wind blowing through a window into a room at the top of a hill by the sea.

He felt resentment. It was unfair that he should have to bear all the responsibility. He should consult others. Geoff Hutton must have an opinion. Where was he? He should telephone Frank Edelstein again. Let the law settle this; it was not a question for a single man to answer. Where was Cliff McOwen? This was no time to run. This woman was his wife.

The nurse was at his side again, an inquiring look on her face.

"Doctor?"

"Sister?"

"Are you going to be long? Can I get you a chair?"

"Don't bother, thank you."

She said automatically: "No bother." Then: "Mr. Edwards-White phoned while you were away."

"Oh? What did he want?"

"Just to ask about Dr. Case's condition. I told him you had been and gone again. I hope that was all right?"

"Quite all right, Sister."

"I didn't know you were coming back, you see."

"Quite all right," he repeated. He carefully avoided looking at her.

Would Sister Roos be called as a witness on that day when he was compelled to account for his actions and motives? He pictured her giving evidence: nervous in the unfamiliar surroundings of a courtroom but determined to give clear and concise answers. She would be a little worried by the knowledge that her words were causing the ruin of a man's life, but she would speak up forthrightly nonetheless. For she could never understand, let alone forgive, what he had done.

"Oh, Sister." He made his voice deliberately casual. "If you feel like a quick cup of tea or a cigarette . . . I'll probably be here for a while yet. I'll keep an eye on the patients."

She looked dubious. "Leave the patients?"

"I assume you don't stay here all night, do you?"

"No, Doctor. But I don't normally go till midnight, after the night matron has done her round. She relieves me then for half an hour or so, so that I can have supper."

"All right. I'll be your relief tonight. Go and have your tea and I'll look after things."

She still seemed uncertain, so he turned away sharply, putting the matter beyond dispute. She lingered a moment, shuffling with a pile of medicament charts on her desk, leaning over to check a drip rate control, pulling straight a cover which hung askew. Then, reluctantly and with a final doubting look which he ignored, she went out. He heard the outer door close behind her but did not turn. He was watching the machines, trying to concentrate on what their levers and gauges told him. But his eyes kept being drawn to the motionless figure on the bed.

You must be calm and impersonal, he told himself. This is no more than any other medical procedure: like causing a small pain in order to cure a larger one; making a wound in order to heal.

Nevertheless, five minutes or more had gone by before he was able to move.

He knew exactly what had to be done.

He leaned forward and freed the clip which attached the tube from the machine to the tracheal tube which led into the body. Then he stood back.

The bellows still moved: once, twice, then a third time, more sluggishly. The fourth time they rose only halfway up the chamber. The bubbling in the water trap ceased.

His eyes turned to the green zigzag on the cardiac monitor. It had become irregular, steeper, as the distressed heart sought to overcome the sudden lack of air.

But the body on the bed was motionless.

257

A red light the size of a button glowed on the control panel of the respirator. A warning signal began to sound, regularly, insistently: "Beep. Beep. Beep."

Swearing in startled panic, he fumbled with the controls. Where the devil did you switch it off?

The shrill alarm continued. "Beep. Beep. Beep."

He leaned against the bed, aghast. He felt weak at the knees and suddenly overcome by the magnitude of what he had done. The body was unable to protest at his intrusion. It was left to a machine to cry out against the ugliness of his act.

The cricket call of the alarm sounded in his ears.

"Beep. Beep. Beep."

And a warning signal echoed in his own mind. Every instinct, and not only those conditioned reflexes which medicine had drilled into him, rebelled against this coming death.

No, he thought. No.

His hands were trembling uncontrollably. He clumsily reconnected the breathing tube and the tracheal line. He refastened the clamp.

The alarm stopped. The warning light went out.

There was a taste of decay in his mouth, as if he had sucked on a bad tooth. He did not dare look at the figure on the bed. No. No. No.

The respirator was operating smoothly again. The gases which sustained life went in and came out, regularly and undisturbed. The volume control needle flickered across its dial, then back again, ceaselessly to and fro. The bellows rose up, fell down.

The pneumatic doorstop sighed behind him. Sister Roos came back into the room. How long had she been gone? Ten minutes. Half an hour? Time had no meaning.

For a moment he wondered guiltily if she had heard the alarm. Would she come storming at him, casting away her deference to him as doctor, seeing him only as a man and a potential murderer? Would she demand explanations and make shrill denunciations?

The nurse did not appear to notice anything amiss. She stood beside him.

258

"Everything all right, Doctor?"

"Everything's all right, Sister."

"It's probably time I give her another suck-down."

"Yes."

She gave him a puzzled look and turned to the suction machine. She stopped. She was staring at the screen against the wall.

"Doctor . . . ?"

"What is it?"

"There's something odd about . . . "

He looked up at the monitor, too. A small flashing light beside the screen indicated the moment of cardiac contraction.

It flashed. Flashed again. Flashed. Flashed. More and more quickly.

The pattern on the screen had changed. The jagged, church-steeple leaps of the QRS waves were squeezed closely together, and between them were uneven valleys of violent motion. He estimated the rate at which the light was flashing. The heartbeat had speeded up to more than 120, probably closer to 150, a minute.

Tachycardia. Evidence, probably, of cardiac failure and imminent cardiac standstill.

For a mind-numbing instant he was convinced that the blame was his, that cutting off the respirator had brought about this sudden crisis. Then reason and good sense argued differently. The duration of anoxia had been too short, hardly more than a few seconds, a quarter of a minute at the utmost, to have caused the heart to go into failure. But would he ever be sure? Could anyone be sure? Would this moment return to haunt him?

No time, now, for speculation. He had to slow down that racing heart. Pressure on the carotid sinus. His hands were already reaching out, almost before his mind had made its instantaneous decision.

What else? Cut off the air so that she could breathe pure oxygen. Digitalization. A shock to the flagging heart muscle.

"Coramine," he said urgently. "Have you got it here?"

"Yes, Doctor." She moved fast, almost, but not quite, at a run. She reached into the drug cupboard. She had a syringe ready in a kidney bowl.

Then he said: "No."

He lifted his hands away from the still body.

He said again: "No."

The nurse looked at him silently.

He could not find words for the thought which had come to him. But he saw it with utter clarity, as if it was a great globe of light, crystal pure and peaceful. A little while before, as he had worked desperately to reconnect the lifeline he had broken, his movements had been rough with the gracelessness of panic and guilt. These had vanished, replaced by certainty. But still there were no words to express the vision. No words except the one he had already spoken.

He shook his head.

"No."

The church-steeple landscape of the ECG on the screen had changed to one of rolling hills. The heart had gone into ventricular fibrillation. He and the nurse stood watching it gradually grow flatter. They did not speak.

At last only an even line remained on the screen.

Jay was dead. But was death not a kind of beginning?

Something unidentified was troubling his mind, like a fleck at the edge of vision. Something he had forgotten. Something he had to remember.

It came to him. He turned to the nurse.

"There was a patient I had to see today. A little girl."

She stared at him.

"A meningitis case. Baby by the name of Erasmus. She's in isolation in the Children's Ward. Will you please phone and find out her condition?"

She was puzzled, but went obediently to the telephone. He heard her speaking.

Yesterday he had stood under the old grapevine and had seen it, in his mind's eye, collapsing and in ruins. It had seemed to him that nothing, once broken down, could ever be built up again. Now, however, he knew that it was possible to rebuild; painstakingly to restore a vine or a life to what it had been, in all its intricacy of winding and clinging. And with the new season would come the new fruit.

Sister Roos cupped the telephone receiver with one hand.

"I've got the night sister on the line, Doctor. She says the Erasmus baby is fine. She's conscious."

"Good."

"Do you want to speak to Sister?"

"No. Tell her I'm coming round to see the child. I'll be there shortly."

He turned again to look at the cardiac monitor. He watched the flat green line on the screen as if its unvarying shape concealed a vital message.